Prolecto: Genesis

Volume I: Turn the Wheel

Witten and Created by Matthew MacDonald

Part of the Prolecto Universe

A High Roller Entertainment Production

ISBN-13: 978-0615926216 (High Roller Entertainment)

HIGH ROLLER
ENTERTAINMENT ™

TABLE OF CONTENTS

Contents

Episode One

Origins

Written and Created by Matthew MacDonald

Preface, a letter to you, dear traveler

It has often been asked by many souls across many times in many ways, what the future holds. What will tomorrow bring? What lies in wait on the path ahead? These questions persist long beyond the day to day, stretching into eternity. Who will I fall in love with? Will I ever find lasting love? What will become of me, what will become of my life, my future? Will I have a family? And perhaps most importantly, what happens when we die? All sentient life yearns for answers to these questions, and in wanting to know, we create fables, myths, stories. Grand tales of epic proportions, stretching the very definition of the human condition, or other conditions therein… We create elaborate religions in attempt to explain the unexplainable. We amass grand tales of heroes, legends, and monsters. These unknowable forces make up our understanding of the supernatural, and in our darkest hours come echoing back. We each respond in our own ways, in our own time, with our own drive to find meaning to our lives.

There are many paths on the road of life. Some seek to do good in this world for the sake of what is right, others choose to protect those closest to them, and seek out their own path. While even still, others take the road less traveled, and work beyond the duplicitous understanding of good and evil, and even more, there are millions who simply exist to survive.

I wish you the best on your journeys, and in time you will learn I am and ever will be your friend. We will meet again dear traveler, much further down the road. I would warn you that life is most certainly a journey, from which you will never return, but it is already far too late. Once you set out down that road, there is no stopping, you cannot wait, you cannot pause, if even for a moment. Like the ticking of a clock, or the turning of a wheel, life marches onward. In time we learn that we do not need to know what tomorrow brings, but only prepare ourselves to meet that next morning head on. The book has been opened, the key has been turned, the wheel has begun to spin. And with that we begin our fable, a tale beyond the human condition, a story beyond good and evil. Who is right? Who is wrong? Does it really matter?

After all, one person's sin is another's salvation, in time, traveler; you will learn that ultimately all life… is a matter of Prolecto,

A subject of allure.

Safe journeys, until we meet again,

-Bo-Tan, the spirit of death.

Prologue

15 miles off the coast of Italy

The Silverlight Research Vessel Arkay

The Mediterranean Sea

Rune Midguard, the center level, known also as Earth

February 3rd, 2011

2:41 AM

The Journal of Damien Focht, Knight Commander of the Silverlight Guild's Squad Thirty Z Seven

Our 65 foot research vessel had been searching for over 9 months, combing the silt and sand of the Mediterranean, finding nothing, absolutely nothing. Sweeping to no avail, acquiring permit after permit from increasingly belligerent countries in our efforts, braving the harsher winds and cold weather of the early year by the Strait of Gibraltar. Even as I speak the waves batter against our hull.

But it doesn't matter, none of that matters.

"I've found it." I said finally into the receiver of my satellite phone, amidst the icy spray of the sea as the bow of the ship leapt and crashed among the waves at night.

"Are you certain?"

I could hear his excitement over the satellite phone's static, even with his professional and almost monotone voice, through the wind and rain of the rough February weather as our white research vessel bobbed in the 14 foot waves I knew I had made the Chairman proud.

I finally feel as if I am performing my father's duties well… I may make a good Knight Commander yet.

"Absolutely sir, the Laevatien scans are reading off the charts, there's even residual Laplacian activity, looks like Valefor's checked up on it from time to time." I radioed back, trying to keep my own excitement at bay. It's been a long and arduous uphill battle. The past several years in getting to this moment have been nothing but sin and circumstance… but now, finally now, we have won.

"Good. It's time for you to get out of that ridiculous façade, a *Gemini* will be there to take you down to the *New R'yleh,* make sure your crew get a channel marker on it so we can begin extraction. And Damien…" Chairman Daniel Gilden, the man who had my undying respect, stopped to say my name.

"Good work." He added, I could almost hear him nod to me.

"Thank you sir." I replied, as I hung up, I looked to the ebb of the sea.

"The wheel has begun to turn." I said aloud to no one.

The salt and pepper haired, and lightly bearded Dr. Cambray came out of our small research vessel's cabin, eager to hear what the Chairman had said.

"Was that him? W-w-hat did he say? Are you going to tell me what this was all for now?" He asked me, rubbing his shoulders to keep circulation flowing, he's out here in a polo shirt and a lab jacket. I know he's an expert on Xenodimensonal studies, but honestly, the man should have enough sense to wear a proper coat.

I turned to look at him. Even with my warm attire, wearing a wool peacoat with the collar drawn up and a black woolen cap to cover my short shaved hair I made sure I still stared with as much stern attention as I could as I focused my dark brown eyes on him. Letting the scar on my upper lip flair white against my otherwise middle-dark skin. "Are you absolutely sure you want to know? I'm only going to ask this one more time. If you want to remain a professor at Cambridge, if you want to go to sleep knowing everything is ok, that everything will continue on tomorrow as it always has… then I tell you, stop here."

I just wanted to be perfectly sure.

The frail, aging professor nodded still cowering slightly from the waves, hiding from my eyes.

He nodded.

So did I, I would not press the matter further. I immediately started walking towards the ship's center, to make sure I could keep an eye on him as he informed the rest of our crew.

"Indeed, have your assistant prepare her interns for a new datafeed, and inform them we are moving the site to the University. We have to leave, a helicopter will be arriving shortly." I instructed as I briskly walked with him to head to the under quarters. Dr. Cambray's youthful understudy sat at the galley table, sipping hot chocolate with her young interns, two girls working through their master's degree. They have proven very adept, and useful, if not slightly quirky in their personalities. I am used to working with soldiers, not children, but Mr. Gilden requested them, and that was good enough for me.

"Cynthia, we have success." Dr. Cambray admonished to his young assistants with outstretched arms and a happy grin. "We've located the site and we are getting another team to extract it. Is your new laboratory in Baltimore ready to receive it?" He asked the graceful professor in her mid thirties. She was a pretty woman, auburn hair kept in a ponytail and a slender face with blue eyes. Her light skin spoke of many hours behind books, and her constant poise reminded me of her English upbringing.

"It is actually in Kingsport, just south of Baltimore, in one of the new re-zoned Silverlight districts but of course Doctor, our new on-site module has been installed a month ago, we simply need to have the item to observe." Dr. Cynthia Agnew purred back in her posh English accent. She turned back to her students, the younger one, the American with bright red hair kept in a short ponytail that flared out in every direction and more energy then I cared to deal with, immediately replied.

"Woohoo! Now we don't gotta be on this crappy boat anymore!" Vivian Maybell, one of her teaching interns chimed up happily. I rolled my eyes, despite the fact that she and I were nearly the same age I could not help but think that children are horribly spoiled these days. This was hardly a simple boat, this was a new-type research vessel, fitted with amenities far nicer than whatever this expectant student was receiving in a college dorm, yet she complains still, always complaining. I will be glad to be rid of her.

"Yes." I spoke up, "I need all of you to get the scanners ready to transmit data to my coordinates, the Doctor and I are leaving in a moment, but we will return." I explained, cutting to the point I had instructed Dr. Cambray to make but he was simply to slow to get to it.

"Where are you going?" Claudia Brashear, Dr. Agnew's more adept intern of Indian decent questioned me.

"Out." I answered, as I turned with the Doctor to leave.

Once we were outside, I heard the rapid footfalls of someone following us closely behind, I didn't even have to look to know who it was. I turned quickly to see the sharp Indian girl leaning on the frame to the rear exit of the cabin, looking at me with a clearly disapproving stare. I sighed, realizing that it would be impossible not to address her. She's smart, smart enough to know that one doesn't simply step out while in the middle of the Mediterranean. I looked back at her, realizing that I would have to come up with something to placate her before my partners arrived. Explaining now would be far easier than when the *Gemini* approached.

I turned around and walked up to Claudia, as she began to tense her lip, ready to fight me on whatever I had to say.

"Miss Brashear… I understand you're curious about the findings but I assure you, for your own safety, it is best you do not inquire further into this. I greatly appreciate all of the hard work and effort you have put into…" I began to explain before her curt, direct, highly accented yet extremely clear tone started into me quicker than I could reply.

"Mr. Focht, if even that is your name, I have been on a small vessel, working day in, day out, for over *six months*. I am told that we are searching for something, and I'll know what it is when I see it. I'm supposed to provide my expertise in the field, but not receive any feedback, and I'm supposed to uncover a great treasure of humankind, yet I can't even know what it is?! Now we have apparently found 'it' and you have no desire to even inform me of what it is then? I understand corporate secrecy but it's clearly at the point where I cannot do my job without getting a smokescreen of bullcrap from you! I *need* to know what's going on here Damien… and I'm not leaving your sight until I do."

To punctuate her point, she folded her arms and flicked her long black braided ponytail, letting the full four feet of it reverberate down her back, almost like how a rattlesnake would threaten a would be attacker. I sighed again, realizing the futility, a concession must be made.

"Claudia…" I began, attempting courtesy but realizing that I could hold back the details no longer. She was correct, if she was to continue working past this point, she would need to know some semblance of what is going on. "All right…" I began. She immediately relaxed, as her expression turned curious.

"I offer a deal, a peace agreement if you will…" I started, she tensed once more.

"Now, just wait…" I continued, "The item we are bringing up is a site, a relic site, preserved from a great deal of time ago. This site has been long forgotten by most, precious by all. Claudia… I would go into more, but I can't because I don't know fully myself." I lied, but in my time with this company, I've become very good at it.

"You don't even know?" Claudia asked, sympathizing.

"Not entirely, but what Mr. Gilden has informed me is this… that whatever lies down there, the secrets that await within… is the greatest treasure mankind has ever seen, and understanding it, and its many secrets… will change this world forever."

If I only knew then… I was telling the truth.

"Then when will I know more?" Claudia asked.

"Soon." I answered, "You and your fellow interns back at Kingsport University will be studying this site at great length, I expect you… and Vivian… to be working on it readily, around the clock if possible… I have requested to leave this in your capable hands, because I respect you as a fellow academic. I know Dr. Agnew and her adept interns can find the answers to almost anything… now… Claudia… I'm trusting you with this…" I lowered my hand on her shoulder to bring my point home.

She tensed to fight me, but sighed.

"All right Damien… but when I find something, I expect to be kept within the loop." Claudia added her condition, of course, it wasn't unreasonable, unable to be helped, but not unreasonable.

"You have my word." I nodded.

She nodded back to me, and turned to walk back down the stairs.

She stopped about three steps in, and looked back with a concerned gaze, "Really? You're leaving it in our hands? You do know that Vivian will likely break something in the process… and Mr. Gilden's daughter Kayla isn't exactly the paragon of academia…"

I sighed and nodded, thinking of Miss Gilden, the young woman I've protected from an early age. And of course, as always, Claudia was right.

"I understand, but this is what Mr. Gilden wishes." I answered.

And with that, she retired down the stairs.

I took a breath as the door closed… that was very, very close.

"You handled that well…" Dr. Cambray said, rubbing his shoulders again as he once more was standing in the cold without a jacket. I let out a blast of air, letting the contrails curl on the cuff of my jacket as I turned back to him.

"I don't like lying to her, doctor…" I admitted as I stared at the door.

"Then you should have had a different job." Dr. Cambray noted, turning to look at me with an unsympathetic grin. I narrowed my eyes, as I turned back to the sea as a new wind began to blow.

The thrum of an approaching aircraft called forth my recollected memories, for the last nine months I have had to play at being a mere manager of the Silverlight Corporation's research department, a collector of cultural artifacts. Needless to say my patience with people of my own respective age yet not my maturity is not eternal, and found the days staggeringly long. But as the rotorless *Gemini* attack transit VTOL appeared on the horizon...

I knew I'd soon be home.

Dr. Cambray looked slightly amazed as the craft, something akin to a silver blend between an AH-64 Apache and a Blackhawk helicopter, gently flew through the rough winds to turn sideways at our port, allowing us to enter, as a long grey hand slid open the door.

The doctor gasped as got a glimpse of the woman who opened the door for us. Her skin was grey, her eyes a milky white, her hair long and the color of snow. She sat in a lab coat and long dress pants but it was clear that her body was long and lanky underneath, she tapped at a data pad with her long fingers, each digit around 9 inches. She leaned back her head as she looked down at us. Her brow lowered slightly as her slender if not strangely beautiful facial structure seemed to add an air of arrogance to her gaze as she looked back at Dr. Cambray.

"Get in." The woman commanded to the doctor as I entered, and immediately walked past her to get to the equipment locker moving past the two bench-like seats that acted as the main cabin. The doctor sat across from the grey skinned woman, eying her with great caution.

I simply got ready to return to the ship.

I opened my locker, taking a look at myself. Even through my mixed skin tone of my black father and white mother I could see my stubble was really beginning to show, my normally clean shaven appearance had begun to grow out in the weeks of sea bound solitude, but my defined and toned body was still as fit as ever as I hopped out of my foolish sweatpants and donned the silver and black jumpsuit of my under armor. I clipped on plate after plate of my *Silhouette* power armor. The plates clacked in place as the smooth, form fitting power armor clipped on around me, covering my body up to my neck, as I donned the cloak of the Silverlight guild, the turquoise mantle that allowed my suit to vanish at will.

I took a moment to look at myself before I affixed my mask. In my twenty five years of life I have been on missions that most people would never dare dream of, and for my trouble I have received a single scar just above my lip, a marker of my single mistake. But there was no time to dwell, I pulled the hood atop my head as I affixed the hockey mask like front, the iconic white mask of our order with no features other than two yellow illuminated eyes, as the head's up display showed me all the information I would need.

It's good to be back.

"Nice to see you in uniform Knight Commander." Dr. Albertie Toft, the woman of grey said to me as I sat down next to the nervous Dr. Cambray.

The old doctor's curiosity got the better of him, he blurted out suddenly "Madam… what *are* you?"

Dr. Toft brought back her head slightly, letting out a slight chuckle as folded her unnaturally long arms, letting a nine inch long finger tap on the edge of the bench-like seat she rested in.

"If you must know… I am what is known among your kind as a 'zombie', but I find that term rather grotesque wouldn't you agree?" Dr. Toft answered in a… deadpan, tone.

"Sir… is it safe to…" He whispered to me.

"Have a Zombie on board? Dr. Toft, is one of our lead researchers, I value her unlife well over yours Dr. Cambray, I suggest you keep your comments to yourself." I replied coldly, nodding to the good Doctor, who calmly nodded back in acceptance.

"So… where are we going?" Dr. Cambray asked, glancing repetitively over to Dr. Toft as I pointed for him to look out the window.

As he did, the Gemini plunged down into the sea, gently gliding through the dark water as easily as it would through air. The filtered light from the overhead research vessel cast a spotlight through the sea. The multitude of plankton and flotsam in the ocean created a backscatter of debris in the column of light as our silver craft glided towards darkness.

"What… how does your technology…" Dr. Cambray began.

"You will find, Dr. Cambray, that the Silverlight Guild is equipped to tend to your every need, now in return we ask only for your silence in the revelations you uncover. We are meeting with the *New Ry'leh* a vessel more than capable of extracting the site from the bottom of the ocean. Now, *you* will tell us how to harness the power within it." I explained plainly as the VTOL descended through the water. I could hear him gasp as he witnessed the huge 400 meter visage of the *New Ry'leh* rise up from the depths to receive us. The craft was only visible as a massive shadow, but it's not wise to give up all our secrets at once to Dr. Cambray.

"If what you say is true, and this is not a fable or legend… then I doubt you will like how this power is used." Dr. Cambray warned me.

"I'm willing to take that risk." I said then, something I regret even now.

"Wh… what if the world finds out you're hiding this all from them?" Dr. Cambray nervously asked me.

"They won't, besides, everyone has enough skeletons in their own closet to worry about." I answered.

Now it was Dr. Toft's turn to question me.

"What if the angels find out we've moved the site, surely they have some method of detecting this." Dr. Toft asked, more out of concern of success than anything else.

"We've prepared for that contingency." I answered. "We're letting the Kingsport University study this one, they won't be so quick to make a public appearance." Comfortable with the explanation she nodded and leaned back to relax once more.

"Wh..." Dr. Cambray began again, becoming increasingly disconcerted. "Angels!? Zombies!? Ships and helicopters that go underwater, and fly without rotors... what? How long? How long has this gone without my notice!? What secrets have you been hiding from the world!? What is the meaning of all this, what is in this site that has your interest... what is so dangerous!?" He demanded in ignorant anger. I stood and turned to face out the side window. He joined me and glanced outside as well.

We passed by the item we would soon be transposing, I smiled beneath my visor as I read the inscription to myself.

'Azazel, being of darkness'.

"Oh, don't you worry yourself Dr. Cambray" I said with a consoling tone.

"You really have no idea."

Chapter One

Kingsport University Archeology Laboratory

Kingsport University, Maryland

United States of America, Earth

The Journal of Vivian Maybell

August 15th, 2011

5:25 PM

"The sun taunted them, dancing and sparkling against the glittering pane of glass as if enticing them outside to do something much more desirable than what they were doing now. Other students yelled and hooted as they made their way to the campus' pool, laughing and enjoying the warm summer evening, savoring the last moments of the sun's nourishing rays before it bids its sweet adieu..." I dramatically gasped as I reached out with my hand, pressing it against the tinted window as I clutched my free hand to my chest.

"But not us, oh good lord, not us." I stared downward, letting my bangs fall before my eyes.

"We were, as we were always doomed to be,

inside."

A deep sigh rolled off my professor as she patiently waited for me to complete my melodrama.

"Miss Maybell, if you are quite done with your soliloquy of self-loathing, I need more GPR on quadrant A-24." Professor Cynthia Agnew ordered behind dark rimmed glasses with her very posh English accent as she looked over to me in her most certainly 'not certified for Archeology' eveningwear, it was 5:30 in the afternoon at Kingsport University, Maryland, on August the 15th, 2011...

And all of us, were doomed.

It was the last day of our world as we knew it…

Even now, I look back on it with fondness.

"But of course masssterrr, I will get zee machinneee" I chided in my best "Igor" impression, as I went to grab the, in my opinion, unnecessarily heavy Ground Penetrating Radar. Dr. Agnew hid a giggle under her hand at my antics as I walked over to the large stack of expensive archeological devices piled high on the far wall by the lockers, grabbed the device that resembled a large discus with an industrial sized weed whacker attached to the top, and proceeded to complain to myself as I hauled the device onward.

You know, as I lugged that machine around the desks and workstations towards my worksite, I pondered as to *why* I felt so particularly inclined to become an Archeologist. After all I knew the job would yield little pay. It would be hours and hours of hard work, and incessantly I kept coming up against a brick wall of being a woman in such an academic career without any money. It's amazing how many people assume I'm here to pick up a "Ms." Not a "MS", and it gets a little old over time.

But it was all about history, the past has always fascinated me. I wanted to know yesterday, I spent my childhood in worlds found only in time and literature, and to feel parts of it, work in a world outside of this one… I suppose that draw is stronger for some.

Allow me to introduce myself, my name was Vivian Maybell. Oh hey, that didn't change, it's still Vivian, or Vivi for short. I suppose looking back on it; I look like my mother, and my mother is very pretty. I had dyed bright red hair I kept at about shoulder length, but I tied it all up in a ponytail that was kept tight with my naturally springy hair keeping it flamboyant in every direction, like a firework. I sometimes held it in place with a chopstick or pen, I liked that look, also, it's how I knew where to find my pen. My choppy and jagged bangs often fell in a random assortment across my forehead but when I smiled my forehead always wrinkled to make the bangs fall almost over my eyes. I like movies, and comics, and video games, you'll find me referencing them, from time to time when it's not appropriate thanks to my all prevailing attention deficit disorder. Oh, but right, I gotta get back to what I look like! I have a rounded face with a narrow chin, a thin, athletic frame (around 5 and a half feet tall) with a decent bit of an hourglass figure to myself, bright green eyes, and more importantly one of the highest grades in my class, despite my social stupidity. All in all, I had a lot of natural gifts to be thankful for.

But for an overworked college student, my major task was complaining.

"Ugh…" I said as I threw off the lab coat I was wearing, showing off my gray KPU Archeology Department T-Shirt and blue jeans so I could place on the GPR's harness. I secured the machine, and proceeded to schlep my way to what we in the department called 'the site'.

"Mmmmmm, heavy…" I whimpered like a puppy, fishing for help, as I started to operate the machine, which felt like playing minesweeper more than science. It's heavy and awkward in case I did not emphasize the impracticality of the design enough. As I pushed the mammoth machine I looked around me, listening to the electrical motor echo off the large interior of the lab.

I really should explain our lab. When I refer to Kingsport University's Archeology lab, I do not mean a small facility with some heavy black tables and test tubes here and there, although such things do exist here... I mean a dome shaped facility that annexes to another building hall, but the lab is so large that we could probably host a few Olympic events in here if we only managed to move the 'site' held within.

Further, the 'site' was a removed portion of land, perfectly intact, from an underwater shelf in the Strait of Gibraltar. I remember the day they brought it, just a couple days after we got back from our research mission. The dome shaped roof opened up to accept this gigantic hunk of dirt that was lowered down by helicopter into the massive sublevels that made up the space below our lab as it was set in place. Essentially bringing outside, in, allowing us to work in a climate controlled, relatively clean environment. Away from prying eyes. Silverlight LTD had strict instructions on making sure we don't talk about the site outside of class, and our wing has an armed guard in the daytime to keep out snoopers, but that just adds to the intrigue. We get to work on a secret archeological project, how cool is that!? Now I, Vivian Maybell, girlventuer, will uncover the secrets that lie within and bring knowledge and understanding of the lost to the surface, and new light!

And by light, I mean tiny, fragmented images taken by dozens of college students with ground penetrating radars. We're not allowed to dig. That's right, an archeological site that you're not allowed to dig at. Now, I understand that minimal disturbance is preferred in my field, because if you mess with one area of the site, you might lose critical clues like how objects were used. Things like where they were located in reference to the area, and other critical things like imprints and even gas pocket data, but honestly… they won't even tell us what's down there! And it's starting to get old…

Almost a year ago now, Claudia and I were invited to join Dr. Cynthia Agnew, our professor, on an expedition to uncover… something. That was literally it. The Professor wished she could have told us more, but our project financers, Silverlight, the private owners of Kingsport University, our school, have a tendency to keep us in the dark. We have been given heavy ground penetrating radars, and a few new Silverlight LTD new-type holo-computers to work with, but for the most part we're supposed to uncover an unknown object in the dark. Silverlight's number one and only major rule… was that we never, *ever* dig below the surface of this site. But to understand an order like that, you'd first need to understand Silverlight.

Silverlight LTD, established around 30 years ago, was originally a weapons company. They made fighter jets that competed with Lockheed-Martin, and came up with some electronics that put other corporations to shame, fantastic new technology that really revolutionized the world. Then Silverlight branched out, they started making computers, cell phones, cars, and even came up with a new, experimental power source after Doctors Kerensky and Fushida, here at this university, discovered how to keep and stabilize cold fusion around ten years ago. They actually make this area so prevalent, and so wanted by academics and well to do people, that Baltimore actually re-zoned the area south of Curtis bay to rename the area township,

Kingsport, in honor of the university. So this school, and everyone in it, are considered tied to the company in some way, shape or form.

How does a poor girl like me get into an awesome university like this? No idea. I got a full ride scholarship two weeks before graduation from high school… long story. But right now, miss future super scientist has to still use 40 year old minesweeper radar.

"I don't see why you are complaining so much miss arrives late." chided Claudia Brashear, my Indian counterpart. "Some of us have been here since this morning and I've nearly got this entire quadrant done!" She informed in a very forward yet soft enough tone to show she was not scolding. She let her own GPR flop to the ground as she stretched. Claudia had been my fellow teaching assistant to Dr. Agnew for the past year, and yeah she's pretty cool. She's a pretty girl too, dark Indian skin, black hair that was long and braided, and this amazing air of intelligence and calm around her. She has very kind brown eyes. You know, that gentle kind of stare that makes you feel like you're going to be all right. Even though she tells me that her entire family is from Mumbai, former Calcutta, her face has a very Caucasian look to it, making me think that part of it was from somewhere else. My mom likes Genealogy… I can't help but analyze people. Claudia definitely has a way of cutting to the point though… some call her arrogant but I think she's simply not afraid of being smart. She can be a bit of a know-it-all from time to time though, and I admit I sometimes get a bit tired of being corrected, but Claudia's cool. I like her, she's really the only friend here my age I've got that doesn't also bug the heck out of me, like Kayla.

Speaking of friends, here comes one who certainly wasn't.

"And some of us don't really want to be here at all!" whined Sonya Shannon, a rich Silverlight Corporate spook's daughter. I hated Sonya, I really did. She was dumb yet arrogant, popular and beautiful. She had long blonde hair, bright blue eyes, an amazing form that kept her high in the rankings of men's 'women they would most like to sleep with' lists, but she would just use them to get whatever she wanted. I know she's only here because of her father. She's not smart, she's not academic, and above all she never even *tries* to do anything, she always gets someone else to do her bidding. She's even managed to climb her way to the top of the Cheerleading ladder and having been a cheerleader in high school, I know that's one clique you can't just edge in on anywhere, under that I know there lies someone I'm not seeing, because she can turn on you in a second.

I wished she'd leave. I wondered why she was even *in* college, that woman will never have to work a day in her life. I thought this fact over to myself as I watched her struggle along with her GPR, roughing up the surface soil as she trudged through with no care or concern for scientific process or any kind of delicate method.

"Don't worry Sonya… if it's too heavy I can help you do it." Natalie Rayborn assisted in a conscientious tone finishing up a text message on her new Silverlight LTD cell phone and putting the slim black rectangle carefully away in her backpack. Natalie was Sonya's aid de camp in all things, cheerleading and otherwise, but Natalie was the much more realistic of the two. Brown hair kept in a clean and classic 'just past the shoulders cut' with a nice little hairband and an extremely kind "girl next door" look to her with a cute green jumper skirt with her grey Kingsport Cheerleading t-shirt, and her *KPU Knights* letterman jacket she always stole from her boyfriend, classically one of the members of the football team. She had just the right amount of freckles for it to be considered "cute", with green eyes and a pretty build one would expect from someone who devoted their extracurricular hours to gymnastics and cheerleading. Natalie actually was here in the medical program, but she got involved in our project when she was dragged into it by Sonya. Even though her circles and mine would be so far apart, I'm actually pretty glad she was here. Natalie's a very kind person, she sports that cross necklace she's always wearing very well.

As I zoned out and Claudia and Sonya traded words, the Professor finally stepped in.

"Ladies, please, you don't have time to argue. We need to make some progress this evening or I am afraid that our funding might just get cut. You girls are here for the long haul tonight, for better or worse. I'd prefer very much to give some hint of progress within our progress report to corporate, they already bug us enough and Mr. Focht will be here again to check up on us tomorrow and I would like to have something to tell him, thank you very much." Professor Agnew said in that professorial mix of concern and coercion as she put on her coat and grabbed her purse.

Sonya Shannon immediately started to straighten her tight white button down long-sleeve shirt and fixed her collar to make sure there was a nice window of her cleavage as she fussed, "Oh… Damien is coming here!?" She asked with a raised pitch.

"Not in until tomorrow, you can wait to flirt with him…" Claudia sighed as shook out the dust from her Kingsport University Archeology Department grey tee shirt, and shook out some clinging dirt to her slightly bell bottomed jeans. I realized as I watched Claudia an important thing, the professor wasn't going to be here!

"WAIT you mean you aren't staying?" I cried out, she may be our teacher but Claudia and I also relied on her for most of our social interaction and friendship, what can I say though, we *are* nerds.

"Nope, I already got my PhD. You ladies need to earn some credits and I've already put in over 60 hours! By tomorrow you girls better find something good, because with all of your bickering and procrastinating, you have managed to make this little project go down to the wire, pull an all-nighter if you have too, I don't care, just don't break anything, and *get it done*. Goodnight everyone, I will see you in class on Monday." Professor Agnew said in a stern but very concerned and caring tone with a smile, gave a slight bow, and was out the door. It was clear *she* was the professor, her clothing was completely dirt free, and she looked absolutely stunning in her evening wear, her curled auburn hair was in a fine short ponytail, and her little black dress practically screamed "I have a date".

The college students, myself included, wished they were her.

"Oh!" Professor Agnew returned suddenly, showing back up for a moment at the door. "I am leaving you all with my TI for the night, ciao!"

"NOOOOO!" The entire group cried in anguish as a short girl sporting a long hair cut colored turquoise with strait bangs jumped into the room with a giddy hop. Her outfit was that of a classic maid, but not a normal French maid, no, that would only be fringe or weird at best. She was dressed like an *anime* maid, with a gigantic bow in the back. She finished the look with black and white arm socks and matching… sock socks, to add to the supreme amount of vertigo one might experience getting lost in the outfit that was nearly as loud as her voice...

It could only be one person.

"oooooaaaaahhhhHHHHHH YESSSS!" Kayla Gilden, overzealous teaching intern, daughter of Daniel Gilden, founder and owner of Silverlight LTD, retorted in her usual 'Wave' voice.

For some reason, Kayla found it incredibly boring to keep things at one volume, so she would often gravitate between extremes whenever she could, just one of the many habits the rest of the group found amazingly irritating. But no one could touch her, not at all. Silverlight was not only a major corporation, a weapons manufacturer, and world known philanthropic organization, it also has a *private military contractor*. And rumor has it, if anyone so much as lays a hand on Miss Kayla Gilden, you'll be toast by the hour. She has done nothing to inform us this is not so, so in short, whatever Kayla wants, Kayla gets.

"Wellllllllll…" Kayla began, giving incredibly exaggerated leaning gestures in her ridiculous clothing, "I see you all are having TONS OF FUN playing in the dirt so ima gonna sit here and look at kitty pictures until I drop. Okey dokey!" She skipped across the room to the professor's computer and proceeded to do exactly as she had dictated. Kayla was cute, very cute. Little rounded face, similar build to me but just in fun-size, and had that kind of toothy smile that made you suddenly want to forgive her… right until she opened her mouth.

We all stared at Kayla for a moment before Claudia destroyed our dubious trance with a shake of her head and a clap of her hands, naturally taking charge of things once more, "Well, I suppose there is no use complaining now. Vivian, would you start on the A quadrants with Sonya? And Natalie, can you get me the scan/not scanned charts so I am not repeating my work?" Claudia ordered to all of us. I found her plan sensible, and proceeded to set out to my task as Sonya grumbled behind me.

"Sure thing" Natalie replied, walking over to fetch the one of the Silverlight Datapads off the wall, the cool almost paper thin black slate that generated glowing cyan text when you held it up to you. Natalie made a little grin as the text lit up and started displaying the information she and Claudia just talked about, it was clear she thought it was cool too. Natalie and Claudia had been getting on well in the past few days, Natalie had the sense about her to make friends with the people she worked with, and I have to say it was nice to have her here. I really liked spending time with her, even if I did feel a little jealous that Claudia spent more time with her than me.

With Sonya, this was less so.

"Ugh stuck with the friggin nerds all night… friggin Claudia Brashear 'oh I'm so perfect because I'm from India, my whole family is nothing but doctors and lawyers and I'll take all your jobs'." Sonya grumbled with borderline racism as she struggled hopelessly with the GPR, her blonde hair and classic preppy cheerleader build did nothing for her when it came to actually doing real work for herself.

"Not my fault if I'm just better than you at everything" Claudia insulted right back with her clipped accent and a bob of her head. Claudia didn't even miss a bit of work as she did it, finishing a scan and checking it off with a swipe of her finger across the display of the datapad as she completed another quadrant. "At this rate I'll be done with my work in no time while you can certainly spend the rest of the evening with Miss Gilden here, I'm sure you'll enjoy that" Claudia threatened to the blonde.

"That'll be awesome, we can watch *Buffy*! You'll relate!" Kayla shouted over to Sonya.

Sonya looked ready to hit someone.

"C'mon Sony it's not so bad, look, the night is young and maybe we can find something really cool and still have our Friday, so let's play nice, get this done, and we can all go home." Natalie stated with deep reason, acting the natural peacekeeper as she handed more charts over to Claudia.

Sonya sighed, seeing Natalie's argument as too logical to pass up. We all decided to simply do as we were told for a few hours, but as the sun finally set, Sonya's patience ran out.

It was now past midnight… we had been working diligently, scanning, getting dust on ourselves, and getting tired, sweaty, and frustrated… with absolutely nothing to show for it.

"It's been forever, and we're not even allowed to see what's down here just by looking at it!? I mean, we don't even *know*, what are we actually scanning for anyway! This is getting ridiculous, and I'm not going to sit here and keep putting together stupid puzzle piece images when you can just go and look yourself! I don't even know, so what the heck is *supposed* to be down here anyway?" She sighed in exasperation as she took another step onto the dirt grid below. Although impossible from her vantage point, if one could look from a high point within the laboratory, they would see that she was actually standing at the center point of what looked to be a large, and rather ominous pentagon of dirt, from the surface it looked like we had an indoor garden or large flat dirt site, but in reality it was merely the tip of the iceberg, receding down several stories below.

I felt it necessary to explain it to her. I really, really wanted to have my own archeology television show one day, I always took the chance to be Miss Exposition, "We are standing on a dirt slab roughly 20 tons, a single rough sheet excavated by multiple ships from the Mediterranean, and we were one of them! It was really cool except for the whole it took months thing!" I explained, getting excited about the find without realizing it. "We don't know exactly what it is, but we know it was once the holy site of a cult over 2,000 years ago. The only text we have refers to it as Rosier's Temple".

A loud voice heralded my information with auxiliary details, "And in case any of you's guys were wondering, Rosier is the DEMON LADY of seduction and allure, pretty cool amiright?" Kayla contributed to the conversation.

"Yes, we know Kayla…" Claudia purred in a lackluster tone.

"So… is there… treasure, or something down here? I know the Silverlight Corporation, and as nice as they seem publically, they don't do anything unless there's a payoff… both of you know more than you're letting on… so I wanna know… spill it." Sonya pointed at Claudia and I as she took a slow spin around the site to point out the five point star with an eye at the center emblazoned on all of our gear.

Claudia looked to me as I glanced back at Claudia… I didn't know what to say and Claudia clearly was caught between wanting to share and not knowing what was part of the Nondisclosure Agreement we had with Silverlight LTD. Even though it wasn't much.

Kayla smiled as her long turquoise hair seemed to blend in the cyan holograms that projected the many screens of entertainment and random social media around her. Her green eyes accented her nefarious smile as she let her cute nearly level bangs drop just above her eyes as she tilted back towards us. "They don't know a dang thing! I'm the only one that knows what's going on here and even then not the whole thing!" she shouted from where she was across the room. She made a coy, Cheshire cat grin as she arched her fingers and made a smug shrug stretching her hands out over her holographic keyboards. "My daddy funds pretty much this whole college so we get all this sweet future super-duper tech! Like this PC! Oooh, 64 bit kitties…" Kayla went back into her little world, thumbing through random images on a web search.

"Ok, so tell me. Now." Sonya demanded as she turned to face Kayla, her tone dropped a couple octaves quicker than I would have ever expected. The lead cheerleader sounded harsh… I know she could be catty, but that was downright evil.

Kayla responded by smiling and tilting her head as she went back to what she was doing. She kicked her feet in her little black boots a bit more at her computer desk… if you can even call them that. Computers, ever since Silverlight really started to mass produce them, are completely different from what they used to be. Holographic technology became more tangible after cold fusion was miniaturized. Most of the computers were just a little slit that sat on a desk. Like a triangular bar the size of a ruler. They would project a keyboard and occasionally interfaces for games or certain programs that you could hold. Like light, tangible light, that you could move and feel it pull and push. The screens were called up as needed, windows that could be expanded or broken up as you needed them. In Kayla's case she pulled her Facebook off to one side as she looked at funny kitty pictures and her nerdy /b/ internet forums. Her turquoise hair, cut in choppy little raver's bangs dropped a bit to accent a little sneer.

"Oh? You wanna know daddy's project huh?" She asked with a slight chuckle as she slinked back in her chair.

"Yes." Sonya said plainly, "I wanna know what the hell is going on!"

She was clearly losing her temper, which wasn't hard.

"Indeed." Kayla answered, with a very cute shrug.

"What!?" Sonya answered, not understanding what Kayla meant by that, and getting upset at the lack of knowing.

Kayla, however, was being cryptic. At that moment, Claudia and I realized she DID know something, now we wanted to know too.

"C'mon Kayla clue us in, we have to make a finding for this evening or we will be in trouble, if there's anything you can tell us please help us out. I mean it." I asked honestly.

She hopped off her computer desk, and walked over to us, folding her arms behind her back as she took a breath, and let all her little anime maid outfit accoutrements jiggle a bit as she made a single exaggerated step onto the site.

"Ok… I'll tell you what I know… but you gotta promise it doesn't leave this room… ok?" Kayla offered like a child that knew what everyone was getting for Christmas, and like the spoiled brat she was, she was holding out for the last possible minute.

"Fine." Claudia agreed for us. Sonya said nothing, her version of consent. Natalie, on the other hand, started to get nervous. She likes to follow the rules, and if someone told her no, she accepts it.

Kayla stepped out onto the dirt and started to pace around us as she made her big reveal.

"You said it yourself Vivi, we're standing over the Temple of Rosier, this is an ancient site from sometime around year one, Anno Dommini. This was a special site, according to lost legend, this site houses the greatest treasure in all mankind, it was believed to be a gatehouse to somewhere else… or it could have been a seal, Dr. Cambray isn't very good at reading runes so there could be some mistakes, I don't know. Either way, dad says there's a power source in here that could revolutionize the way we look at the world. Isn't that worth continuing? I mean, look at the last time dad found something cool. We all were better for it."

Kayla held out her hands, closed her eyes and shook her head, making an argument of encouragement for us to continue work on her father's behalf.

"The discovery of cold fusion in the 1970's was a huge benefit, I mean… the world is switching off of oil, we will soon have new vessels that can take us places we never could go before… average people might have flying cars someday. All of the things we always thought of as science fiction like cell phones, holographic images, and whatever… look, it's coming to pass. It's neat, it's the future, but it's because of careful work and not giving away all the corporate secrets that this information doesn't all fall in the wrong hands. Dad was very clear that he could only tell us what we would need to keep going… Sometimes it's better not to ask. Claudia, Vivian, we just need to find something, like a power spike or any sign that what's supposed to be down here, is, and we can bring in Silverlight and then see some new inventions soon. Plus we'll all get our names in the paper for the discovery. I think that's pretty neat." She explained, but not really. Kayla clearly knows what we're dealing with, but she's keeping her father's secrets well.

"So all we need is a little something. That's all I'm looking for, if we so much as find the slightest hint of a power spike on any of our readings, that'll be enough to call Damien in and we'll have our discovery and next project. This is supposed to be open and shut. No more questions now… just keep scanning, ok?" She coerced us in the most polite voice possible as she sweetly folded her hands and tilted her head.

"So… a power source…" Claudia noted, now getting more information than we had before. "That gives us a start… thank you Kayla… there might be another way to go about this without radar… Vivian… do we still have the equipment from the *Arkay*?" She asked, motioning for something as she started going through her datapad.

I thought about it for a moment, remembering all the high tech gear that Silverlight had furnished us with, then remembering suddenly that I had crammed it all in a locker next to our TA offices. "Yeah!" I answered suddenly, knowing what she was getting at and bolting for the locker, "Yeah you want the thing that goes doodly wamp?" I asked her as I pressed my thumb on the biometric lock, now interested at getting somewhere.

"The what?" Natalie asked.

"You were supposed to hand back all the stuff leant to you for the trip…" Kayla narrowed her eyes at me. I made a big grin and shrugged.

"Vivian likes to keep things." Claudia stated in a neutral tone, neither for nor against me.

Kayla raised an eyebrow, very concerned at what I've kept.

"She means a hand-scanner, Silverlight gave us one for doing some dives in shallow water, we were looking for particles of something called Laevatien energy. It's apparently an energy source made from sub particles of matter, Dr. Cambray knew a great deal about it, but he wouldn't tell the professor. We still have the device though, Vivian forgot to hand it all back." Claudia explained.

Ok… so, privately… maybe I didn't *forget* completely… but… more, strategically misplaced.

Kayla folded her sock covered arms and leaned back in her unable-to-be-taken-serious outfit. I continued, fishing for what I was looking for.

I pulled out the small handheld device, a small silver tool that looked like a speed gun with a display on the back. I turned on the thumb pad to start the display, as the Silverlight star appeared on the image, the booting up sequence for the device.

"Got it here!" I said as I trotted back to Claudia. Natalie looked worried, she's always been one for following the rules. Claudia and Sonya were more than willing to help me figure this out though, as Kayla decidedly said nothing as we started to walk around. The short corporate brat toddled several steps behind us as we started walking around the site, trying to peek over our collective shoulders.

"Curious?" Sonya purred as she suddenly turned around and surprised the young corporate spook. Kayla immediately folded her hands and turned her head away, jutting out her bottom lip as she retorted quickly.

"I want to see what you're doing with my father's stolen property…" She said in a quick passing of the buck.

I, however, was completely distracted.

"Oh!" I noted quickly, as a reading of energy started to spike as we walked together, slightly startling Claudia and Sonya as Natalie continued to fold her arms and pretend we weren't doing this.

"It's to the left!" Sonya excitedly pointed, angling me with my device to the stronger signal.

"To the left, to the left…" Natalie sang to herself to avoid her nervousness.

"I know, I can read it too!" I shouted, shrugging her arms off me as I started following the signal.

"Shhh... shhh… just keep following!" Claudia hushed the argument, ushering me forward with her hands gently on my back.

"Stoooop! Everyone stop rushing me, I'm being rushed. This is you, rushing me." I complained as Claudia and Sonya prodded me onward. My voice deteriorating into defensive cute mode, getting closer and closer to an endearing baby talk.

"So… you found something huh?" Kayla asked, with a dainty little shrug as she tip toed behind us.

The signal read 80% saturation, I've never seen levels that high, the energy was everywhere! Why didn't they say it was a power source!? We could have been done *ages* ago!

I excitedly reported my findings, "Yes! It's that energy we were supposed to look for… that Laevatien energy! Say it with me, Lay- va – tee –en! Whoa look at that spike… it's ginormous!"

"That's base metal… your scanner is showing base metals…" Claudia gasped, pointing to the area we were standing over, then tapping on my scanner's screen, "Look AU, W, and… that composite… is that reading carbon fiber? It's reading advanced grade aircraft composites! What the… what the heck is down here?"

"There isn't supposed to be any metal in the structure… It's supposed to be sandstone…" I mused, "Claudia there's no way our scans could have been so far off… This scanner has to be broken, there's no way these materials could have been down there, our GPR would have picked it up ages ago. Metals give off the biggest signatures… yet we didn't see these? I don't know Claudia… something seems wrong."

"What do we do now?" Natalie asked, with growing concern.

Sonya stepped in to answer.

"We dig." She stated with a harsh tone at the back of her throat. Grinning like a jackal before prey.

Natalie shook her head as Sonya proceeded to explain.

The very coy and conniving Sonya paced around in front of us, slinking in her walk like a cat. "Look, we need to look, see it with our eyes, confirm what is right here in front of us. Supposed to be sandstone, but it's all metal… don't sit around looking like idiots, just open this up. I'll get a shovel, and we'll see it for ourselves."

There was one rule Silverlight LTD was adamant about this entire time. That under no circumstance, at no time, should we ever, *dig*.

We stared at each other, saying nothing, doing nothing.

"We *really* aren't supposed to be diggin!" Kayla warned, pacing around behind us yet infinitely curious. I could tell as she held up her chin on her black and white arm sock covered hand that she was stuck between her desire to listen to her father, and her want to know.

Sonya stepped forward from Natalie, hands on her hip. Tapping on her tight black slacks as she pulled down her tight white button down shirt to adjust herself almost out of instinct as she strode up to intimidate the diminutive Kayla Gilden by standing over her. Sonya brushed aside her long blonde hair as she met eyes with our entitled TI.

"Then tell me what's down there." Sonya stated plainly, she motioned for Natalie to grab one of the shovels off the wall. Natalie, again acting almost on instinct, obeyed Sonya, running and grabbing the shovel and handing it off to the tall blonde.

"I told you… I *don't* know." Kayla answered with a more serious tone than I've ever heard her speak. She's always known for acting as silly as she looks, for her to drop her tone an octave like that means she is starting to get upset at Sonya. The jury was still out for me… as much as I don't like her way of doing things… I had to admit, Sonya was very close to getting results.

"Then…" Sonya returned, grabbing the shovel firmly in both hands, standing to where the signal was strongest, and ramming the shovel into the ground, leaving it standing right up and down, imbedded in the soil. "Let's… find out."

Claudia paced around the shovel still implanted into the ground, she decidedly has said nothing this entire time. I imagine she was in the same boat I was, caught between wanting and worrying.

We all really wanted to see what was down there… even Kayla.

Kayla put her hands to her side and stared at Sonya through her turquoise bangs. "If my father finds out we disobeyed his direct orders…"

"Kayla's right, it's not wise to upset Mr. Gilden. He could have us expelled Sonya… or worse…" Natalie warned, tugging on Sonya's shirt to try to get her to stand away from the shovel.

"It's always easier to ask for forgiveness than permission Natalie. You want results, you wanna go out on the weekend instead of stay in every damn night, doing this? Then we dig, we dig and get the answers, right here, right now. If anyone is going to stop me, bring it, stop me right now. Otherwise help me, or get the hell out of my way." Sonya delivered her ultimatum with a confident, purring tone, clearly taking charge of things and very openly stating her intentions. She had in more ways than one drawn a line in the sand… and left us to where we stood.

Help her break the rules, and find out what we've been working on for almost a year…

Or just walk away, and give yet another report of "we don't know" to the company and school.

As always when I got nervous, my mind wandered, a part of my ADD. One thought leads to another, and to another, and eventually I arrive at some abstract concept that pulls me back to where I am.

I pondered the words of *Isaac Asimov*, the first law of his three laws of robotics,

'A robot may not injure a human being, or through inaction, allow a human being to come to harm'.

Yes, we're not robots, yes, that doesn't seem relevant… but it was… it reminded me that inaction… was an action.

And so I chose not to stop Sonya.

I chose to allow all that would follow from it.

And so we watched her dig.

Sonya dug for only a moment, just a few simple scoops to upturn the soil… and there it was.

What we were looking for all along.

In the small area of uncovered soil was a patch of ornate and jeweled gold, brass, and iron, with a symbol sticking out of part of the side of the exposed area. It was still glittering, without any sign of a patina over all the years. An item like this should have been tarnished over completely, but here it sat, as if it was perfectly polished...

Waiting.

Kayla's sillier, curious side got the better of her, as she immediately flipped back into being completely into the event, "Whoa that's REALLY cool!" Kayla shouted happily, leaning over in her in her maid outfit. Her black and white striped socks got a bit of dirt on them as she leaned over without concern for how much of her dress she was displaying to anyone behind her. She patted around the hole on all fours. I admit she looked a little cute in her matching black and white arm socks as she tried moving around the hole to see it from more angles. I could see all the little gears in her mind churning as she worked at what this small glimpse of an image could be, before turning back to me with a sigh and a stare of determination.

"I have to see the rest of this thing..." She said finally.

"Ah, dangit me too..." Claudia reluctantly agreed.

"Gold... I see gold..." Sonya purred. She smirked as she narrowed her eyes proud and happy at getting her way, and seeing the results that came from it.

I didn't answer, I just ran to get more shovels.

Everyone except Natalie hurriedly dug around the surface of the initial hole, carefully removing the layers of dirt, one by one, as we made out the shape. The more we dug the more we realized that the surface underneath was a large slab of smooth metal. A very beautiful piece of metal, silver with gilded bronze and gold. The filigree lines continued towards a focal point, so we started digging towards that middle point. Upon finding it, we discovered that at the center we were uncovering was two peculiar six point stars, made of clockwork, and appeared to be made for one to roll into another, like a wheel made of brass, bronze and gold. And despite not being cleaned or polished in multiple millennia, was shining in full luster without any sign of oxidation of any kind in over two thousand years.

"Whoa..." Sonya admonished, staring at the insignia, "It's one of those goth things" she breathed with ignorant amazement.

Claudia sighed at the comment.

"Pentagram, it's called a pentagram Sonya, and the word you're looking for is pagan, not goth. But not even is it truly pagan, and that's not a pentagram, it has six points, pentagrams have five. But this is neither... this symbol is originally of the Judeo-Christian faiths. This symbol dates back all the way to the original Jerusalem in the days of King Sol..." Claudia began to explain, making the hand gestures an academic normally does when they are speaking about something they are interested in.

"Whoa, don't care" Sonya cut her off with a dismissive wave and classic 'talk to the hand' gesture.

Kayla certainly seemed to care, as she started muttering to herself as she stood over it, carefully feeling the golden clockwork gears as she admired the symbolic wheel.

"Oh this is so sweet... it's the seal of King Solomon... just like in dad's bedtime stories... There's the seven layers... and the nine circles... and here at the center is the cross... that's us... Oh! Oh this is so cool... this is it..." Kayla gushed.

Claudia leaned in, being coy but polite as she put her hands on her knees and bent over, "This is what, Kayla? What does this mean?" she encouraged the happy 19 year old to start gushing information.

Kayla shook her head, "I don't know... I just... my favorite bedtime stories... fables... tales... I don't know... it's just...this is totally wicked cool!" Kayla stood up and made a little happy dance, stamping her feet as she coiled her hands in. "Oh this is awesome!"

She was off in her world, we would be getting no answers from her.

"Wh... what do we do?" Natalie stammered, slightly scared.

"What is the matter with you? You've been spooked all evening!" I asked, noticing Natalie was shaking like a leaf.

"Oh I don't know, take your pick... a perfectly sparkling gold clockwork seal unearthed after thousands of years under the cover of darkness in a massive university laboratory. Deliberately defying explicit orders of an all-encompassing weapon's company. Or the fact that there's clearly a metal structure here that no one can detect... What's to be afraid of?" Natalie retorted shrugging and giving a small, very nervous giggle as she continued to shirk backwards slowly. She glanced up at the room and immediately looked even more nervous as she practically jumped. We all glanced skyward to see something we certainly don't remember being in this laboratory before now clearly focused on us.

Cameras, many, many cameras, each of them with that little telltale logo of the Silverlight Corporation.

Ok, she had a point.

We all looked at each other, and pondered our position. Kayla and I were frozen with the same "busted" look on our face, lips pursed as we looked to each other.

Sonya sighed, looked at the cameras, looked at the wheel and the seal that was clearly built to allow it to roll into, and nodded to herself.

Natalie shivered in a nervous state of panic, just hoping we wouldn't mess with anything more.

Claudia looked at me, as we realized how bad this looked.

"I'm good for the night" I said with an uneasy smile and bowing away from the clockwork device in the floor, my palms outstretched to show I was washing my hands of the matter.

"Me too" Claudia added

"Agreed" Natalie stated.

"Uh huh" Sonya nodded.

"IMA GONNA TURN IT!" Kayla said in her deepest voice possible, as she thrust her hand into the dial of the symbol and rolled the clockwork pieces to click into place.

"OH... WHY WOULD YOU DO THAT!?" Claudia shouted, completely at a loss for all explanation as she turned to Kayla.

Kayla put out her fist in front of her triumphantly, grabbing onto her upper arm and assuming a proud pose. "Because true courage is doing right, when all others have done wrong!"

"But that was wrong… as a matter of fact, this whole thing was wrong. You said it yourself we weren't supposed to be messing with it, and you turned the device!" Claudia explained, still holding her palms up before her in in complete disbelief.

"Oh…" Kayla realized, placing a finger to her lip and tilting her head as the floor began to rumble. She jumped, leaping towards Claudia for support as the ground below us rocked with an earthquake like force.

"I immediately regret this decision!" Kayla shouted to the exasperated Claudia as we all bolted in every direction away from the site. As I dashed I glanced up to see the red lights on the security cameras click on, as I felt the swell of something coming up out of the former seabed rock below. The ground beneath me began to lift as I made my best speed for the periphery, but as I felt myself being lifted my dash became a leap as I barely made it off the edge of the site lines before a rapid and heavy force came shooting out of the ground towards the dome shaped vaulted ceiling, knocking out the power generator on the overhead lights in the process…

Leaving us in total darkness.

"AHHH!" Natalie screamed in the pitch black.

"Shush! That's me!" I explained as I accidently touched her while fumbling for the light switch.

"I'm afeared!" Kayla shouted, resorting to cuteness to protect her from danger.

I could hear a hard smack followed by Sonya's extremely perturbed tone, followed by a very steady stream of obscenity. After a moment of cursing she recuperated long enough to start scolding the rest of us, "Someone turn on some friggin lights!" she ordered, as I saw the outline of her rub the back of her head.

"Oh god girls, really… ok… I got the lights." Claudia stated with exasperation and a singing tone as the backup overhead lighting flickered on.

"Oh…" Claudia gasped, at a loss for words as she turned around. We all had similar responses as we discovered what was hiding in the sands all this time.

Before us, floating around a foot off the ground, hovering above a sunken portion of earth without sound, without any form of emission, just floating, was a small island. Around fifty feet in circumference, give or take a few feet here or there to make up for the jagged and natural looking cliff face edge, the island levitated over the displaced sand around it, that filled in to a deep funnel shaped depression below it. On top of this island, there wait a single structure. Around a story and a half tall, domed, with Romanesque columns lining its front entrance. The building itself was a dome, made not of stone or any such period make… but of a gleaming metallic compound. The rim of every silver hexagon was a gold gilded band, made with a brass filigree that shimmered without any patina… it was beautiful, impossible… but right in front of us. Had I not seen it myself, I'd have doubted myself too.

It looked almost like a temple… or tomb.

"W… what is that!?" Natalie shouted, pointing at the floating island, afraid to move closer to it as we gawked and stared.

"I…" Claudia attempted to describe it, but failed as she lacked the words that accurately described the completely impossible phenomenon that lay before us.

"That's… this… no… no way…" Kayla gasped, still externalizing her mental conversation.

"I think we found your power source." Sonya stated the obvious, pointing at the levitating island.

"This… is… awesome…" I stated excitedly, finding I was the only one brave enough to walk closer to the edge of the site.

"Vivian… what are you doing?" Claudia worried for me, reaching out to stop me from getting closer.

I turned around to look at her, my eyes wide with excitement. "Don't you want to go? To see what this is and answer all those nagging questions? This is it Claudia… this is what they were after! Look at it, this is completely fantastic!"

Claudia shook her head, concerned and nervous that she was in for much more than she had bargained for. But I was committed, we went this far, it would be wrong not to see this through to the end.

"Won't anyone else go with me? Sonya I know you wanted to see what was down here, now let's go and get those answers!" I tried to encourage, but she stepped away, providing a small amount of comfort to Natalie who continued to maintain maximum distance from the floating platform-like island.

"Kayla?" I asked, seeking some sort of company.

She snapped out of her daze as she shook her head, blinking and focusing on me.

"This… yes! I need to see more of this… Vivian… do you know what this is!?" She said as she skipped closer to the edge of the line between the solid ground and the sands at the edge of the site.

There was a collective look of no. Followed by a series of stares at Kayla.

She fell back on cuteness to avoid us getting to upset at her for withholding information. Taking her black and white arm-sock covered hands and poking her index fingers at each other as she raised her pitch and continued explaining. "Vivian… when I was little… dad used to tell me stories. He told me of fantastic places with floating islands that could hold cities, beautiful kingdoms and palaces just beyond human reach… this is exactly as he described. His stories were all I had to go on for most of my life… to see it in front of me…" She turned back to look at me, her blue eyes shined as she grinned a most curious grin.

"It's another matter entirely, the allure is without question. I'm going."

I looked out at the gap between where I stood and where the beginning of the hovering island's edge began. It was barely a two foot gap, I could make it with a little leap.

For all my life, I've dreamed of experiencing something fantastic, outside the normal realm… now it was right in front of me, there was no way I was passing this up.

"Claudia… do we have any flashlights or things here?" I asked, turning back to her. She looked to the dome structure then back to me. Snapping out of her concern in order to help me.

"Yes… yes. Vivian, if you're going in, you're going to need some assistance. I…" She pondered as she began to pace back to the equipment lockers on the far wall, "I'll set up monitoring! We'll set you and Kayla up with the remote cameras we used in the *Arkay* expedition, I'll keep watch at the computer here and record what I can!" She said as she began to collect equipment from the locker, grabbing out a pair of equipment harnesses and testing the walkie-talkies on each shoulder. I could tell she was feeling a little better about not going with me by helping, and she's right… we're archeologists, we need to record all we can of this.

"W-what will we do?" Natalie asked, getting closer to talk to Kayla and I, but not close enough to near the edge. Sonya stayed with her, obviously a little nervous about all this.

"Stay with Claudia, help her with whatever she needs to do at the computers." I instructed. The two cheerleaders nodded, happy to be given an out of the situation.

Claudia came back, to me, handing off the harnesses to Kayla and I. "Ok… now I've got the camera, walkie-talkie, and there should be a few things left in there you hopefully won't need, like carabineers and flares…" She instructed as we snapped on the harnesses, putting a black strap across both shoulders and clipping the waist belt tight. I turned on my flashlight on my left shoulder, and the radio on my right.

I helped Kayla get hers on over the silly flared shoulder pieces of her dress.

I turned back to Claudia as I realized she was still fussing, "Now I'll want you to keep reporting in regularly, I'm going to do my best to keep an eye on you and the minute you see something you don't like you just come right back here Vivian. Don't you dare get yourself hurt or…" her tone got more and more worried as I halted the concerned rant by dropping my hands on her shoulders and making her meet me eye to eye.

"We're good." I said stared Claudia, smiling as I made my nose and forehead wrinkle, my smile made her smile as I tilted my head and tucked my lips into one corner to make a funny face.

Claudia sighed, still worried for me, reaching over and straightening out my harness before turning on the camera right below the flashlight. She then motioned for Natalie and Sonya to join her as she walked over to the holographic computer. "Ok, so Kayla and Vivian are going inside, we can keep track of them through this. See Kayla's camera on this screen and Vivian's here? And we'll keep in touch on the walkie-talkie." She said as she picked up one of the mentioned devices on the computer desk. Natalie and Sonya nodded and took a seat on folding chairs around Claudia's seat. Claudia nodded to me as Kayla and I stood at the edge of the long sloping gap between the lab and the floating island…

It's time.

Kayla and I gave one more look to each other, clenched our fists, and steeled our gaze…

And leapt across the gap.

Chapter Two

Kingsport Archeology Laboratory

The floating island

Kingsport, Maryland

United States of America, Earth

August 16th, 2011

12:24 AM

The Journal of Vivian Maybell

After that initial moment of landing, I realized I had been holding my breath. I don't know what I expected when I set foot on this mysterious island, but what experienced was like any other form of ground. It didn't rock, it didn't waver when we landed… it just stayed, like it was supposed to be there.

I looked to Kayla and she glanced back to me, we were obviously on a similar line of thought as we walked to the entryway of the building, the archway, with a large gilded door bearing King Solomon's Seal.

"Kayla, look at this!" I said, seeing amazing glyphs along the exterior of the seal. I motioned her over as Claudia and her group looked up from the computer.

Kayla squinted as she tried to make out the markings on the door. "So how do we open it?" She asked me.

"Don't you want to know what it says first?" I asked. Kayla didn't seem particularly interested.

Claudia walked over to help.

"Vivian, what kind of runes are those? Are those any kind you recognize?" She asked, trying to prompt my memory. I have a love of language, and studying dead and ancient languages has been a personal pastime to my studies.

"I'm looking at the runes now… these aren't runes though, these are glyphs." I said as I reached out and put my hand on some of the text, feeling the embossed edge of the metalworking, "It's interesting, the glyphs are spaced to clearly have a defined grammar… so it's almost… modern. Modern English prose but… but the shape, the styling… I want to say Greek but with heavy elements of Norse runes with a very strong hint of Sumerian script. It's…" I struggled to come up with a way to say it that didn't sound crazy.

"It's like an underlying precursor to all of them. Every part of this appears almost like a protolanguage, but the way they are spaced denotes dictation… Claudia… I think we may be looking at an ancient developed language. But not one I've ever seen before." I said finally, turning around.

Kayla continued to look around other areas while I talked, looking for another entrance to the building, but found something worth my attention as she did, "Hey! Vivian! Here!" She shouted as she motioned for me from the far side of the Romanesque column to the right of the entrance. I quickly ran around to see what she was pointing at, to discover some etchings into the metal… made in Latin… likely made by explorers past.

"I don't think we were the first people here." Kayla noted as she pointed to the scrawling. Now Latin… that was something I could read, even if it was partially worn off.

I bent down to read off what I could, "By sealing her away… we seal away the three…" I started, as Natalie and Sonya came closer to listen. "It's all scratched off and messed with… it probably eroded in time. Most of this text is unintelligible." I said with a sigh.

Kayla thought about it for a moment, and looked at the gilded structure.

"How did it erode if none of the other metals are touched? More likely someone buffed it out." She said with a raised pitch of curiosity. She narrowed her eyes as she thought about it. "Vivi look for tool marks…"

I did as she instructed as I put my hand on the worn out space… sure enough there was markings… circular markings overlapping… like… someone buffed it out with a circular tool. Like, modern power tool markings.

Now that, opened up more questions than answers…

There was a bit of text at the bottom I could read, "Should ever this gate be opened, what was once three shall become one again, and when that day comes…" I stopped, realizing what was written, "We shall be welcome in Valhalla no longer."

Once again we all became quiet.

This was surreal.

"Guys… I don't think we're dealing with a normal ancient ruin…" I said aloud.

I heard Claudia, Sonya, and Kayla sigh.

"So what tipped you off?" Sonya asked with a crass tone. "No, really, because I'm completely taken aback here… was it the floating temple part of the gleaming metal island?"

I turned back and shot her a look. She raised her eyebrows at me.

"Vivian… I think you should come back off the thing, we need to call Silverlight and have a professional team come down and investigate." Claudia cautioned, motioning for me to come back to her.

"I, I want to check out a couple more things." I said as I stood back at the doorway, placing my hand on the center of the seal and looking upward, just wondering what sort of civilization this was from. Claudia put her hands on her hips, I tried to avoid her eyes to pretend like I didn't see her worrying.

As I laid my hand on it, the seal began to glow. The ring of text along the edge of the seal illuminated and projected a holographic image of itself forward, then rotated once before joining to form a square projected screen, a perfectly 2D floating holographic screen, just like our new computers.

Just like our new computers.

I looked around to the side of the image to see it was just flat. On the rectangular orange glowing screen I saw a line of black text of the strange runes. They read like this:

"Vivian…" Claudia beckoned sharply this time, growing more concerned for me as she waved her hand, "I'm sorry, Rosier, and her temple will have to wait. This is getting far too dangerous, now please… come… *back*." Claudia really emphasized her last words, it's as close to real anger I've ever seen her. She must have been really worried, I should have listened.

But as she spoke the first three words, the screen changed.

Immediately after, the wheel of the seal began to turn, as the door slid upward, revealing a pitch black darkness within.

Kayla immediately perked up as the door opened, seeing it slide up and taking advantage of the moment. She ran for the interior, but I was in the way, so regardless of if I wanted too, I was pushed inside.

No sooner had we went in, the door slammed shut behind us, leaving Kayla and I in the dark…

Alone.

I looked around in the darkness, as I struggled to turn back on my flashlight, panicked, I had reached up the first time and flicked it off instead of on, now I can't seem to find the switch.

The radio crackled of my walkie-talkie on my shoulder, "Vivian! Vivian can you hear me!?" Claudia's voice was clearly in distress as she made her call.

I flicked on the flashlight then held down the talk button, "Yeah, I can hear you Claudia. I just got light in here I'm trying to figure out where I am. "

I panned the light around… finding anything but what I expected to see.

I was expecting hallways, I was expecting possibly altars or perhaps rows of lit torches and what have you. But what I got instead was something else entirely. I saw countertop like structures along the wall with a waist high top slope that curved down in 45 degrees, almost like the same angle a writing desk would rest. The interior dome seemed to be split into two large antechambers, the one we were in, and a dividing wall at the middle point. I went to walk over to Kayla, who was pressing on parts of the dividing barrier wall, when I stubbed my toe hard on a circular metal dais about waist high. I cursed and grabbed my leg as I looked over to Kayla, who found a small alcove on the wall that she could rest her hand within.

"Don't fiddle with stuff Kayla, we're not messing with anything! We're just finding a way out and leaving!" I ordered to Kayla, who glanced back at me with a shrug.

"Hey you were all 'let's explore this' now you don't want to? C'mon Vivian, we got this far let's see how this goes. Look I'm starting to figure this out." Kayla said as she pressed her hand down on the alcove she was toying with. There was a hum of power starting up through the dome. Within an instant Claudia started radioing me.

"Vivian what are you doing in there?" She demanded, "The outside of the dome just lit up. It's glowing orange and blue around the edge of it, doesn't look like anything dangerous but it doesn't look like something you should be fiddling with, now get out of there."

Inside, Kayla and I were taking a momentary mental breather to just comprehend what was going on inside the structure, because after Kayla turned the power on…

The dome came alive…

Overhead lighting chimed in, filling the interior darkness with a bright white light. Holographic consoles with full keyboards projected all over from each of the sloped structures as more data began to stream through the alcoves beside them. This wasn't a ruin…

This was an outpost.

Computers… from two thousand years ago.

"Kayla… do you know what any of this…" I began.

"No." She cut me off as she shook her head, backing up to me.

The circular dais at the center of the room lit up, turning our focus as it displayed a circular holo image, two white feathered wings spread out over the circle as seven stars flew in to complete a start-up graphic. After the symbol hung there a moment it switched over to an image. We saw earth… with two other bodies rotating around it, I thought at first it was the moon, but as I looked at it, that wasn't what it seemed to be displaying. In orbit around it, nine rings of equal size almost stacked on top of each other rotated on one side, while on the other seven symbols like a crescent moon radiated out away from the planet. Around the image of earth an overlay of some kind of energy seemed to wrap the entire planet. More of this alien text appeared all over the edges of the image, likely providing data to the images shown, if only I could have understood it then.

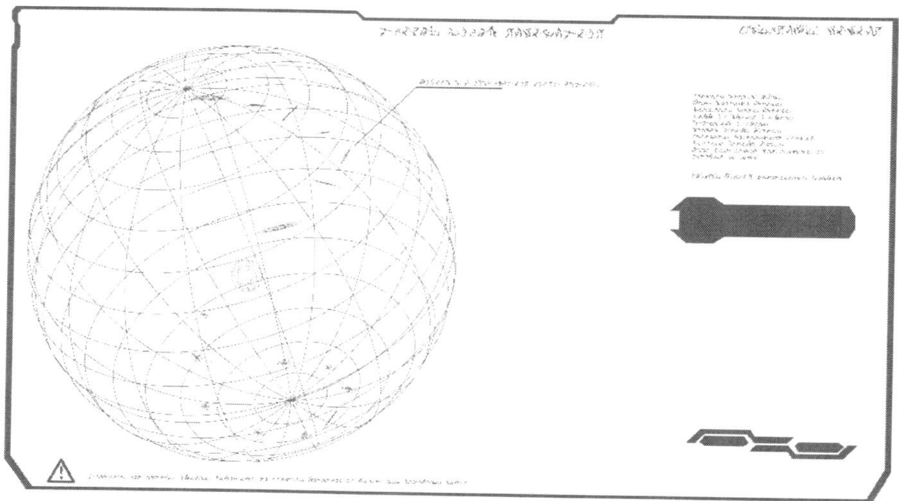

"Claudia, are you seeing this?" I asked into the radio.

"Yeah Vivian… not believing it, but I'm seeing it." She replied.

Two large buttons, swoops of light that appeared like arrows rested at the bottom of the display. Kayla leaned over, letting her hair drape over one shoulder and the side of her face as she tested a few buttons on the bottom, pressing on the arrow bars. As she did, the image shifted, the image in turn shifted to another item entirely.

This image was very different, the image was that of a woman… but not a human woman. She lay at rest, upright, hands held outstretched, possibly in suspended animation, or dead. She was beautiful. Humanlike in general shape with a slender nose and shallow chin to her facial features, and a very serene expression as she rest. Her image was in orange like the rest of the monochromatic holo-display, but I could tell she had long dark hair that trailed down her back with short front bangs. Her head had two small horns that protruded from the top right above the hairline, her ears were long, and pointed. On her hands she possessed clawed tips that had no fingertip, just a single continuous layer of very smooth skin, five fingers, just like mine. I raised my own hand to compare. The woman's figure was very exaggerated, her feminine features very pronounced with a large bust and hip to waist ratio, her feet had the same clawed ends as her hands, just toes, formed to be a little more ferocious. The most striking feature of all though, was the tail. A long whip-like tail, with an arrow point on the end. Around four feet long, it trailed down from the end of the spine.

That's not human.

"Claudia…" I said in almost a gasp as I realized I might be looking at the member of the race that built this ruin. This wasn't a human structure, that wasn't a human being… This… I realized what I was saying to myself as I was saying it. It was impossible, there was no way. I mean, I've often dreamed of meeting extraterrestrial life, of seeing things and people from lands far removed from here… but it was always a dream.

Just a dream, away, removed.

Where it can't hurt you.

"Vivian I see it." Claudia reported. "Now, I'm going to say this one more time..." She geared up.

"Get. Out. Of. There."

I looked to Kayla, "We really should get out of here." I said to her, Kayla nodded, now fully as scared of this place as I was.

"Ok..." Kayla said, agreeing. "How?"

Good point, I had to come up with a way.

I looked at the buttons below the dais, and tried to extrapolate a plan.

"Ok... so you found a control to turn on the lights and the systems, so there must be a control to operate the door. Help me look! Kayla, I know you can figure this out, I'll start looking here as you look around the room, we'll find something." I ordered, trying to take charge of the situation.

"Hey." Natalie radioed to us, "We're trying to find a way to get you out from out here, I'm on the island, I'll try working on something through the door."

I pressed down the button, "Thanks Nat, I'll let you know if we have any progress on this end."

Kayla started looking at controls around the door while I worked on the panel at the dais. There was something about the image of the woman that I found alluring... something that seemed to capture my gaze and wouldn't let it go. I kept looking back to her, letting that image just flicker and stand. I wanted to know more about her, what was she like, what about her civilization? Were there more? Was the history channel right and we're all from aliens? Probably not, but it was an entertaining thought. There were so many clichés running through my mind I couldn't help but let my ADD wander.

I pressed one of the buttons to the side of the arrow bars. Another box appeared on the screen, I was getting somewhere.

Now, that looked like a ton of text that had to do with a decision. Perhaps that decision was 'would you like to stop all this nonsense and go outside now?' but… probably not. Two boxes appeared where my hand was working, one with a… squiggly… and the other with… another squiggly. I went with my gut and pressed the left squiggly, hoping that would just get me out of this menu so I can do something else. The box went back to a single word for several seconds as the outline around the woman ebbed in light, after a moment it went back to the monitor of her… but this time it had much more data to it. A pulse and heart-rate monitor in the top left of the image. Both read zero, or what I assumed to be zero. A small amorphous blob seemed to rest in the midsection of the woman now, possibly a focus point of some kind?

"Vivian, how are you doing over there?" Kayla asked me, bent over and trying to fiddle with the door.

"I'm…" I looked at all the things I had messed with in a short time. "I'm doing fine… I think I'm done looking at this thing, I'm going to go do something else now..." I said as I stepped away to the dividing wall at the center of the room. Perhaps I could find something here, after all, this is where Kayla found the light-switch. Nervous, and my mind wandering, I started to fiddle with the console Kayla used to turn on the lights as I started to sing to myself to pass the time.

~♪" Blue canary in the outlet by the light switch, who watches over you! Make a little birdhouse in your soul…"♫~ I sang to myself, it comforted me as I nervously pressed buttons on the panel.

With a rush of air, a door opened, but not the door I wanted.

The dividing wall between us and the second antechamber was now open. Kayla looked back over to me with a narrowed gaze. I shrugged my shoulders.

"Vivian…" Kayla began, leaning around the corner before she could scold me to look into the next room out of curiosity.

I heard Claudia's voice on the radio, "What was that, we heard a sound Vivian, is everything ok in there?"

Kayla walked to the open doorway and motioned me to join her, Kayla answered for me, "Vivian's going to have to call you back." She said as she cut the line.

"What are you doing?" I asked Kayla, as she waved at me faster and pointed into the next room. I sighed as I trotted up to the door and glanced around the corner…

And there she was.

The woman, the creature, was at rest, held upright in place on the far wall. On the wall opposite her rest a beautiful and ornate mirror, the gilded mirror looked ancient, actually out of place with the advanced technology around her. She seemed to be locked in permanent stasis of some kind. She floated just off the ground, with a bright light below and above her, radiating against her dark blue skin. She wore a black jumpsuit that almost resembled a modern wetsuit, covering her from the neck to her ankles and wrists. Over the right breast on the lapel, another symbol, a red hexagon with a white four point star rest. Yet another piece of a story I've not yet come to understand.

"Oh…" I gasped, stepping into the room with an empowered and all-encompassing feeling of curiosity and elation as I found myself going towards her. It… she… was real… it's another life-form, away from humankind. A sentient, sapient, being, kept here in some type of suspended animation. I wanted to meet her, I wanted to speak with her, understand her… this was exactly what I wanted. This was exactly the type of thing I've always dreamed of… to see a glimpse of a world beyond mine. To step away from the ordinary and experience something new… I realized it was dangerous to go close…

But there was something that drew me towards her…

The allure was incredible.

"Vivian…" Claudia radioed, I cut her off.

"Claudia, Natalie, everyone get back to the computer! You have to see this! Look at my camera feed!" I ordered as I stepped closer, Kayla hid along the edge of the doorframe.

I was now standing almost alongside her. Just seeing the being resting there, in a complete state of serenity. A woman of unknown race and origin, trapped in permanent sleep like a fairy tale…

But this wasn't a fairy tale… this is modern life.

"Oh… my…" Natalie breathed into the radio as they picked up what I was seeing.

"What is it?" Sonya asked.

I smiled as I stood in front of the woman. "It's…" I began as I walked around to look behind her, seeing something I didn't witness in the holographic feed. On the woman's back, she had two small wings about a foot and a half in length, shaped like an angular bat wing. They jutted out between the shoulder blades and kept at a 45 degree angle. It was only then did I realize what she was.

"A Succubus." I concluded. Using my love of myth and folklore to put words to what I was seeing.

"The 16th century demon?" Claudia asked. Kayla had more to say as she stared from the door.

"Yes… my dad used to tell stories of them, the succubus and its male counterpart, the incubus, are very strong, and had some surprises to them that made you want to stay at a safe distance… this creature matches his description of them almost perfectly…" Kayla still didn't want to go into the room. I turned around to question Kayla more, when I glanced across the mirror opposite me, a hint of movement caught my eye.

Kayla stopped as I stiffened at the sight, the woman's tail had begun to curl.

I turned quickly as I checked on the actual being when the arrow point tail shot forward and stabbed me! I groaned as the sharp arrow point end dove right into my gut through my grey T-Shirt. I gasped in horror and pain as I watched a dark red stain creep out around the stab site. Suddenly the tail went taught, as I began to feel a new sensation…

Pressure.

"Unn..." I moaned in discomfort as the pain began to subside, I reached for the tail to try and pull it out of me, but as I did I found my hands stopping before I could yank it. The pain was gone now, and in its stead, the feeling began to switch over to being very… very, good. I… I didn't have the ability to stop whatever was happening, every part of me wanted to keep going where I was. I couldn't stop! "…help…" I eked out weakly, my voice almost a whisper.

But Kayla just watched. She held onto the door frame, peeking out around the corner…

And watched me.

I could only glance down to observe as I looked at the spot of skin exposed from the stab wound, expecting to see blood but instead found only my skin… as I watched it discolor to blue.

The skin around the wound became darker and darker as the color began to spread out around the site. The feeling was becoming better as it continued, not painful but wanted, I wasn't sure if I was ok with that. I reached down and lifted up my shirt a little to see that the blue color had taken over most of my belly and was moving outward across my body. I began to feel tingling sensations as it moved across me. I felt the tingling speed up as it shot down my legs, I heard the sound of my bones popping as I watched my hips begin to widen, seeing more dark blue skin emerge as my jeans were forced a little further down. It was only then as I began to feel a most incredible sensation. A feeling of becoming lighter… like something inside me was going away! I attempted to gasp as I realized what was occurring! Glancing back to Kayla, she was as fascinated as I was curious…

So we both sat back to watch my transformation.

I heard the sound of my bones beginning to snap and pop, you would think that would be painful but instead I found it very desirable, like every part of my brain was telling me this was a good thing. Something in this transformation must be messing with my head because every part of my mind wanted nothing more than this to continue. I felt a heavy pressure in my feet as they began stretching, pushing on the limits of my sneakers. I reached up one foot, being careful not to tug on the tail still imbedded in me as I threw off my first shoe, as I did, my toes came ripping through my socks, as new dark blue feet appeared, equipped with sharp claw like toes. Just like the woman, the claws had no nail, just solid skin forming a point. As I touched my toes, I felt the ends were still sharp… It was curious… but I realized…

I was becoming like her.

I didn't have time to remove the other shoe as my foot came ripping through the material. I just kicked off the rest as my pants went tight from my changing form underneath. My waist cinched in as I felt the tingling moving up. I knew it was transforming my upper body now. I felt a powerful bit of pressure on my lower back right before a sharp point ruptured from the base of my spine, as an arrow pointed, dark blue and whip-like tail came shooting out, whipping in the space behind me as it did. The tingling moved up to my chest as I watched my shirt strain as my bust started gaining considerable size as I felt hard pressure on my back, as I heard the ripping of my grey T-shirt as two small bat-like wings emerged and started to flex and shimmer against the overhead light.

I put forward my right hand as I watched the color slide down, as it did I noticed my hairs disappeared from my skin, making the feeling very smooth. My fingers started to stretch as the nails disappeared and the ends of each finger became pointed sharply. I realized now that only one part of me remained unchanged as I quickly began to panic once more.

Like someone drowning at open sea I struggled to crane my neck away in futility. As the color moved up my chin I could feel my teeth begin to tingle, fangs were coming, I knew it. I thought to myself. "What will happen to me? Is this the last sentient thought I will have? Will I become a feral creature, killing and murdering? How is this even happening? Will Dr. Agnew still give me semester credit?" All of these questions unnecessary yet comforting in some strange way came flooding inward as my fangs grew in, they provided the familiar against the new as my ears grew pointed and long as my hair cascaded down my back, clattering the pen I had stuck in my ponytail against the metal floor, the sound of it falling helped me cling to humanity as my eyes became yellow and serpentine, and two black horns sprouted from my head. At the very end of the process, I looked down to see a large knot travelling down the tail, I felt a small bit of pain as the knot pushed open more of my wound, as it forced its way inside me.

And then she released me, the tail immediately went limp and my wound sealed closed. I stumbled back a couple steps in quick recoil, fluttering my wings as I did. I realized that I had been transformed into her image, the form of a Succubus…

A demon.

I realized I was holding my breath, and gasped quickly, exposing my teeth as I leaned. Kayla immediately jumped backwards and screamed, scared of me and my jerky motion. I turned quickly and shouted back, waving my hands.

"NO! Kayla! Kayla! It's ok!" I shouted to her as she turned and shouted back.

"Then why did you make the evil monster 'ahhh' sound when you finished monsterfying!" She shouted at me, panicking as she threw her arm sock covered hands out to the side and shouted.

"I didn't mean to when I finished monsterfying! I was holding my…" I tried to counter but she was still hysterical and yelling.

"Oh my gosh Vivian you got turned into a demon lady!" Kayla exclaimed.

"I know! Stop yelling at me!" I shouted back, flaring out my wings and making my tail stand on end. Ending our argument with both of us staring at once another in silence. Kayla hid back behind the doorframe, peeking out with a cute worried stare as she poked her head out into the hall just enough to keep two eyes on me.

She finally built up enough courage to ask, "Are you ...*sure* you're not evil?" she asked with a worried gaze.

I looked over at myself in the mirror. Whoa, that's a sight to behold. To see yourself after you've left your humanity behind. I can tell you I wasn't really ready for it.

I walked over to the mirror, checking myself out. I felt really light as I took a step, like nothing weighed anything, clothing, the equipment harness, nothing, not even me. I... well... my face shape looked like me still, I could recognize me, but there were modifications. Everything looked a little more even, and my nose was a little better formed and looked a little cuter, actually most of me was made prettier, my hair that grew in was a light white, with my fire red tips left over from my dyed hair, it flowed down my back with an almost perfect wave, I pushed aside a lock over my eye with a blast of air.

I played with myself a moment by poking at my horns, and fluttering my wings, hee... I have wings, how is one supposed to react to this? I flicked my tail... I have a tail too! As I made a pleased smile from this my ears flicked up and down quickly in a natural motion. I surprised myself at this and perked up, making my ears flip up higher. I have flippy ears too!

I put my hands on my now completely curvy hips as I looked at my very exaggerated female figure in the mirror. I smiled to myself, showing my fangs... I realized...

This might seriously be ok...

"I don't think I'm evil... I still feel like me!" I shouted over to Kayla. I took one finger and poked my stomach, realizing my skin continued to give way, pressing further and further in as I kept applying pressure. I kept going until I felt the skin touch the skin on my back... I... don't think I have anything in me anymore... I'm... hollow. I pressed quickly.

As I did, I made a squeaking sound.

I surprised myself, fluttering my wings.

"And…" I added, "I'm pretty sure evil doesn't squeak!" I shouted to Kayla.

"That's just what evil wants you to think!" Kayla shot back.

"Quit being a butt, we still need to get out of here… I figured out what this room is for! It's the lady demonizing room!" I reported back.

"Vivian… is that you?" Claudia asked me over the radio as Kayla stepped into the room.

"Yeppers. All 100% grade A me." I answered, "I mean look at me!" I was kind of jazzed on the moment. I realize that I was just transformed into a monster, but… honestly every nerdy bone… hehe, well I guess not bone but… you know. I liked it, I really liked it.

"Claudia this is great!" I noted, "Check it out I am all light and I feel all strong and stuff, look at me go, a cha, cha, cha, cha, cha-cha!" I started making some smooth karate moves into the surrounding area, turning to my left to make a sweet power kick when…

I realized how close I was to the mirror.

My foot went right on through.

The mirror, being true to mirror-dom, shattered.

"Ooooooo…." I groaned, seeing the pieces of the mirror continue to break as they fell off the frame onto the floor.

Kayla slapped her hand on her forehead. "Yep… confirmed, demon is still Vivian, repeat, demon is still Vivian." She reported into the radio.

I jutted forward my lower jaw as I scratched my head, "I sorry…" I apologized as I looked at the broken mirror all over the floor.

"Way to go Vivian…" Kayla scolded, "You managed to break the one ancient thing in the room, way to archeology."

"Oh way to rub it in." I complained, folding my arms and raising my little bat-like wings indignantly as I flicked my tail. Looking up and away from Kayla as she let slip a slightly pouting expression. I thoroughly enjoyed how expressive I could be with my new wings and tail.

I looked back at her as I caught her pouting, "Are you… jealous?" I asked. And watched her face flush as she shook her hair letting her bangs hide her eyes, "…no." She answered as she stepped back into the main room. I smiled coyly as I tiptoed after her.

"You are aren't you! You're totally jealous I'm a succubus now and you're not." I asked with an ever increasingly smug grin. She started working on another console around the door when I tickled her a bit, making her jump.

"Stop!" she shouted, "Ok maybe a little!" She admitted.

"Ha! I knew it!" I pointed at her, "See this is totally cool and you know it!" I put my hands on my hips and gave a swish of my tail to show how good I was feeling after the transformation. I mean, I just got supernatural up in here, this is a nerdy girl's dream come true and besides, woo! Look at me!

"Ok… but we still need to get out of here." Kayla reinforced.

"Ok, ok!" I waved at her, trying to calm down, "I'll help you, just give me a moment to think…" I said as I started focusing on the door. Kayla worked on making a wheel like hologram appear over the right side of the door.

"Ugh!" I grunted as I placed both hands on my stomach as my wings and tail whipped out involuntarily, I felt a horrible feeling in my gut that just wouldn't let go. And I don't mean that metaphorically, there was a literal grinding, bubbling sensation in my gut, like I had eaten something that didn't agree with me. Or as if something was moving within me. Oh yuck, yes it feels like something was moving inside me and it didn't feel good.

"Vivi you ok?" Kayla asked, worrying for me, I realized something as I glanced up to her… I could actually feel and understand her emotion. I could feel the genuine concern under her tone, I knew she was worried about me. I let my eyebrows relax with the realization as the pain came back with a vengeance. The feeling kept building as I felt a sharp pain, I doubled over and grabbed my stomach.

"uurk! Yep… Yeah, doin'… doin' great…" I lied obviously as I tried not to completely fall forward on the floor and throw up.

"You're not turning evil now and gonna eat me are you!?" Kayla worried.

"Stop with the eating people! Help me… ack!" I shouted back as another sharp pain popped up as I felt something seem to latch onto some part within me. Like something was climbing me. Oh, gross, what was that thing that went in me at the end!? I think it's the thing… oh please don't be the thing.

"Hang on! We're about to get out of here!" Kayla shouted as she hit the right sequence of buttons to open the door. She ran back over to me and grabbed my shoulders, lifting me under her arm and carrying me outside as I continued to feel that strange pain. As I lifted off the ground without trouble I realized how light I was now, I imagine the heaviest thing on my person now was my jeans, Kayla could carry me without trouble. She came running out of the gateway with me and leapt across the gap, bringing us safely out of the temple as she laid me down on the floor. I stared upward at the ceiling lights as the room started to spin. Something was really wrong and I didn't know what, I was starting to really get scared.

"Vivian!" Claudia shouted, running from the console over to me with Sonya and Natalie in tow. Natalie rushed over to the wall to grab the emergency first aid kit as I groaned and bent my left knee to help me turn to see Claudia approaching as she kneeled down to see me, I felt her hand on my forehead as she brushed aside some hair. She spoke, but I couldn't hear her. My eyes wanted to close but I fluttered them open, trying to focus on the people around me, but instead I could only feel the sensation within.

Moving, sliding, I felt something working its way up my back… from the inside. I could feel something lash forward following by the sensation of a larger mass dragging its way inside me. It was a horrifying thought, I didn't know how to deal with it, or what to do! I could feel it at my upper back, then at my shoulders, I started to choke as I felt it moving into my neck. I reached up for support, as Natalie started to undo her medical kit in attempt to check my vitals with the portable AED/Pulse Oxygen reader, Claudia looked at me with a very concerned and worried expression. I wish I could have said something to comfort her, but all I could do was choke.

Kayla shook her head as she looked down at me, trying to think of what to do. I felt whatever was harming me moving up, pressing further up my body… almost into my…

The room spun out of focus as it pressed into my head, I think I might have gasped or screamed, I don't know, I can't remember. The next thing I knew I felt the stretching and pressure sensations I experienced when I first changed. I felt my body starting to grow as my form became taller and taller. I looked at my right hand as a black fluid started to appear on my fingertips, moving outward to cover my hand. I looked down as my form shifted outward, my form flared, my feet clenched tight as they reformed into thick and heavy hooves. My wings started stretching further and further out, becoming longer and more angular.

This wasn't like the last change at all, none of this was welcome and none of it wanted, I felt pain as I was forced into changing more, I felt pressure as my growing body ripped through the equipment harness across my body, I struggled as I felt something slipping across my consciousness, inputting wants, desires, taking over. I glanced down once more as my body started to stand, my shirt started to rip as I saw my dark blue skin underneath. Small veins of black began to etch their way across my body in the open areas, as I lost more and more of myself. I looked down at my hands, now standing at around seven feet tall, flexing my fingers as I saw the black tar-like ichor begin to harden around my hands, Azazel's improvements have begun to set in.

Az-az-el? Where did that name come from!? What was happening!?

No! This isn't what I want… this isn't me! I tried to cry for help but the words wouldn't come. I felt my lips becoming fuller as my mouth smiled on its own accord. I stood up and… no! Ah… this was feeling better… I… I… could get used to this. I tilted my head as I let the changes continue, letting Vivian take a back seat to the action as I looked at my current prey. Four girls… all capable of becoming succubus, the succubae will make for a better minion than human beings, humans are far too fragile for my taste…

That one! The one with the turquoise hair! It's Gilden's daughter, I know it, I can feel his lineage flowing through her! Yes... she will make a nice addition. I flipped around my powerful tail and stabbed the small human as her friends ran scampering off in every direction. No matter, I will find them later. The young woman in the garish black and white outfit gasped as I lifted her up on my tail, like a stuck pig being lifted on a spit. She struggled as a light blue color began to wash over her, she was beginning to transform. I forced more of my power over this host, as I felt my face begin to shift, becoming smoother, more beautiful, with an angular face shape that just exuded my calm and serene grace...

She would soon become a succubus, one of my favorite races to make a minion of. If I am trapped on Rune Midguard I shall have to make use of them as much as possible until I can find more powerful stock.

Oh... for too long I have been kept at bay by the angels and demons, hounded by human investigators and cast aside into stasis... Oh Rosier... to think I no longer need you, I will miss you my beautiful Succubus, but this is a new world, and a new generation.

I pulled my near complete prey close to my face as I sneered.

"Did your father ever warn you about me, Miss Kayla Gilden?" I asked with my deep and purring tone as her left eye turned yellow, her turquoise dyed hair growing outward and longer showing off black roots as her body stretched and filled into the more sultry proportions of the succubus. Her hands and feet grew their claws as her wings and tail emerged. It would only be a matter of time until I could input some of myself into her, and then like this host, she shall become me. For now this small dose will have to do, I am back at square one once more.

"My father will get you..." Kayla promised as her horns emerged from her head.

I smiled.

"Oh... he certainly is welcome to try... but if Gabriel and his angels could not end me... what hope does the feeble race of humanity have to come against me?" I returned with a coy and toothy grin. Oh... for two thousand years I have been captive, and for longer than I remember I have been forced to do the bidding of those less worthy than I. Now I, Azazel, have returned upon this world. I will have my revenge on the fools who have trifled with me... and when chaos once again enters this plane...

I will return home once and for all.

Ah... Daniel Gilden and your Silverlight cult have my warmest regards, thank you, dear Gilden, for freeing me.

It is good to be back again.

Chapter Three

Kingsport University Verne Building of Earth Sciences

Kingsport University, Maryland

United States of America, Earth

The Journal of Claudia Brashear

August 16th, 2011

12:47 AM

Well, this evening has turned out differently from what I had expected. By now, I was hoping to be enjoying a nice warm bubble bath in my less than perfect graduate dorm room. I had even prepared my evening incense sticks for such the occasion, first lavender to calm the senses, then sandalwood to unwind, and finally a bit of cinnamon, I know that cinnamon normally awakens you but to me it puts me out like none other. What a wonderful evening after working through the dirt and lifting that horrifically heavy ground penetrating radar.

But tonight's warm bath will not be had tonight, no, tonight we will be running screaming from my quirky counterpart who has managed to make a real monster out of herself.

Literally.

Now, being a woman of science I do not believe in such things as monsters, ghosts and what have you, but in that very same breath, I must believe what occurs directly in front of me. And well… the level of evidence that what is occurring right now is… very hard to dismiss, so I am actually quite certain Vivian has become a blue skinned, bat winged, creature. I'm certain she has now converted Kayla, and now the two of them are in pursuit to do the very same to us.

That's something definitely not in the course description for our archeology lab.

As we ran I received a hard tap on my shoulder from one of the two cheerleaders I was dragging along with me. Sonya. I turned to see that the two of them were very much out of breath, their pale skin showing the bright red lines of exhaustion from a mere jog from a couple hundred feet, so I turned a corner with them and came to a stop. We had bolted from the laboratory to attempt to get out of the building in a way that wouldn't put us past the monstrous Vivian and the recently captured Kayla, but where would that get us? The building is surrounded with open flat ground, and I have a feeling a winged creature would have a serious advantage on us in such a situation.

"Really? Are we tired already?" I asked in an honest mix of panic and disbelief. I knew Americans weren't really in the best of shape but honestly girls, really? This is life and death. They wouldn't hold up for long in Mumbai, that's for certain. Both of the supposed to be fit members of the cheerleading team were doubled over against the large plate glass windows that made up our second story exterior.

"Screw… you…" Sonya insulted as she dropped forward, putting her hands on her knees as she glared up at me, clearly still out of breath.

"At least it can't get much worse than this." Natalie gasped, out of breath as everyone took a moment of respite from the oncoming demon women. I just shook my head.

"You realize that such a phrase usually yields some sort of…" I began. Yes, I may be a woman of sound science, but that does not mean I'm not a little bit superstitious. What can I say though? I was raised in a traditional Indian family. My mother was certain that mysterious sometimes transparent people known as Jinn caused her toaster to stop functioning, how does one shake an upbringing like that?

I do digress, because no sooner had I begun to explain the reasons why one should not make absolute statements, the lights went out across the entire building.

"They cut the power." Natalie nervously acknowledged as she backed up against the wall.

Sonya glanced at the frightened Natalie, and in a selfish spat turned her own fear into unnecessary rage at her compatriot. "What do you mean *they* cut the power? They're like animals woman!"

I heard a scream across the building at night… the distinct cry of Vivian shouting no…

She was hurting… we needed to do something to help her, fast.

"Enough!" I stopped the squabble before it could start, taking charge. "If we have any hope of getting out of here we have got to make our way down to the south entrance. That should simply be another left and straight shot from there. With any luck, Vivian will head towards the north entrance, and we will be on our way."

My companions both looked at me like I had three heads or something.

"Why the south entrance?" Sonya asked with a firm tone of rebellion. "What makes you think Vivian and Kayla will go north?"

"Because that's the same stupid way Vivian always goes home, she has it in her head wrong that it's a faster way to go, then immediately forgets that she has to walk the length of the building to go south again…" I found myself smiling as I explained it. I don't know why I've always found Vivian's warped sense of reality to be so appealing, but it was frightfully cute.

Natalie had the most inane smile as she attempted to hold back a comment.

"What's so funny?" I asked, my curiosity was killing me.

"You're sweet on Vivian aren't you? And I like the way you say things." She admitted. Great, I am glad everyone can enjoy my accent and my ambiguous sexual preference. But now is not the time or place to discuss such things.

"I say things properly! Now get on with it! We don't have much time before…" I started to say when I was interrupted by a light and insidious cackle.

"Kekeke" a voice obviously belonging to Kayla giggled from no direction at all, her tone was hers, cute, and very much un-augmented.

"Oh crap they've spotted us!" Sonya shouted as she backed up to me, now suddenly relying on me for leadership.

"Hey! How'd you know I'm here!?" Kayla asked from the shadows. Her glowing eyes gave away her position, hiding in the stucco panels on the ceiling with a plate pried back. She was indeed a succubus now, dark blue but with her turquoise dyed hair still prevalent. I could only see the top of her head, but already I could tell she's become much taller, grown out to a larger size like Vivian.

"Do you has the night visions too?" She asked in her normal, almost infantile tone.

"Kayla… is that still you in there?" I asked with genuine curiosity.

"Yes! I mean no! No, not at all! Azazel is driving my actions but I still have my mind, it comes and goes in spurts, Vivian's fighting with it, I don't think whatever this is likes her very much, but seriously just go! Go somewhere other than here!" Kayla shouted back to me.

"Ok then, try to fight it I'll see if I can do something to help you! Now run girls, run!" I instructed at I nodded to Kayla. The three of us bolted as Kayla started to growl as whatever was possessing them began to take control once more. We had only run a short while when we heard a shriek and the sound of beating wings I knew she wasn't far behind. Even from feeling alone I knew she was closing the gap on us, we wouldn't be able to escape in a straight run. I needed to think of something fast.

We passed the classroom Vivian and I teach our Saturday Greco-Roman archeology course, and I still had my keys.

"Girls, quickly, in here!" I shouted, diving into the room and holding the door for my companions. With a decent sprint, Sonya managed to get in shortly after me, but immediately ran around to slam the door behind her. I found myself struggling with Sonya as Natalie was still sprinting for the door.

"Leave her!" Sonya shouted.

"No!" I shouted back, pushing her off me and giving enough time for Natalie to enter, and then I quickly slammed the door behind her and locked it firmly with my keys.

Natalie caught her breath as her auburn hair was left disheveled in every direction; she glanced up at Sonya with a nasty gaze. "Leave her?" she asked between heaves. Sonya just shrugged in defense.

Kayla, outside, raged at our apparent escape. She paced in full view of the large windows to the hallway, she certainly looked different from the little cute demon girl that poked her head out a few moments ago. Now she was very tall, even more buxom, and possessed hooved feet. She flicked her tail back and forth, the little heart shaped spade at the end glittered in the low light.

"Man, doors, my ultimate weakness!" She complained out in the hall.

"What!?" I asked her from the other side, standing at the large window as she looked at me from the other side.

"What!?" Kayla said to herself as she turned, angrily staring into the glass and speaking with a more fearsome tone.

"You know, doors! Every monster movie the monster can't open doors, so I'm not even gonna try!" She complained to herself in Kayla's own voice, not the voice of her possessor.

I understood… she's talking to whatever is controlling her, she's being annoying… and if there's one thing she's good at…

I shook my head in disbelief of how ridiculous that sounded. "Well that's not going to get you anywhere because I locked it anyway, so run along now so we can get out of here." I hoped that perhaps Kayla would just give up the pursuit of us.

Kayla fell at a halfway point between control of herself and domination from the outside force.

"I can't do that, I gotta convert all of you, like really really. And besides, I've got super strength, don't you guys want super strength?" She attempted to bait us into coming out.

"Yes!" Kayla shouted to herself in the more upset voice, "The succubus are among one of the strongest races in all the worlds, now smash that window and convert them!"

"I can't." Kayla answered herself.

"Why?" The sinister side of her asked in near exasperation.

"Because I don't wanna break the school, that's wrong. Plus this is dad's school, I don't think he'd appreciate that one bit." Kayla explained politely.

"But capturing us against our will and turning us into living monsters is perfectly acceptable. C'mon Kayla can't you see this is wrong? Fight this thing within you and help us out!" I argued trying to appeal to Kayla's moral side, but all I got was backlash from both parts.

"No Claudia, once I get this thing out of me I'm so still converting you, this is awesome!" Kayla retorted, she leaned against the opposite side of the window from me and shot me a coy glance over her shoulder, and ran her hands down her curves. "Besides..."

I knew I wasn't going to like whatever was coming after that word.

"We all know you want this anyway."

I huffed as I put my hands on my hips and scolded the seven foot tall demoness "What's that supposed to mean?" I demanded.

"Nothin…" Kayla shrugged in an obvious deflection, her glowing white eyes flickered as her fangs glimmered in the moonlight from outside.

You know what? No. Demons and dread spirits aside this conversation is a long time in coming. Kayla needs to fess up right now.

"No, not this time, you've been making sideways comments like that for weeks now, ever since Vivian and I got back from our trip to the Mediterranean! What exactly are you insinuating!?" It didn't matter what was happening, and you know despite the size and monstrous adaptations, that's still that little brat Kayla in there, I demand answers.

"Whoa hey, rude! I'm not like insulting you or anything!" Kayla spun around to say as she put one clawed hand on her sternum in a defending stance to my verbal assault. I couldn't help but notice that the power that exuded over her retreated back, as her eyes turned back to being yellow and serpentine instead of a glowing white. "I'm just saying I think it's pretty clear you at least swing both sides of the plate!"

"What!?" I shouted, turning to the cheerleaders for support in the conversation, but Sonya just stared at the ceiling while Natalie shrugged.

I hung my mouth open, speechless. They thought that of me as well…

Natalie tried to elaborate on Kayla's behalf, "It's just kind of your way. You know, like how you're always looking out for her and the way you respond to Vivian's jokes, even when they so aren't funny, I did that for a boyfriend I had in high school. So it's like the same thing. There's nothing wrong with it or anything it's just…" She shrugged, failing to come up with more words to describe the situation.

Quickly, Kayla came to Natalie's ideological defense, tapping on the glass with her pointed finger to get my attention. I looked to her with narrowed gaze, she waved her hands and continued.

"Ok, right so level with me here, If I'm super off base, I'm sorry and I apologize, but in the nine months you and Vivian shared a bed, a room, and a bathroom on a tight ship, you didn't once take a peek and think that maybe you kinda sorta…"

I cut her off.

"THAT is none of your business!" I shouted, pointing at her, then quickly throwing up my hands and pacing away from the window, realizing what I was doing and with whom I was speaking, "I can't believe I'm having this conversation right now!" I honestly stated. The large light blue skinned demoness shrugged in a responsibility shirking manner as Natalie ran up to pat my shoulder in comfort, obviously feeling terrible at making me feel bad.

"Where the heck is Vivian anyway?" Sonya asked over to Kayla.

I spun around again "Yes, Kayla, where *is* Vivian anyway!? You seem like you're finally beating that thing within you. Perhaps if you're both under control again we can all gather together and sort this business out like the educated people we are."

Kayla huffed and rolled her bright yellow serpentine eyes at me.

"Whoa don't let this chill stuff fool you…" Kayla quickly stated as she waved her hands, "I totally have no control over myself right now, if you guys open that door I'm so all over you like a hobo on a ham sandwich, but the ability to have sort of control like right now comes and goes in waves. Honestly it's been pretty easy but I feel something building up. I lost track of Vivi back at the temple thingy when we suddenly turned seven feet tall and sexy. I have to constantly concentrate on being me or Azazel takes over, that's the name of the thing inside me by the way, see I'm helpful. You're welcome."

The seven foot tall demoness that was once Kayla Gilden sighed as she pouted towards us, losing control a bit again and trying to pull herself away.

"But seriously guys, look, being a succubus is awesome, I mean look at these hooves they're like permanent high heels! But yeah, I dunno where Vivi is, I should probably go check, anyways, I'll probably be back when I lose sanity again, so see you guys later!" She waved and took back off into the stucco roof, apparently breaking stucco tiles wasn't against her convoluted moral compass either.

I shrugged, "Right let's go." I stated plainly as I motioned for my still human companions to get up and move.

"We're not going to wait for Vivian?" Natalie asked.

"Kayla said it herself she's on the verge of losing control, perhaps next time she might attempt opening doors, then we're all doomed." I explained. That was all that was needed to get the women to follow me out the door, and on our way to freedom.

No sooner had we stepped outside, we heard a sound that rocked the building foundations, and I mean that very literally.

It was a substantial roar.

This Azazel being does not like being trifled with, that, I know.

"Time to go." I stated briskly as we began a running pace for the stairs.

That had to be Vivian. Whatever has gotten a hold of her really has done a number on her psyche, I do hope she's all right. I pondered to myself as we ran down the long corridors towards the stairway, unable to stop my wandering mind from putting together the pieces of what has occurred this night. Things were starting to add up, and I didn't like them.

We knew we were gathering a cultural artifact from two thousand years ago. We knew the endeavor was funded entirely from the Silverlight Corporation, a company that produces modern weapons, computer systems, and mostly military technology. There should really be no reason besides raw philanthropic means to finance the mission, but the stipend more than paid for my TA ship, so I didn't bother to ask. Kayla said there was a power source down there… we saw it, the levitating island. No doubt that power was something Silverlight intended to use, but where we deviated is they did not expect Kayla and Vivian to make as big of a mess as they did. We broke the rules, we touched the ruin.

But was that intended? Was the rule in place for us to break? After all, the cameras descended and started to record in the laboratory *after* the temple rose, they knew what this temple did, and they knew what would happen. But why? And to what end?

Foolishly I had decided to worry about details like this as I was descending the stairs to the first level, and in doing so missed a step completely, then in my moment of trying to recover I stepped down and bent my right ankle very unnaturally, causing myself to fall. I slapped my head hard against the concrete wall, as Sonya sprinted ahead. Natalie caught up and stopped, seeing my tumble. She glanced up the stairs for just a second, and then felt the small golden cross necklace she kept with her always. Without missing a beat Natalie got down and lifted me up using her shoulder.

"You can do it Claudia, we're going to make it out of here." She encouraged me kindly.

I couldn't help but feel slightly moved at the selfless act of bravery Natalie was showing at that moment.

"You're really quite a good cheerleader, you know that?" I smiled as I once more found my feet.

"My dad's a marine, he tells me you never leave a man behind." Natalie said with a twinge of pride. I found myself grinning a bit as she let slip a southern accent.

"Let's go, I'm good to run again." I partially lied, I wanted to make sure Natalie made it out, and I was certain I could at least keep a brisk pace even with the wounded ankle. She risked herself in saving me, but I don't think I could stand the guilt if she was harmed because of it. We needed to leave now, then I can focus on saving Vivian.

Then we heard a second roar.

"That was from outside!" Sonya shouted as she reached the end of the next hallway. She quickly began to backpedal towards us as a large demonic form descended from the skies above the double doors at the end of the hall. Her whip-like tail flicked in the low light, as a very much transformed Vivian Maybell began to walk towards us from the far hall. We turned to run back, but Kayla appeared at the base of the stairs.

Trapped. No… wait, no we're not!

"The classrooms, we can escape through a window!" I shouted as we ran to converge at the center classroom. Sonya was first inside, Natalie followed quickly after, and in a move I really should have expected, Sonya slammed shut the door. As I flopped against it with my wounded ankle, I heard the handle lock.

"Claudia!" I heard Natalie shout from the other side. I could see their forms through the frosted glass door, arguing, as shadows descended around me. Sonya grabbed onto Natalie and forced her out the window… Sonya was using me as a pawn to sacrifice… in order to buy them time.

Hurt, battered, and betrayed, as the two girls forced their way outside, I turned around, slumping to the bottom of the door as I resigned myself to my fate.

Kayla's hooves clacked on the linoleum floor as she closed in, her smile wicked, clearly no longer in control, but I was most surprised with Vivian… poor Vivian. Her darker blue skin, which, actually was rather beautiful, was now scarred with lines of black coursing through her, like visible veins. Her form was even more exaggerated than I had seen previously, and her wings were huge and bat-like. Her face wasn't hers anymore, it was more slender, with a different brow line that was smoothed and very pretty, but absent. Like the effigy of an attractive woman, with no personality to lie within.

"This one is useless…" Vivian, no, that's not Vivian talking, whoever is talking through Vivian said with deep malice.

"And I would have expected the daughter of Gilden to be more powerful, she is overly emotional, concerned, and worthless." Kayla acknowledged. I realized they were speaking of themselves.

"Perhaps this one will make better stock." Vivian mused, tilting her head, she raised her tail, pointing the sharp end at me and preparing to strike.

I winced, preparing myself for the pain.

"No!" Vivian suddenly shouted, as the tail shot forward the path was altered to smash into the window frame on the door behind me, shattering the frosted glass as Vivian pulled away from me, reaching with one hand and trying to rip the black tar off her hands, "I don't want you! I want to be me! Get out of me!" Vivian shouted to herself as she flung some of the black ichor off of her, dropping back as her face started to shift back to who she really was.

"Useless!" Kayla shouted as she pushed Vivian aside, still controlled by the parasite within them as she stabbed into my side with her blue, arrow pointed tail.

The pain was quite incredible. Vivian dropped to the floor as struggled, trying to fight with herself long enough to save me.

It's all right Vivian… you tried.

I reached up to grab out Kayla's tail, trying to get her off of me, when I felt a powerful pressure under my skin. My hands stopped moments from grasping the tail to yank it out of me when I found I could not… I didn't want too, the feeling that washed over me was pleasant, calming, wanted. I was simultaneously disturbed by this fact, and in that same breath, not.

I let out a surprised gasp as my already worn tennis shoes cracked and gave way to angular claw-edged toes as my feet stretched and turned the same light-blue hue as Kayla. I felt my legs and body beginning to fill and form to the new shape of the succubus. The tingle of the tail emerging caught me off guard. I turned quickly to see it begin to move back and forth, as mentally I found the capacity to move it on my own accord.

I saw Vivian struggling with something, as the black lines receded from her. Vivian became shorter as her wings lessened and her form receded to a more reasonable figure as she regained her normal height. I myself started to move in the other direction as I gasped my clothing strained, I felt the skin color alterations wash over my face as my eyes started to turn. Horns grew on my head as my ears and teeth lengthened, my claws grew in on my hands.

"I'll deal with you later…" Kayla sneered at Vivian as my partner stood up using her palms.

"Don't take Claudia! Let her go!" Vivian shouted to Kayla as I felt something hard and painful deposit inside me from Kayla's tail. As it did, Kayla began to shrink, decreasing in size like Vivian as she returned to herself.

"Ah!" Kayla shouted as she pulled her tail out of me. "Claudia! Are you ok!?" She asked me with genuine concern. I knew she was being sincere because… I could feel it. I understood her emotions very plainly, being able to interpret them without question.

"I'm…" I checked myself over, turning to look at myself in the remainder of the reflective door behind me. "…ok…" I said with surprise as I caught a glimpse of what I now was.

I'm beautiful…

There was no sign of any blemish on my light blue skin. My hair had fallen out of its braid and now had a metallic blue hue to it, but that can certainly be fixed, the color, to be honest, was rather desirable. My yellow serpentine eyes had an alluring effect, I couldn't look away. I… I looked almost like some of the deities of Indian Hindu tradition, I brought my hand to my face, just to feel my new smooth skin to see if it was real, and it certainly was. I turned back to see Vivian sitting near me on her knees with her hands on her legs, looking over with a concerned expression.

"Hey… you look great!" Vivian encouraged kindly with a smile, letting her now long bangs fall over one eye as she tilted her head for her smile. I could feel a powerful wave of concern for me. I felt moved, I've never felt such a strong emotion from someone before. I couldn't help but stutter a bit as I replied.

"Y-you really think so?" I asked, slightly nervous as I pulled up my slightly tattered tee shirt to try and be as presentable as possible.

"Mmmhmm." Vivian nodded with a large exaggerated expression. "We didn't hurt you, did we?" she asked, worried.

"No, Vivian... neither you nor Kayla are doing anything wrong, that much is certain... it's this other being here... Azazel was it? Where did it go?" I asked, Kayla helped me stand as we all took a moment of reprieve, just standing in the hallway for a while.

Kayla sighed as she rest against the wall, curling her tail and letting it flop as she thought.

"Azazel..." She said the name with an exasperated sigh, "My dad told me about her...", finally, Kayla was willing to talk about this.

"Good gracious, you knew!?" I spoke up, "You knew she was down there?"

"No!" Kayla shot back, folding her arms, "I just knew she existed. Dad said she was an evil spirit, he told me about her in bedtime stories... to scare me. She was supposed to be a corruptor, a dark power that possessed people, but he didn't tell me she was real! And he especially didn't tell me that she'd exist within the ruins we have been standing over for months! I don't think my dad would put us in danger like that! I think somewhere in here, we made a big mistake..." Kayla let her folded arms drop as she sighed.

"This is all my fault..." She blamed herself.

I walked over to her with Vivian as we moved to comfort her.

"No, Kayla, we all share this blame..." I began, "We were curious, we wanted to know... and now..." I stopped mid-sentence as I felt a rising, churning sensation in my gut. I gasped, grabbing my sides for support.

"No! Claudia! You have to fight it, that's Azazel!" Vivian explained.

Oh my word... now I understood what Vivian was up against, this power, creeping up into my mind... it's overwhelming. As my body changed and turned on the outside I felt internally the force of all my being slipping away! Like someone else was coming in as I was leaving. That terrible sensation of losing yourself, like being drunk or under the influence of a drug, you were aware of what was going on, yet had no power to decide otherwise. As it continued... I felt more and more the sensation of enjoying the changes, like I was being forced to accept the new me as Azazel's force became dominant. I remember feeling my lips move to a smile as I looked down on Vivian and Kayla, turning to the window, and remembering my mission.

My prey had still eluded me, I had to ensure I caught them.

And then like Vivian and Kayla before me… I was Azazel.

Claudia existed no more.

Chapter Four

Kingsport University Verne Building of Earth Sciences

Kingsport University, Maryland

United States of America, Earth

The Journal of Kayla Gilden

August 16th, 2011

1:01 AM

"No! Claudia come back! Please!" Vivian shouted as she trotted after Claudia. Her attempt was stopped suddenly as she walked onto the shattered glass with her now more humanlike foot, our hooves vanished when Azazel stopped influencing us, the way Vivian grabbed her foot suggested real pain. I ran over to her and grabbed her, bringing her around to look at me so she could focus.

"Vivi think! You know she can't hear us!" I shouted with concern for her, this night has been more dangerous than anyone could have expected. I didn't even have to ask Vivian what she wanted, I could *feel* the powerful desire to go after Claudia. There was no use fighting it, and we didn't want Azazel to get out in the open. I sighed and pulled her along with me to head outside through the south door of the building.

"What are we going to do?" Vivian asked as I pressed on the door, walking out into the cool and calm later summer night. The smell of wet grass from the night's dew permeated the area as the half-moon provided light to the darkened campus area. I provided what answers I could as we walked along the grass, our demonic outlines silhouetted against the rolling fields of flat Maryland grass as the moon cast its silver light upon the two of us as I trudged ahead, trying to get a hold of the situation before things could get any more out of hand.

"I don't know, but we managed to be released from Azazel that means that Claudia can do it as well. I don't think my father would have let us walk into such danger without support, I expect a Silverlight team will be here at any moment. So basically, I want us to stall for time…" I explained as we walked forward. Tonight, was terrible… for years, I have built myself up as a normal girl, with a normal life. Yes, I was a corporate tycoon's daughter, but many people at the Kingsport University were. It's a well to do school for well to do people, this is expected, it would be the one place we could blend in.

But my life has been anything *but* normal.

My father, commands Silverlight LTD, the largest corporate power of the modern age. Everyone knows it, and by now everyone accepts it as the true might of the human race. My father's company had improved the lives of billions through new breakthrough technologies and the new cold fusion power source that has weaned much of the world off of gasoline and other fossil fuels as the primary power source. We've secured our spot at the top of the corporate ladder, rivaling the giants of the modern era. Silverlight computers are number one, Silverlight cars, jets, and all the modern conveniences that people have come to expect from life.

All we asked in return was that no one ask us how we got there.

And now, that secrecy will be soundly out the window if what we have done here tonight is allowed to escape, both literally and figuratively. Dad had told me, mostly in the form of bedtime stories, about other worlds. Other realms, outside of our own, not exactly alien, but variants of Earth, where beings and cultures seemingly impossible here exist and thrive in the day to day. Most of these creatures make up our limited understanding of our mythologies, and now I, Kayla Gilden, am now a Succubus, one of the races of the realm of Rune Lowguard, known to modern humanity as hell.

How will the world react to this? Will I have to be hidden away? Is there a cure? Do I want to be cured? I kept pondering the questions to myself as we heard a scream and scuffle up ahead, jarring me away from my thoughts as Vivian and I started sprinting at a speed I could have never attained before my conversion, then took flight. I noticed something I hadn't before, when we are at rest, our wings are small, cute, little bat-like wings, but while aloft, our wings stretch and take on a larger and more intimidating size and shape, more V shaped, with the same bat-like flair.

We soared high over the area, seeing over the nearest building to the Verne Building of Earth Sciences, where the Archeology Laboratory was located. Past the Bradbury Building of Literature and Science, we could see that Claudia had found Natalie and Sonya, and still under the power of Azazel, had tried to corner them off before the two could sprint to Sonya's car, an easily recognizable red Camaro in the parking lot. Claudia reached forward with her clawed hand and grabbed Natalie by the arm, I saw Natalie kick and scream as Claudia dragged her back towards the ground. Natalie screamed for Sonya, but Sonya ran inside her car and slammed the door.

Vivian dove, immediately moving to rescue Natalie, I myself found it more interesting to watch Sonya…

I saw her lock the door.

It's amazing, I might have been under the influence of some ancient power, but tonight I've seen her sacrifice myself, Claudia, and now Natalie, her supposed best friend, all in order to get away. As I watched Sonya stare impassively at Natalie's transformation, as I saw Claudia elbow Vivian to send the now very light demoness flying backwards as she pinned Natalie down to deny her escape from her conversion, I felt Azazel stir…

She was still within me.

And she was focused on Sonya.

I noticed that Claudia was staring up to Sonya as well. We may be separate bodies, but it was clear that Azazel worked as a hive-mind, she was focused, so we all were. Natalie's clothing creaked and stretched as her form altered under Claudia's powerful grip as she was forced face down on the Kentucky bluegrass, Natalie's hand shot forward to attempt to grasp something to get away, as I watched the light blue skin of her new form slide up her arm, and turn her fingertips into claws.

"No!" I heard Natalie shout as her horns emerged and her eyes changed, the solid knot of Azazel moving from being to being could be seen even from my high vantage point as it slid around and entered Natalie, she would be influenced soon as well.

Sonya took Natalie's conversion as a sign to leave, pulling back hard on her car's transmission and peeling out backwards in reverse. The car then lurched forward as she drove headlong forward at high speed in the parking lot, cutting across spaces until she neglected to look ahead, likely staring back at the demons on the front lawn, as her bright red car went slamming into the only other parked car in the area…

Natalie's blue sedan.

I dropped down by Claudia and Natalie as Claudia began to revert to herself. Vivian was quick to catch Claudia from toppling back, as she supported her friend to her feet. I bent down and picked up Natalie, and helped her get some of the dirt off her little sweater vest. Trying to be as modest as possible with her succubae form.

"I…" Natalie stammered as she looked at her hands then back over to Sonya, she clearly was still in regret of being turned, but I wasn't really feeling all that sympathetic, I for one think this transformation is incredible. The amount of raw power I have now mixed with the fact I will never have to worry about looking good, I will have so much time to do what I want now…

Plus, if the legends are true… this means I am now immortal.

"You're fine." I said as I helped her left wing get out of its confine, being stuck around some of the woven threads of her shirt's back. "Don't worry about it, you look great." I said as Natalie tucked her now long dark blue hair behind her ear. Vivian was quick to help Natalie to her feet and try to care for her. Vivian's caring nature would take care of this. Meanwhile, Sonya was in a bad way. Her car's front was shattered against the side of Natalie's sedan, I could see Sonya's hand dangling from the side of the open driver's side door.

"I'm going to look, stay here…" I cautioned to Vivian as she held onto Natalie as Claudia comforted the both of them. I straightened what was left of my nice maid's cosplay attire, which looked more like the rags of someone who had washed ashore, as I pulled up my black and white arm-socks and proceeded towards the shattered Camero.

Honestly from the impact of the crash, and the way Sonya's hand hung from the door. I expected her to be dead.

I steeled myself for the worst as I walked the short distance of the car park, and approached the battered red car's driver side door. Sonya lay there, crumpled over the steering wheel as her legs contorted unnaturally in a mangled state. Her beautiful white skin and blonde hair were tarnished by spray of car fluid, scrapes, and blood. Her eyes were closed as she lay motionless, only held up by the seatbelt that confined her.

Claudia caught up to me, worried, "Kayla… is she?" She asked me as she approached, not wanting to look at our last human companion if she had indeed expired. I shook my head. Claudia halted her approach. I looked back to Sonya…

And watched a line of blood recede…

"What the…" I gasped as I looked at Sonya beginning to heal... wounds were sealing as her horribly broken hand flexed, allowing her fingers to realign with a series of sickening pops.

Claudia ran around beside me, "What, what's gone… oh… my…" She worried along with me as Sonya cracked her neck as she started to stir again, reaching up and ripping the steering wheel out of the column and throwing it aside as she reached up and grasped her head.

"Uunnngh… friggin… car… popped up…" Sonya moaned and complained as she flopped back in her seat. She slowly became more aware of her surroundings as she shook her head and looked over to me.

The stare from Claudia and I must have been something, because as soon as she met eye contact, she started to laugh.

"Heh… hahahahahaha… oh… you saw it did you? My… 'gifts'?" Sonya asked as she tried to stand up, kneeing her crumpled dashboard as she did and jerking her knee up swiftly to strike it, smashing the car more and freeing herself. "Don't even start with me Gilden, you should recognize it Kayla… after all… this is ultimately your father's doing…" Sonya sneered as she stood out of the car, straightening out her stained and blood soaked white button down shirt as she dusted off her pants. "Or are you surprised that I *survived*? Well… miss *Gilden*, you will soon find that you're not the only one with a daddy who cares… if you're rich enough, you can get the right treatments… in this case, from our dear Silverlight's nanotechnology wing… a project you might be familiar with… remember the Survivalist project?"

Claudia looked to me, I narrowed my gaze as I stared at Sonya.

"That's classified." I answered, unwilling to continue.

There's some things *more* important to keep secret then what's happening tonight, that's definitely one of them.

"Classified doesn't mean gone away. Well, I'm better than your normal human now, I'm stronger, more powerful… I heal… and above all, I'm tougher than you even as you are now…" She strutted up to me and gave me a sneering grin as she shook her head, "So what are you gonna do, you got my ride, now are you going to try to impale me with your little tails, add me to your silly group?"

No… Sonya can't become a Succubus. If she's already this strong, and this nasty, I shudder to think what would happen if…

I started to feel a heavy strain within… Azazel…

No!

"That…" Vivian, Natalie, Claudia and I myself said in unison as Azazel spoke from within us.

"That is the power I seek… give it to me!"

And with that, I felt a horrible lurch… Azazel was growing again, climbing… trying to take over me!

I did the most expedient thing and ran, ran as far away and as fast as I could, but as I did I heard Claudia groan, as her form started to flair and turn into the tall, hooved, and powerful Azazel controlled version of herself. Sonya just held her ground and smiled.

This. Wasn't. Right.

How!? How is Sonya one of the *survivalists*? How did I not know that? Why would my father have one of them out, let alone near me!? He couldn't have known… he wouldn't…

And right then, it all made sense.

This was a trap.

Sonya wants to be turned.

"Natalie, Vivian, you have to keep control!" I ordered, as I watched the two of them struggle with themselves.

Vivian tried to encourage Natalie to keep control, "Natalie, it's ok… just stay calm and think about who you really are! Don't let her…" Vivian's statement stopped mid-sentence as she arched her back and allowed herself to turn. "Coming… Natalie?" Vivian purred in a new and deeper voice.

"Crap this isn't…" Natalie complained as she suddenly shot up in size and form as her hooved feet ripped through the last of her footwear. "Me…" She completed with a smile as she joined the converted.

I needed to stop this, they could catch Sonya… if I could fly down and grab her I could…

I felt the sick, black ichor of Azazel slide up my throat and into my…

I tumbled to the ground as my form flared and turned, I stood up and relaxed, feeling empowered by Azazel's sweet embrace.

"Ahh… better." I said as I stood, "Now where was I?" I said with all my bodies as the one known as Claudia held Sonya aloft…

At last… I've found my host…

The one I would return to this world through…

Nanotechnology, advanced science…

Unlimited power.

I used all of my bodies to lance into the still screaming Sonya Shannon, she complained and cried to not turn, something about her beauty and being normal, petty human affairs that would soon have nothing to do with her. I let all but the smallest vestige of me slide out of my hosts and into Sonya, I sneered from many angles as I watched Sonya's form turn. Her body flair as her already beautiful form became even more aggrandized as the powerful Succubae DNA took control. Midnight violet, almost black skin emerged as her blonde hair turned to white. Her eyes turned serpentine as the color burned an almost glowing dark green. She gasped as the changes became favorable… she felt my power…

And wanted it.

What?

No! No this can't be happening! I watched my form shrink back down to me as Sonya neared completion. The other girls standing around her, doing the same, Azazel was being pulled out, transferring herself completely into Sonya! I wanted to stop her but I could do nothing…. As Sonya's black wings burst from the back of her now incredibly strained white shirt, as her tail emerged, bearing a razor sharp end, like a scythe. As Sonya's clawed hand reached the sky, her horns emerged, her body… turned.

I realized, we had taken the most power hungry member of our party…

And gave her all she's ever wanted.

"No!" I shouted aloud as our tails pulled back, and Sonya flopped to the ground on her knees.

"Oh my gosh!" Vivian gasped, "That thing is now inside of Sonya!"

Natalie bent down to help up her friend.

"Sonya… Sony… are… are you all right?" Natalie asked with genuine concern, feeling overwhelming remorse at her actions, something we all could now easily feel emanating from her.

Sonya slowly picked up her head as her voice attained a deeper, raspier and harsher tone that would stay with me, and become a bane to my existence for years to come. "Why would you care…" She said as her bright green eyes locked with Natalie's, letting her new serpentine irises undulate as she focused. "Demon." She spat her final word as she smiled and let her disheveled bangs fall about her eyes in a wild fashion.

The word struck Natalie as she made an immediate and sudden realization. "Oh… Oh my God!" Natalie shouted as she backed away, crawling backwards on her hands and knees as she pulled the cross pendant out and thumbing it over quickly as if it would somehow protect her. "No… I'm not…" Natalie protested, looking back at Sonya as Miss Sonya Shannon finally stood, rising high and flexing her knew demonic wings.

"Now… look at what you've done… you've destroyed me, ruined me… made me look like a monster…" Sonya started laying into everyone, but stopped as she realized a curious slip in her words.

"Ha…hahahaha…hehehehehehehe…" Sonya giggled to herself in a crazed and shambling way as she reached up and brushed back her hair to let it all flop back as she rest her hand against the top of her head, leaning back and teetering as she let her wings flap and tail crack like a whip. "*Look*, like a monster… oh… oh that's rich…"

Vivian stood and waved her hands, "Sonya, be calm, you're not acting right! I know that Azazel's trying to influence you, but you need to try to…" Vivian tried to help Sonya and placate her, but Sonya simply lashed out with her hand and raked Vivian across the abdomen with her claws, making Vivi double back in pain.

"Enough! You have done quite enough for one night Miss Vivian Maybell… look at what you've unleashed on this world… And it doesn't matter what being this is, this Azazel or whatever… She is nothing compared to me. I am Sonya Shannon, the winner… the survivor, and you've given me even more. I am more than just a queen to all I see, I am a monster, and you made me this way." She laughed as she lifted off into the air, letting her wings stretch to their full demonic form as she silhouetted herself against the half-moon behind her.

"I am reborn, renewed, but really I'm all the same. I'm on the outside what I always was within. I am a monster, a demon… just like all of you… I do not need your pity, your concern,

I do not need anyone,

Any*thing*,

Anymore."

She cackled as she let her hands out to the side, showing off her claws as she let her scythe edged tail dangle. She pointed at us with a clawed hand, challenging us with her usual biting and harsh reality she loves to do, "You see, I'm going to be just fine, I have places to hide, summer homes to escape too, and people I could always just kill… but you? Oh all of you are royally screwed. Tomorrow's a brand new day, and people will have to accept you or burn you where they stand. But me? I'm a winner, I'll find a way through this, I'll survive, because at the end of the day, I always win. Now ciao suckers, I got a whole new take on life to ponder. I'm more than Sonya Shannon… I have become the defiler of worlds, and there's so much to do… and all the time in the world to do it."

And with that, she tore off into the sky.

And I was left staring, fists clenched as I looked into the portion of sky she had retreated too.

"And I'll be waiting…" I promised to myself, I would not let my father's empire fall to a little brat like her…

My father…

"Tch…" I gritted my teeth as I clenched my fist. What was I thinking? Look at what I've done… I'm… not human anymore. I mean, I've always been a little different. But this is not something I can hide…tomorrow the sun will rise, and my companions as well as myself will have to come to terms with the world, just as the world will have to come to terms with us.

I heard a whimpering cry from behind me as I turned around sharply to see Natalie, on her knees, weeping into her hands as she trembled. Claudia and Vivian were close by her, offering a comforting hand and providing emotional support. I, however, was less empathetic to her perceived plight.

"I'm… I'm a demon… a monster… away from God." Natalie cried, pulling away her hands to see her new color and form, disgusted in what she was, in who she was.

"No." Vivian corrected, staying close beside her. "I don't think that's how it works. You're going to be fine, Natalie, we're here to help you." She tried her best to comfort, but Natalie wasn't having any of it.

Natalie stood up and threw out her hand to the side, clutching the other close to her chest as she wailed, letting slip her southern accent as she protested, "No! Y'all don't understand you're not believers. Vivian I dunno what faith you have and Claudia I know you've told me dozens of times you don't have one! But for me, someone with faith in God, this is *not* going to be ok! This is not acceptable! I'm a demon Vivian, a *demon! Doesn't that mean anything to you?* We're not human anymore! We're the creatures of the damned, we've probably lost our souls! That's not something you just get over! We're dead, we're damned we're…" She shouted, completely out of control and wailing.

Until I stepped in.

"Shut up." I said in the same deadpan tone my father has used to silence so many before. And like him, all turned to face me, as I let my hands rest at my side. Time to see this from another perspective.

"We're demons, yes, the Succubus… which if all my father's stories were true, is only one of many different races of them. If we're now succubus, then so what? All we've done was bring the world back to reality. So we're not alone, and there's obviously more to this than anyone here understands tonight. So be it. It's been a long time since humanity ever had to come to terms with anything, about themselves or anyone else. Perhaps it's time for something like this to occur, perhaps it's time to let this wheel of fate turn, and bring about a new era. We all knew that something new was going to come with the turn of the century, and the start of a new millennia, let it be something *grand*." I explained with a growing fervor.

I'm not ashamed, I'm not upset. And you know what? I have no regrets. If allowed to go back and make my actions again, I will turn that wheel one more time. Yes, my father will be mad, yes, I disobeyed his orders, but in many ways I felt at that moment that this was something that was meant to happen. If not to us, then someone else. You can't keep an entire world hidden away, you can't let something this fantastic exist merely within the realm of fiction. I'm a succubus, I'm here…

I won't be denied.

My name is Kayla Gilden,

The daughter of Silverlight,

I deserve to thrive.

Vivian raised her hand and opened her mouth, clearly about to say something in return, but her comment was cut short by the wail and siren of multiple police vehicles pulling into the parking lot, their bright headlights blinding us as we all raised her hands and recoiled to hide from the light, I myself remember letting out an involuntary hiss. I could hear the slap of car doors and the lock of weapons getting ready, as my eyes adjusted to the new bright lights, I could see we had been surrounded.

"Kingsport Police Department! Lay down your weapons and place your hands where we can see them!" A dark skinned and bald police officer shouted as he raised his pistol and started towards us with a careful, yet still firm pace.

I let my hand drop as the light became more reasonable, as the lights dimmed I saw a police woman with light brown hair in a tight ponytail raise her gun towards my head. I could see the faces of the police all around us, surprised, scared, and above all, curious.

"Ladies… I am Deputy Chief Samuel Morel…" The male police officer introduced, "Can you understand me? Do you know what I am saying?" The man said in a slightly gravel and kind tone as he let one hand off his gun to tap on his chest.

“Yes, we can hear you just fine…” I answered sarcastically as I sighed and rest my hand on my hip. “Me Succubus, you Sam.” I parodied Tarzan as I tapped on my chest.

“We're just students at the school!” Vivian ruined my moment of first contact with honesty.

“Yes!” Natalie joined in. “There's no need to shoot, please! My name is Natalie Rayborn, I'm one of the cheerleaders of KPU… please… I'm just like you… please… let us go…” Natalie was clearly still distraught as she dropped once more to her knees, upset and crying as she reached up to wipe a tear from her yellow, serpentine, eye.

“Oh my God…” Deputy Chief Samuel Morel gasped as he realized who we were, he immediately holstered the gun and spread out his hands, “Put your guns down! Everyone put your guns down!” he shouted to his fellow officers.

“Don't it could be a trap!” The female officer shouted. Relaxing her grip on the gun for a moment before tightening it again.

“Damnit Lea! They're just students, the one in front of me is Kayla Gilden!” Samuel pleaded with his fellow officer, using my local celebrity to show our lack of threat.

“…Take 'em in, we'll figure out what to do later.” Officer Morel, gave the order as he sighed and leaned on his car. I remember the SWAT team rushing in and cuffing us, as Samuel Morel looked on in an expression that could only be described as a loss for words. He didn't know how to handle us, but he was sure that cuffing and imprisoning us was not the way. However, he was not in charge, so humanity reacted as it always does.

In fear.

I made sure to look as many of them in the eye as I could on the way to the back of the squad car. I saw Natalie crying, Claudia comforting Vivian, and finally, I saw my passive stare at my own reflection.

So I'm no longer human, in many ways, I find that liberating. Humanity is such a cowardly race, they react out of fear and panic. But they are the masters of this world, and as it stands, we are now their prisoners.

Sonya is right.

The world will have to deal with us, we are now here. They, are not alone…

And nothing, will ever be the same.

To be continued.

Episode Two

Prologue

Shannon Family Summer Home

Hampton, Virginia

United States of America

Earth

August 16th, 2011

5:21AM

The Journal of Azazel, Being of Darkness

I had it. For a sterling, shining, moment, I had it.

Freedom.

I had what I had wanted for centuries, a chance, an opportunity, to be released. I had control of a small enclave, of succubae no less, one of the strongest of races…

But now… I've made a mistake, and once more I am bound to servitude for it. As if fate has decided I would be robbed of happiness for all of time.

"Oh… don't fret sweetie, I can feel you fussing in there and it's making me not feel as lovely as I should be…" Sonya Shannon, that damned woman, chided me as she brushed her… ***my*** white hair in the view of her full length mirror. As much as I hate to admit it, she *is* beautiful. Her narrow framed face and the flawless symmetry of her form. The bright green eyes and midnight violet, nearly black skin of her Quietus Succubus hue became her, and her body, even before I turned her to a succubus, was at the peak of feminine attraction. I wondered how she got that way, as I had not seen humans so fine occur naturally.

She sat on an ornate stool made of an elegant dark wood, as she sang to herself in a carefree tone, the light alabaster walls and fine high end Victorian era furniture seemed out of place around such a monster… but I can't really talk, after all… I'm a being known to these inferior creatures as a parasite, so who am I to judge?

"Why?" I asked her through her lips, staring at her internally as she smiled. She grinned back at me with her pointed teeth, and made a pose by leaning back and flicking her fingers, looking at their pointed ends as she talked casually to me, like explaining her daily plans to a friend, or a child.

"Why what? Why am I so beautiful? Why am I so powerful? Why am I so much more capable of controlling things than you are? Trick question really, they're all the same reason, and you can thank Uncle Sam for that one Azazel. You were defeated before you ever had the chance to start. But you already know that now… Ah, lalala…" She stopped to look at her nails as she got out her file, and stopped, seeing her pointed claws, and concentrated as her nails started to take shape, lengthening out to form long, eleven inch blades that resembled a wild animal, or a lawnmower's cutting edge.

She's discovering how to use her new form…

"Oh… now that's a fun addition…" Sonya mused as she turned her hand over and flexed her fingers, listening to the sharp edges of her bladed fingers make a small cutting whistle through the air as they moved. "So… what do you call that? And is this mine… or yours?" She asked me.

I would give her as little as possible, there was no way I would simply allow her to use me like a toy. This little brat defies a power she can barely understand, let alone… I… I felt something invading my psyche! Something penetrating me! Azazel! Being of darkness, the first Nexan! No one dares to…

"Yours…" I answered, against my volition, "The succubae and incubi, possess the ability to transmute their bodies in certain points. The teeth and claws can lengthen at will using a natural alchemical process called living-metal. This process allows you to reform broken claws and always keep your edges as sharp as possible, making the succubae one of the most deadly demonic races in hand to hand combat."

"Oh… thank you…" Sonya noted, as she pulled back in her blades to her fingertips, flexing once more to test it out. "Handy…" she noted and got back up to dress herself in a new outfit.

How!? How could she possibly control me like this! I am the possessor, not the possessed! She was accessing my memories, forcing me to recall information for her… no one on this mortal realm can possibly do that! It's beyond reason! Sonya chuckled to herself as she felt my internal struggle, tossing off her old clothing as she fished through her closet for something new. Her demonic silhouette ebbed along the far wall, as the outline failed to capture her eyes and mouth, leaving the startling image of a shadowy form with hollow eyes and a sinister smile.

"Better living through chemicals my dear…" Sonya chided. "You're now an unwilling member of an experiment over 15 years in the making." She began to explain as she put on a seductive set of white lace undergarments. "You think that you've got the drop on humanity, but that's far from the case. In 1936 you tried to escape, didn't you? Trying to get back to some far-flung place… let's see if I remember my homework… R'yleh wasn't it? But you didn't get out did you? You were stopped by a team of investigators, and sealed away once more…" She told her story with great accuracy as she shuffled into a tight set of leather pants, ripping her tail out the back with a hack of her scythe edge.

I kept quiet, she knows that she's right and so do I, there is no need to discuss this.

Naturally, she kept going.

"Well, the part you don't know is that those investigators didn't just go home. They realized what a threat these other worlds could be… so this great nation established a government agency tasked with learning about and preparing humankind for defense against these extradimensional threats. It's called the Department of Paranormal Investigation, or DPI, if you are so inclined, and hehe… like all secret human organizations, it has a major flaw…" Sonya happily explained as she clipped on a tight black belt, and after extending her fingers into blades to construct wing-holes in her shirt, she slid on an off white dress shirt, smirking heavily as she realized she couldn't fasten the top buttons with her new flared and dramatic form.

"Humans are terrible at keeping secrets, you expect me to believe you've hidden an organization away for almost one hundred years?" I returned, pointing a flaw in her fable.

"Of course not, after all, someone has to fund them… so they turned to a corporation that could actually handle the responsibility… someone you might be familiar with…" Sonya purred, and it all made sense.

"Silverlight." I spat from her lips.

"Oh… right again, The Silverlight Cult, now Silverlight LTD, amazing in a new age of corporate dominion how three little letters turn you from an anathema to a respected world leader. And humankind has benefited heavily… we're more advanced, we're basking in a technological revolution! Profits have never dropped below 1100% since Silverlight started exporting its technologies in 1991, my father, Carter Shannon, holds nearly $1/6^{th}$ of the overall company's shares, do you *understand* what power that brings? Oh Azzy… you are just so outdated, this isn't a world fought through raw power. This isn't an age where a monster like you or me can muscle their way into power, it's all through quiet control. You don't walk into someone's home and shoot them to take all they desire. You crawl in their bed a welcome and wanted guest, put them to sleep…"

Sonya pulled tight a choker collar necklace, a little white ribbon with a gilded cross at its center.

"And smother them." She finished as she smiled a wicked grin, her teeth gleamed in the reflection of the morning light upon her fangs, as the shadow on the wall showed the inverse upon the mantle.

I have made the ultimate mistake… I may be a parasite… I may be considered frightening and wicked by these inferior beings…

But this woman,

Is a monster.

She modified a black leather jacket as she threw it on over her other attire, moving quickly through the house with her powerful, lighter form.

"Oh Azzy sit back, relax and simply lend me your power… It's a long time in waiting and eons of wanting so prepare for a new world order. Let the politicians squabble and the media spin, the demons have come to play…" Sonya threw open the front door as the sweet summer wind came blowing through the entryway. She let her white hair flutter in the breeze as she took a deep and drawing breath.

I had sought to reenter this world as a conqueror…

But I have played into her hand.

I was not ready,

And neither, is this world.

Episode Two

Rise of Sonya.

Chapter One

In the back of a Silverlight Limousine

Enroute to the Kingsport Municipal Law Enforcement Office

Baltimore, Maryland

United States of America, Earth

The journal of Damien Focht

August 16th, 2011

6:45AM

There are many situations, lands, combat routines that may make the average man sputter and choke in fear and pain that I may endure without issue or problem.

But silence, in a situation like this.

I cannot stand.

I sat on the fine leather seat of the u shaped rear cabin of the company's luxury cold fusion limousine as I ran my hand down the silver stitching of the seat I resided, as I took a breath, feeling my chest against the confines of my tight black suit, the lapel pin of my company upon my chest pressing into my skin, as if stabbing me for my infraction. As I turned slightly I saw my father sitting across the limousine's aisle. Gideon Focht, his hair kept in very thinly shaved military fashion, his suit perfect, impeccable, the perfect, pure white shirt he wore seemed to glow off of his dark, African skin. The whites of his eyes gleamed as he listened intently to his only superior, the owner of the corporation itself, Daniel Gilden.

And while he listened to Mr. Gilden's concerns. I was forced to sit, and wait. As I stared across to Dr. Albertie Toft, the director of research and development for our company, and the only Zombie I know currently employed at Silverlight LTD. She was in business attire today, with a dark silver dress shirt that allowed glimpses of her lithe body underneath. Her stiletto heels shined with a perfected sheen as she folded one leg across the other, resting her long, 9 inch long fingers across her knees as she looked at me with a cold, dead, stare from her grey, almost milky white eyes.

No one said a word, not one, as Daniel Gilden spoke to my father.

Things, have gone horribly wrong.

"I understand." My father said finally, the accent of his Ivory Coast upbringing prevalent within every word, and the direct and projected tone in which he said it made it clear that he intended me to listen.

"Yes sir, absolutely, we will have all issues resolved and taken care of without question, I am sending our Knight Commander to retrieve your daughter immediately, no sir… they won't be exposed to the public, he is going to get one of our darkened company cars right *now*." My father explained as he glanced up at me, locking his dark brown eyes on mine as he listened to Mr. Gilden's response with his mouth partially open, ready to reply at a moment's notice. The tug at the edge of his mouth gave away the undercurrent of anger sitting directly under that thinly veiled professional veneer. I involuntarily grasped onto the seatbelt as I felt the oncoming wave of reprisal coming towards me from my father. I am not afraid of demons, armies or any horror that may await me in any realm, but the wrath of my father I fear for without question.

"Yes, I can put you on speaker, one moment sir…" My father quickly moved to obey Mr. Gilden's command as he moved the small and thin wallet sized phone away from his ear and laid the device on the small table at the center of the limo carriage. As soon as it was laid on the table the phone immediately began to broadcast sound through the car's internal system.

Dr. Toft unfolded her legs as she leaned forward to listen, letting her grey-white hair fall forward over one shoulder as she carefully moved without making a sound.

"Thank you Gideon." Daniel Gilden's very American and professional voice crackled on the sound system's static, "This, without question, is the largest slip up of any security operation we have ever had as an organization since the beginning. We can go into details on why there wasn't a security team on site or how our Knight Commander failed to respond to the scene in time but for right now we have a bigger problem at hand. We had risks, but now our gamble has failed. You can't reveal something like this and have the world not know about it. There's already video of the girls walking around the campus going viral, they even have the attack on one of the cheerleading girls, Natalie Rayborn, in full footage from the on campus housing. It's a cell phone, but it's pretty obvious the video is not faked. We're in the open ladies and gentlemen, so you know what that means. Both Archlight and Valefor will know we're keeping the Gatehouse of Rosier and exactly where, so expect company. We've received word that the DPI have already activated the Boston Hellgate in Arkham, so expect Valefor Agents in your area soon if not already. I have made various plea bargains with the media, and called in some favors, but an entire blackout is just not going to be possible. So at 3:30 Eastern Standard Time today, the world will learn that we're not alone."

Dr. Toft took a breath in anticipation for what would come next, but I already knew it.

“And now my daughter is now one of these demons. This is beyond unacceptable, the fail safes should have been in place, Damien… where was your team last night?” Daniel Gilden, the father of Kayla, asked me directly. Every eye in the cabin turned to me, but my father’s eyes seemed to stare right through me.

How do I reply!? Do I tell him the truth? I was not stationed that evening, Knight Commander Shannon’s team was supposed to be watching them, but I had not found until this morning that Knight Commander Shannon was back at his mansion in Corpus Christi. But this was my project, my first command situation outside of a combat op. I was the director of the operation, it was my job to keep tabs on the matter, and I had failed.

“They were not on station sir, I accept responsibility for the inaction sir.” I said without any level or layer of excuse. I may not have defended myself, but I did defend my honor. A man takes responsibility for his actions, no matter what.

“I want an investigation into what happened Damien, I know you, and you’re your father’s son. Gideon would have never let me down, and neither would you. Something is very wrong here, and I don’t like being kept in the dark. Where is Knight Commander Shannon? Has he been informed on his daughter’s condition? Does anyone have a location on Sonya?” Daniel Gilden moved right along, and in doing so, may have spared me my father’s wrath. The chairman was upset, but not unkind, in his sideways compliment of me, he showed he still had faith in my ability, and this opportunity to track down Carter's child may yet prove to be a silver lining in all of this.

"No." My father answered plainly, "Sonya Shannon disappeared off all sensors as soon as she left the campus, I have several teams seeking her, but we have found nothing, we know her to be carrying Azazel's central nexus… she may be under the influence of the Nexan lifeform…" He explained with a tone of regret, but was quickly cut off by Daniel Gilden.

"No Gideon. That is not what is occurring here. Azazel is strong, she can corrupt, turn and violate the minds of individuals the world over, but not that mind. Not Carter's daughter. Don't forget Sonya Shannon is a protégé of the DPI's Survivalist program, her mind is incorruptible, something else is going on here Gideon… something that we're not being told and I don't like it. All of you, find out what's going on, and stop it before it gets out of hand…" Daniel completed with a rare candid moment of concern. We all knew that if he was troubled then something was deeply wrong. The man runs a practical shadow government, a man like that does not simply worry without a reason.

"The wheel has begun to turn. If we do not act quickly, the floodgates will open…

And this world will be reunited once more." He said more to himself then all of us.

"Sir?" I asked out of honest curiosity.

"Damien, in time, all will be revealed." My father answered for him.

"That's right, but for now, your responsibility is simple, find Sonya Shannon, and protect my daughter." Daniel Gilden ordered with solemn tone.

"As you wish." I answered, bowing slightly to the phone in reflex as Daniel Gilden hung up the line.

I sat back, and waited for my father's wrath.

But it never came.

"Carter Shannon." He said aloud, as Dr. Toft turned to face him, brushing aside a hanging lock of hair with her long fingers.

"You suspect something as well?" Dr. Toft asked with her slightly rasp and wavering tone.

My father folded his hands and steepled his fingers, resting his elbows on his knees as his wide face and carefully groomed facial hair set an outline with the slowly greying edges of his beard. "The man has always been ambitious, but on this occasion let us hope that his ambition has not driven him to pursue foolish actions. This is not a time for games, Azazel was sealed in the gatehouse for a very good reason, and tampering with such a structure would spell an end to our entire Earth. This is not something for ambitious men to play with..." My father returned as he sat back and poured himself a glass of water from the dispenser at the back of the limo, placing perfectly formed cubes of ice in the stout and heavy glass.

The zombie woman folded her arms and took a breath before looking back to my father with an expectant tone, "Gideon, I need to know... what is this gatehouse, really? What is the purpose of that structure and why is it so important that everyone and anyone will go to great lengths to ensure no one else gets their hands on it? If I am to assist, I need to know. Tell me what this is, *please*." Toft asked with more emotion than I have ever seen from her. Dr. Toft is a strong woman, undead or not she always has a handle on every situation she is a part of. To see her concerned, along with Daniel, the entire situation leaves me ill at ease.

"No." My father answered plainly, "And I mean no disrespect. But that information can only be given from the chairmen directly. It is not my place to say. By the very fact that you have not yet been told, shows the level of secrecy entailed in this. Mr. Gilden trusts you with his life, you know this. Yet he has not told you, do you understand?" My father explained in a way that could not be misinterpreted as cold.

The zombie woman nodded, as we all leaned on whatever was most comfortable, thinking.

The past 12 hours have been nothing but confusion, and chaos, and it looks like the next 12 will be more of the same.

But right now, we know one, all important, thing.

This world, is about to change.

Chapter Two

Kingsport Sheriff's Department Holding area

Kingsport, Maryland

United States of America, Earth

The Journal of Vivian Maybell

August 16th, 2011

8:02 AM

I suppose looking back on it; last night we were kept in a state of cognitive dissonance. I mean, who would believe us after what happened the night before? Where do I start? How could I possibly begin? I found myself strangely unapologetic for the events the night before, but since those first rays of dawn hit our cell window I could not help but feel an oncoming sense of dread.

This was real, this is me now.

Vivian Maybell…

succubus.

Wow…

I tugged on my bright orange jumpsuit and pieced together the night before. The temple, the woman… the transformation, Azazel, the police… and now this. No sooner had we stepped into the public sphere, we were caught and branded as outsiders…

We were not human anymore.

"Well… one thing is for sure…" Kayla whined in a complaining tone, somewhere behind me. "Orange clashes terribly with blue! We've been had Vivi! Caught for being blue on a Friday!" Kayla complained and moaned as she writhed in her baggy prison uniform jumpsuit on her top bunk like an upset toddler. She, like all of us, were covered from neck down. Only our tails were allowed to hang out from cut holes made kindly by one of the policemen here, the deputy chief, Sam Morel.

Last night was a flurry of activity. We were arrested and carried to municipal office. There we were kept out of public eye. No one at the station knew what to do with us. Silverlight LTD had been contacted and they downplayed the incident, saying that it wasn't a major issue but they would send a team to collect us in the morning. It was smart, but the obvious nature of the event was there…

This was a major issue,

We just proved we're not alone in this world.

And that scares the crap out of people.

I remember Natalie crying as Claudia tried to take charge. I felt numb, sitting at the back of the cell and pondering my position. Officers filtered in and out all night, just taking a peek at us, we were like animals, just for their display.

I looked up from my bunk in the prison cell at my companions. Claudia stared at herself in the sink, tugging at her horns and examining her jaw line, testing something probably. She stopped her self-examination to look over at Natalie, running a caring hand through the upset girl's hair. Poor Natalie rocked in her bed, holding her knees and sobbing to herself, clearly in regret of last night's events, and Kayla…

"C'mon cops! This is racism! What am I being held for!? I bought your calendar last year! I pay my traffic tickets! Now lemme go!" She shouted as she leapt onto the prison bars.

Kayla did what she always did, fight and pawn everything off on her sense of humor. Hiding that deep well of thought behind a smile and a silly façade. She's troubled, and deep, but some people embrace their pain, while others, like Kayla, hide it.

As for myself, I just wanted to sit and think. I have never really been the type to just go for something… why did I approach the woman last night? Why did I not fight harder to get away? And more importantly…

Why did I enjoy it so much?

It would be so easy to say that I was and continue to be under the influence of some magical force which controls all my actions from afar, but I know in my heart that's not true. I went to that temple because I wanted what it had to offer, and now I will be damned for it. Now we all will.

Possibly literally.

As I sit and wonder, I realize I do not hold any pity for myself, only sorrow that I dragged others into it.

I'm not ashamed of what I am. As a matter of fact, I like it…

It's what I always wanted. To be away from the normal, the human…

In many ways, I can be me.

Then suddenly, a noise distracted me from my reflection.

I watched Kayla's long ears perk up from her current "perch" half way up the bars of the prison cell. We've found that the succubae have elongated, almost elf-like ears that can tilt up or down slightly at will, almost like a dog's but less extreme. I personally found it rather endearing. She had gripped on with her clawed toes and hands and proceeded to make a demonic monkey out of herself in protest, trying to shake the bars loose, although, I imagine if she really wanted out, she could force the bars open with her newfound strength, all that really held any of us here was our willingness to listen, and the moral obligation to do no harm.

"Hey Vivi, voices I know!" Kayla said suddenly in an excited whisper. I perked up my ears to listen as well, to my surprise I found that I could actually angle my pointed ears, and like animal's, it really did make a difference.

"Sir, I understand. And ma'am, of course we will let you see them, but be warned… they don't look like anything natural, and we will have an armed guard standing watch" explained the deep voice of Samuel Morel, the officer we encountered last night.

"I will be fine, thank you for your concern." Purred the recognizable almost posh English accent of our professor, Dr. Cynthia Agnew.

We could hear the click and the whine of the heavy electronically locked door opening to the containment area, and the click of her heels as she walked up to our cell.

"PROFESSOR!" Kayla cried out happily. Everyone else looked up from where they were at her. Claudia and I sprang to attention. Kayla almost reached through the bars for a hug, but stopped when she realized the professor wasn't alone.

In addition to the two police officers, Professor Agnew was joined by a strong and tall young dark skinned man with a professional buzz cut and a clean shave, wearing a fine suit with a silver star on his lapel.

Damien.

I know I must have narrowed my eyes, because the corporate man tightened his tie and attempted to professionally look away.

I took the professor in, trying to gauge her reaction. Her auburn hair was back to its normal position, in a large wadded ponytail with one curl flipped forward. Her cool sunglasses of yesterday were replaced with the standard, nerd-approved variety, and she was once again in her lab coat with a red button down shirt and black dress pants.

But smiled as I noticed she still kept the heels.

Her face was completely unreadable. I couldn't see anything past that impassive face or a single hint in her hazel eyes. Were we in trouble? Or did she intend to help us? My heart also stopped with the realization she could find us appalling now, we could be seen as creatures, no longer her trusted students, and what of Damien? I knew he would know more about this then he was letting on, that much was obvious, but for him to just calmly accept us as we are?

That's something else entirely.

"Kayla… I saw all the videos from both the security cameras, and the radio recordings…" the Professor began, composing herself, "What were you thinking? You were supposed to be in charge, that's why I made you my TI. Digging in an archeology site? Actually touching relics with your bare hands? I expected so much more from you!" she laid into Kayla, technically our superior as the Professor's TI. We didn't expect a rebuke so harshly or so quickly, honestly I didn't know what to expect. It was clear Dr. Agnew was upset, but upset at what we did not know. She looked to Damien, who looked to the officers with an apologetic gaze, as if we were misbehaving children and he was embarrassed on our behalf.

Kayla released her grip from the bars in shame, slowly sliding to the floor as her ears and tail drooped. I know Kayla was feeling distraught at letting Dr. Agnew down, but I felt relief. If she cared enough to scold that meant she wasn't afraid of us. Further, it meant she still was willing to be our teacher.

"I'm… I'm sorry professor… please don't expel me." Kayla apologized in a voice far more sweet than I had ever heard from her. She glanced up at the professor with her big yellow eyes, tears forming at both sides.

"Oh… oh, no dear, that's not going to happen, not by me." The professor sighed, immediately feeling sympathy for Kayla as the professor put her hand to her head. She turned to Officer Morel, "What have they been charged with? Damien, can't we do something?" She passively postulated to Damien and the officers, who were standing just outside of view until now.

Officer Morel offered his answer in a very conscientious and deep gravel tone.

"Disturbing the peace, they were simply deemed a public threat…" The dark skinned officer listed, scratching his thinly shaved head. "Nothing really worth holding them any longer over, if you are certain they aren't going to do anything…" I took a moment to study the officer that seemed to be caring for us all evening and this morning. He had been kind, conscientious, and understanding, and the only real sign of humanity we've seen through the night, away from the gawkers and scathing remarks. He had a wide brow and a kind set of brown eyes. He was in good physical fitness and looked to be in his early thirties. Everything about him seemed calm and inviting, almost a complete juxtaposition to the cold and calculative Damien.

"We never were a threat!" Kayla protested, pouting up at the officer.

"Miss Gilden you will be quiet!" Professor Agnew snapped, Kayla immediately folded back her ears and retreated her hands under her chest, drawing back her tail as close to herself as possible.

Another officer stepped forward; she clearly had some reservations about letting us out. I had seen her several times as well, often in close proximity to Officer Morel. Several times during the night she took Natalie away from us to talk to her. Natalie always seemed placated, and the woman didn't seem to have a grudge against us, but from what I had heard from Natalie, the woman wasn't worried about us, she was worried *for* us.

"I don't know if we should… I mean… look at them. Do you think the people of Kingsport are going to be just fine with them walking around?" Came the curt and concerned voice of the second officer, a fair skinned woman in her early 30's with a slender face, brown hair with short bangs, and a cropped ponytail, most likely shoulder length if she took out the band that held it in place. She looked tired, exhausted emotionally as well as physically. I could tell she'd been talking to Natalie most of the night.

"Lea, they are just kids, college students, that's it" Replied the male officer, getting his keys and opening the cell door.

"You're free to go girls" he said warmly.

"Thank you for your understanding Officer…?" Professor Agnew thanked, offering her hand and tilting to ask for his name.

"Deputy Chief Sam Morel, you know, like more-el oh and this is Lea Therrien, my partner." Mr. Morel explained, returning the handshake with a smile. I managed to catch 'Lea' slightly cringe at the word 'partner', and from that look in her eye, it's not hard at all to assume she wanted a little more than that.

"The Silverlight corporation thanks you and your fellow officers for your discretion in this matter." Damien politely enforced as he shook the officer's hand.

"Uh, sir, we might not have said anything but…" Officer Lea began, I could already see Officer Morel tense.

"But?" Damien asked.

"Yes, I should be frank with you sir, there was local media on the scene when we took them away, not much news occurs in Kingsport in recent history and the media have a habit of following us out of the driveway." Officer Morel stated in an apologetic tone.

"We are aware, thank you for informing me anyway." Damien nodded as he mentally processed the information. I could tell he wasn't happy but he was willing to be professional about it.

"What's important is that the girls are safe." Officer Morel kindly added.

Damien looked up at the Deputy Sheriff and smiled an empty grin. "Yes, you're right." He nodded as he immediately went back to forming whatever plans he had cooked up in there. I know I can read emotions now but you have to *have* emotions in the first place in order to read them.

Officer Lea sighed, and walked over to Natalie, "Hey, are you going to be ok?" she asked Natalie with a kind tone as she pulled out Natalie's cross necklace from her pocket and handed it back to her.

Natalie nodded, Officer Lea sighed as she leaned over to give the poor girl a hug. "You're going to be just fine." Officer Lea kindly assured as she patted the back of our Christian demoness. Once more Natalie nodded in unwilling acceptance.

We all filed out; thanking the officers for letting us go as we did.

"I suggest you girls pick up a change of clothes on the way home, the clothing you were in was nothing but tattered rags, I can't in good faith send you off like that, so just have someone drop off the jumpsuits later. Girls I don't know quite how you got this way, nor do I really care, but… just take care of yourselves, no more scaring people into calling us down there, you hear?" Mr. Morel advised in a kind tone with a bit of a laugh.

"We understand… thank you…" We said with the drone of schoolchildren.

As soon as we got outside into the parking lot, we saw the Professor's slightly dingy white Hyundai, and Damien's clean jet black Escalade sitting right next to it. I imagine they arrived at exactly the same time, convenient. I didn't know if Kayla or Natalie knew Damien, but the proximity that Damien kept to Kayla on the way out seemed to suggest they knew each other, and once the police office door was shut and Damien was certain things were out of the way. The very educated, smooth talking corporate spook set to work immediately.

Or so I thought.

"Now you've gone and done it Kayla." He said with utter rebuke in a more casual English accent, my jaw must have visibly dropped because they both turned to look at me for a moment.

Not what I was expecting at all.

"Damien, if you think even for a moment any of this is my fault you will have my father here so fast…" Kayla started to threaten back, ok. So she does know Damien.

"Your father will be here at three." Damien cut her off.

The conversation stopped dead for an electric moment.

"Dad's coming here?" Kayla said, getting worried, her tail and wings betrayed her feelings instantaneously.

"As I've said, you've really done it, I am off doing damage control, apparently the media already knows of your…" Damien panned his eyes up and down Kayla's body, something she responded too by turning as to not present her newly enhanced chest. "New forms, and now I have to talk to the Supporting Dean about our next moves. Soon parents will be questioning sending their children to Kingsport, you've really gone and made a mess of things…"

I cut in.

"Now wait just a minute…" I said as I walked over and stood between Kayla and Damien. "No way dude, no way!" I scolded as I wagged my finger at him. My tail flicked back and forth as my little bat-like wings stood on end. "There is no way you're so cool at seeing us. You know what we can do, you know what we look like! We're totally scary now to the average person, I'm a freakin demon now for crying out loud! You're being way, way too cool about this, which means you know. Or knew, what was going to happen. You knew that site would do this to us and you just let it happen. No! Worse, you actually wanted to stop and film it! I saw the cameras don't deny your men put them in!"

But Damien, being the same corporate spook I had to deal with for the entirety of our little nine month field trip, deflected like a champ.

"Yes, the Silverlight Corporation DID put in those security cameras, they are for preventing theft and tampering with the site, something you, Miss Vivian Maybell, did. I did not know that the Temple of Rosier would transform you into a succubus, but I did know the temple was down there, so did you." He spat back coldly.

"But you did know Succubae existed. Otherwise you wouldn't have identified us so quickly." Claudia concluded, folding her hands and standing at my back. I folded my arms to do just the same pose she did, but with more gusto.

"It was a lucky guess." Damien answered.

"Stop!" Kayla shouted, stopping our dual inquisition.

Damien to my surprise stopped completely for Kayla.

"I still can't believe you'd do that to yourself." Damien said as he looked her over once more.

"I like being like this, thank you." Kayla replied, sticking out her tongue as she folded her arms and made a single indignant wag of her tail dismissively.

"Either way, I'm going to have to ask you all to come with me." Damien said as he pressed a button within his suit coat, making the SUV's door slide open.

"No you will most certainly not." Dr. Agnew finally spoke up.

"I beg your pardon?" Damien asked as he turned to face her.

The professor held onto Kayla's shoulder as she moved me back towards her. Natalie and Claudia closed in behind her, as our teacher went to bat for us. "These girls are my students, they are my responsibility. If anyone deserves blame for what has happened, it would be me for leaving them unattended. Do not punish them or treat them like animals for what they are now. They will be under me, at the University, continuing their studies. I apologize to both you and your company Mr. Focht. But I cannot allow you to take them."

Damien looked at all of us, then the professor, and then nodded. Something I wasn't expecting.

"I can respect that Dr. Agnew." He said with a soldier's honesty. "But if I let you do that, you will have to meet me half way. They have to either be at the campus, or at their homes, they can't gallivant off into public. Not right now anyway, I'm still doing damage control. These women will cause a media blitzkrieg if the news gets a good hold of them. You will have to protect them. We will give you all the equipment you ladies need to keep researching the ruins and yourselves since you are so interested, but in exchange we just ask you not to go on the public airwaves in any form, and please, please do this for me, don't try to convert anyone, especially men." Damien compromised.

"Why not men?" Claudia asked immediately.

"Because your venom would eat them from the inside out Miss Brashear." Damien answered with exact and extreme honestly.

"Oh!" Several of us said at once with a rather immediate negative reaction.

"So you do know about us." Natalie spoke up.

"I really can't say ma'am, I'm sorry." Damien answered in as much honesty as he could.

Professor Agnew finished our little discussion for us, "Well, we will find what answers we can on our own then Mr. Focht, and thank you for providing what tools we need to do so. I think we can abide by your terms, and hopefully will not cause any more trouble for you or Mr. Gilden."

Damien started towards his car and sighed, turning back to us as he stood on the running board, half in, half out, "Remember, he will be there at three, you ladies have a good day, I have many places to be and not much time to do it in. Be careful, and goodbye." Damien said as he got back in his Escalade, and drove away, leaving us with the professor...

And a startling realization of how much trouble we were in.

Chapter Three

In Dr. Cynthia Agnew's Hyundai Sonata

Enroute to Kingsport University, Maryland

United States of America, Earth

The Journal of Claudia Brashear

August 16th, 2011

10:12 AM

I felt the edge of my short sleeved polo shirt, it was white with black trim, and fit me tightly, but it was the only thing that Dr. Agnew could pick up for me in a pinch, and I am very thankful. She had gone into the local general store on our behalf, and picked up a set of clothing for each of us. Mostly jeans and a t-shirt, but it was something nevertheless. Better than prison orange anyway.

But now where do we rest?

What happens now?

I remember reading tales, fairy stories, my favorite. Stories of young men and women becoming strange beings, meeting incredible creatures and having adventures, but real life wasn't anything like that. We're different, feared, and the very thought of what humanity will do with us sends shivers up my no longer existent spine. I looked across the backseat, seeing Kayla's reflection in the window as she stared outside, her yellow eyes reflecting back. Natalie folded her hands and had them tucked into her lap. Just politely and courteously waiting for the ride to end, Vivian chatted with the Professor, excited, with her lap piled high in all the books and various items the professor had moved to accommodate us.

"So, you think there's anything cool about us now?" Vivian asked the professor, eager, curious. Her loving tone and happy smile made me want to smile too. Something I've always loved about her, she's excellent at looking for the good in things, she complains, excessively, but she always finds a way to brighten anyone's day.

"What do you mean Vivian?" The professor asked, a bit of concern in her tone of voice. I knew what Vivian was asking, but only because I understood her way. I'd explain it, but she clearly was bent on doing so herself.

"I mean like super powers! Like do succubus have ice beams or x-ray vision? Maybe super strength or fli… oh right we already fly… we can fly professor! How cool is that!?" Vivian asked like a child, excited and carefree. I don't think she was really thinking about all the negatives this could also cause, but I am glad she is enjoying it while she can.

"Succubae are the demons of lust and envy, we're apparently very good at looking sexy, and having sex." Kayla said impassively, head in her hand and sighing as she looked over to Vivian.

"Laaaaame." Vivian whined as she paddled the tops of the books she was holding for the professor. "I'll discover all my powers yet! Then we will carve a new chapter in succubae history!" She raised a hand to the roof and almost lost her stack of books, quickly catching it with her hand and tail, as she whipped it around and used the arrow point end's broadside to catch the sliding pile.

Natalie turned to Kayla, asking politely, "Kayla… now that we're all changed, is there anything else you can tell us? Your father and his company seem to know a great deal... maybe there's something you can tell us?"

The car grew quiet, even the professor was curious to learn something. As Kayla stretched and tugged on her black and white arm socks, brushing aside turquoise hair as she thought a moment. "I don't know… it's hard to separate fact from fiction anymore…"

I understood what she meant, and nodded to her in agreement as I took a moment to look at my sky blue skin.

"Dad told me…" Kayla began, thinking about it as she waxed nostalgic. Listening to the hollow hum of tires on asphalt as the car drove down the long straight road towards the university, "Dad used to tell me bedtime stories, tales that I loved… It was only when he could pull time away from work to be with me, right before bed. It was my favorite time of day." She said as she smiled, looking back at Vivian, the Professor then turning to Natalie and I before letting that impish grin fade as she continued.

"Well in his stories, he once spoke about the Succubus… started off pretty negative, saying they were annoying and often interfered in plans that didn't concern them. He told me they were very strong, very beautiful, and extremely deadly. But then he would go on and say that they were some of the bravest creatures he ever saw… and they were the only beings that truly understood the nature of Prolecto." Kayla explained with a careful tone, considering her own words as she said them. Natalie perked her ears slightly as she raised an eyebrow. I could already see Dr. Agnew and Vivian turning to ask the question, but Natalie had beaten them too it.

"What's Prolecto?" Natalie asked directly. I smiled, I hadn't heard that word in a long time, a long time…

"Prolecto is a subject of allure." Kayla explained, "It literally means allure in Latin, but more accurately it's the force that guides you. It's the method behind your actions, and the reason and drive that spurs what you do. Dad once said the color of a succubus, or incubus, told the world directly their element. Dad was always on about Prolecto, it was a concept he held dear. Philos, Eros, Quietus, and Agape, four elements, four kinds of love. All guiding forces in the way we act, and experience the world we live in. In many ways, Prolecto is the term for your entire perspective, the what, why and who that you are, and how you see the world."

Natalie nodded, thinking it over, "That's… wow, that's very interesting, I never thought of anything like that before…" She said as the mulled it over. Testing the word on her tongue.

"My mother used to use that word to describe the world." I added, "She told me to understand someone's Prolecto, the subject of their allure, was to understand where they fit in life. Of course being a superstitious woman in Mumbai, that meant she could pin down what was supposed to be people's destiny within the first few moments of meeting them…" I shook my head as I thought of her, mimicking her actions as I wagged my finger at a person that was not there, "See there Claudia, that one is going to be a great doctor! He knew that cat was sick, and it was! You should marry him, he will have money!" I pantomimed my mother's way of speaking as I arched my back to copy her scolding, know it all, way.

And as I did I realized I missed my mother, we were already on poor terms though, I imagine with my transformation now, they would feel their daughter was truly gone...

Natalie giggled at my impression, as Vivian smiled, "Did your mom ever tell you your destiny Claudia? Did she ever explain what kind of person you were to be?"

I looked over to Vivian, she always asked the most cutting questions at the most inopportune time, and was always unaware when she did so. "She did, but we didn't agree... she said I would be a good partner, a loving wife... but I wanted a career. So no luck there I'm afraid." I said with a shrug. There was no way I was going to be an Indian housewife, no thank you.

"Maybe you were meant to help people." Vivian said directly as she looked ahead, focused, watching the school appear as Dr. Agnew pulled onto the campus. "Maybe we were." She mused.

"You're certainly all a help to me." Dr. Agnew said as she glanced up from the rearview mirror to me.

"Really Dr. Agnew? Even after we made such a mess of things?" Natalie asked with some concern.

"Oh Natalie, especially so." The professor continued. "You've given me a glimpse into something I could have never dreamed, and we're going to see this through. Don't fret Natalie, you're among friends."

I felt Natalie relax as we pulled in, which was good, as I was growing tense.

"How shall we proceed professor?" I asked with great trepidation as the car pulled into the parking lot, coming to a stop right outside the Archeology building. "Just... walk to the lab?" I mused, realizing we were about to step out onto morning classes. I was concerned on how the students would react.

"We have too, I don't have another way." Dr. Agnew replied with a shrug. "You will have to experience the world again eventually, personally I'd rather it be sooner than later".

She was right, and I knew it. I looked down and outstretched my hands, looking at my sky blue skin and claw pointed ends to my fingertips, seeing how familiar, yet alien they appeared to me. As I did, I found a dark blue hand in mine, as Vivian reached around her seat and placed one hand in mine, squeezing it closed in support.

I smiled.

"Let's go." I said in false courage, as Dr. Agnew opened her door.

We got out, and as fate would have it, we decided to get out at a time where the classes were changing, students across the campus made their trek to their next building, and next field of study. A torrent of young minds and bodies, some deep in thought, others without a care in the world. Natalie held onto my hand, as I returned the motion. For some reason, caring for someone else always gave me strength, and so I had the courage to go on. Kayla stayed right up front with the professor, brave, strong, and unafraid. Vivian kept as the anchor point to the group, standing middle and making sure everyone was sticking together like a nervous sheepdog, I could see her looking back, performing a headcount every few seconds. It made me smile.

The first group of students we had to pass through barely noticed us, just plodding along in their daily chores. I started to relax, realizing that perhaps the other students didn't think anything of us. After all, there are so many people that will go out in strange costume, or an unusual garb, perhaps we are being seen as that? I could feel the emotions rolling off of Vivian, as she came to the same conclusions as me. I saw her tail flick happily as she realized we were making it through the crowds, but as she did, we heard a scream.

They suddenly noticed us.

The crowd parted instantly, just as we were about to enter the Archeology building we found our way blocked by a sea of gawkers and students who were suddenly too frightened to move. Dr. Agnew put out a hand in a reflex to protect us, as Vivian stepped around and shook her hands out in front of her attempting to calm the crowd.

"No, wait! It's ok! We're just students like you, we're not here to hurt anybody!" Vivian declared as she whipped her tail about and fluttered her wings nervously, an action that quickly backfired.

"Look she has horns!" A student shouted.

"Is that real?" Gawked another.

"Whoa…" gasped a third.

The comments came rolling in. I could hear the chatter of scared and concerned people, growing ever curious as they crowded us in. The situation was getting worse by the second. I saw a couple campus security officers closing in from afar, trying to get through the crowd.

To my surprise, I felt Natalie's hand leave mine, as she pushed between us to stand front and center, putting herself out before us all.

"Sam! Samantha Revel!" She called out, picking out a face in the crowd as she spotted a few cheerleaders among the group.

"It's me Natalie! Natalie Rayborn!" She explained as she put a hand to her chest, tapping twice as she looked to her friends with a pleading expression.

There was a group of seemingly out of place people among the crowd. A beautiful tall blonde cheerleader was with three nerdy looking young men all with lanky builds and varying degrees of brown curly hair. They all seemed to congregate around her as the blonde cheerleader with blue eyes and fair skin and a lanky figure took a step forward. "Natalie?" She asked with a dubious stare as Natalie's friend, Samantha, started to recognize her friend's face among the new body features.

"Oh my god is that you?" Samantha gasped as she reached slightly and stopped, curious and not understanding.

"Yes, it's me!" Natalie shook her head as she fought away tears once more, "I'm… I'm just different now… there was an accident, and…" She struggled to explain, "It's still me, but please, help me calm people down…" Natalie asked in honest tone. The crowd seemed to stop to listen to Natalie and Samantha's conversation. "I don't even know all the details, or if this is permanent or anything but right now we need to get back to the lab and figure some things out… please Sam… guys… help me."

The boys looked around at each other, and shrugged.

"Yeah ok." The one with the darkest hair said as he shrugged and waved his hands, "Nothin to see people, back it up…" he said as his two friends started to do the same in a completely nonchalant tone. I was surprised they were so calm, but I'm beginning to realize that the world is nothing as I thought it was.

"Thank you Justin… Sean, Jack, guys, thanks…" Natalie genuinely thanked with a slight bow.

"I… I don't know what I can do… want me to say something on the air?" Samantha asked, my eyes opened wide when I realized where I recognized her name. Samantha Revel runs the school's radio tower broadcast program as the DJ… she often spoke on Chinese Mythology, I actually listened to her show regularly. The boys with her must be the undergrads that work with her, I hear them from time to time talking about video games and things that don't really interest me, I tend to turn them off when they come on, but they were certainly helpful today.

Then I realized this was the radio group… this could be a problem.

"No Sam, we're trying to keep it low for now… but maybe later… I can do an interview?" Natalie asked with a tone of compromise, raising pitch at the end.

"Yeah… let's do that… for now… go Natalie. We'll help you all we can…" Samantha encouraged as she waved her hand to dismiss us. Samantha and the others directed people away from us, helping us get past the crowd. Dr. Agnew didn't look a gift horse in the mouth and cautioned us onward, prodding us into the building, to the lab, and safety.

We breathed a sigh of relief, looking to one another for a brief moment before we started down the hall.

"First contact achieved…" Vivian sighed, "That was nothing like the movies…"

"Still better than I expected." Kayla returned, "No one threw anything."

"That's a start." I threw in, trying to stay optimistic.

"If they get violent, back in my office I do have a can of bear mace." Dr. Agnew offered, trying to make light of the situation.

"Yaaaay…" Natalie weakly cheered, waving her hands in a lackluster way, "Bear mace." She hung her head as we walked down the empty hall together, Natalie's distraught footsteps left clapping noises with every somber clomp.

Dr. Agnew wrapped her arm around the girl, pulling her close, "Now cheer up dear, you see your friends were still there to help you." Dr. Agnew pointed out to Natalie as she gave a couple conscientious tugs to try and cheer her up.

"Y-yeah… you're right…" Natalie realized, picking up a little.

"Yeah those guys were pretty cool, how come I never see you hang out with them Natalie?" Vivian asked as she slowed her walk to allow the professor and Natalie to catch up. I was curious on this as well. They seemed very different from the type of people Natalie would normally hang out with.

"Samantha and I are on the Cheerleading team together." Natalie explained. "She's very smart, and she often lets me go hang out on top of the radio tower, the tallest building on our campus. I go up there to think a lot… and get away from Sonya." As she finished explaining Dr. Agnew let us all into the lab.

I noticed as we entered that Silverlight had put in some heavier security measures, they put up heavy doors and had a biometric lock installed on the door. Looks like the Professor will have to let us in and out. Very clever Silverlight. I decided to say nothing about it as we walked in, but privately made note of the many new defense systems, darkened windows, and other small additions that cautioned outsiders to keep out.

"Get away from Sonya? I thought you two were best friends?" Vivian asked in a curious tone, as we all found a seat in the small workstation area around us. Kayla draped herself over one of the lab tables, propping herself up on her elbows as the rest of us took a seat like civilized people. Dr. Agnew had a couple things to say on the matter as well.

"I have been meaning to ask you, now that we are away from Silverlight, where is Sonya? She is obviously no longer with you, and she's dropped off Silverlight's radar, so if there's anything you can tell me… it might be crucially important." The professor asked in a tone still kind but clearly with an undercurrent of business.

Natalie sighed as she looked over to the professor from her small black rolling chair, shuffling the chair from side to side as she spoke, a little bit of a nervous habit as she explained what she needed to say, "Sonya… is a friend of necessity." She began, "When I first came to school, I joined cheer because that was how I always met friends. It gave a common ground and let us all rally together. But this school was different. Sonya rules that clique like a military unit. I remember being surprised when she told me how to dress, what parties we would and would not be attending. She constantly uses her sexuality as a weapon, as well as ours... something I've never really been comfortable with. If a boy wasn't doing what she wanted to do, she'd threaten to take the team elsewhere, and all his social credibility with it… I… professor…" She stopped as she folded her hands and looked up at the professor.

"If Sonya Shannon cannot be found, it's because she doesn't *want* to be found." Natalie finished with direct eye contact, making sure her point was brought home. Natalie's serpentine eyes told of volumes of repressed aggression towards Sonya, and the feelings that rolled off of her to all of us told that there was much more we could know about the two of them, but likely would never want too.

The room was quiet for a moment, thinking on what may wait ahead of us. Sonya was always annoying in my opinion, but dangerous? I couldn't see it. But if Natalie is that worried about it, who am I to say otherwise?

Our silence was broken by the click of the entryway as Silverlight personnel began to pour in, carrying more devices and carts full of electronic equipment. They moved into the laboratory with military precision as they began setting up and unloading new equipment and tools right around us. The professor shot to her feet as the rest of us all perched or recoiled in some surprise from the action. I realized before I knew it that I had hopped onto the nearest lab table and gripped onto the edge with my clawed feet and one hand... like a monkey, or other animal. I let my wings and tail droop in self disappointment in my increasingly animal-like behavior as I hopped back to my feet and straightened myself out. Trying to look the proper woman once again.

"What is..." The professor started to say before a tall man in a grey jumpsuit with the Silverlight corporate logo passed off a datapad to the professor with a light-pen, cutting off her statement entirely.

"New equipment and all biometric materials required for studying your demons, now sign here please." The man said curtly.

I bristled at a particular word in his sentence as Dr. Agnew accepted the pen and pad, turning it around and signing on the appropriate area, "*My* demons? Has this happened before? Or elsewhere? Is this specific technology for studying them?"

"I dunno lady" The workman answered in a very New York tone, "I just work here. In the meantime I suggest you keep your demons away from the public eye..." He took a deep breath before continuing, giving a completely lackluster finish to his explanation, "We here at Silverlight realize you have a choice of technology solutions, thank you for choosing Silverlight, if you have any questions contact technical support open twenty four hours a day, seven days a week. Have a good day." He finished explaining, then made a motion for the rest of his men to leave, and so they did... leaving us dumbfounded, with copious amounts of new technology.

"Awww..." Kayla cooed happily as the door slammed, smiling up at the professor, "We're Dr. Aggie's personal demons now!" she laughed at the situation, finding it funny, "Now to heckle you into evilness... Go ahead professor, go get doughnuts, with sprinkles on it... you know you wwwwaaaaaannnaaaa." Kayla purred as she wiggled her fingertips, "tempting" the professor in a most stereotypical way.

Dr. Agnew put her hands on her hips and held back a smile as she looked at Kayla with a roll of her eyes, "Ok you… let's see if we can't learn a thing or two about what's going on. As long as Silverlight is willing to foot the research bill I don't see why we shouldn't learn a thing or two. So… up on the table little miss temptress…" Dr. Agnew patted the new biometric table Silverlight just wheeled in.

"We're going to examine a demon."

Chapter Four

Kingsport University Archeology Lab

Kingsport, Maryland

United States of America, Earth

The Journal of Natalie Rayborn

August 16th, 2011

12:36 PM

"AAAAAeeeeehhhhh" Kayla hammed up her response to the tongue depressor and flash light inserted into her mouth as the professor examined her on the table normally reserved for rock sampling.

I shook my head as Vivian and Claudia both peeked around Dr. Agnew's shoulder, trying to get a glimpse of what's inside. Silverlight had furnished us with all that we would need, giving us a chance to see if we can make sense of ourselves, perhaps learn a thing or two about what we now were… I personally hoped for a cure, but from the way everyone's been talking, this sounds permanent so…

What do I do now?

The Rayborn family has been a military family for as long as we can remember it. It's been a pretty simple existence, live off a fort, boys join the military, girls marry, and church is every Sunday. I had a pretty set life, and a pretty set way, now that's all derailed. I actually spent most of my time down in Virginia and Georgia, and because of that I'm a pretty southern gal, but up here in Maryland I have got to keep my southern ways in check, especially out here in college. People here always interpret southern as dumb and for some, being Christian only makes it worse.

I know I sound a little defensive, but I've always had to be a little defensive about my faith… and for a couple reasons too. If I was not showing it off enough in the south, people would assume I'm unfaithful. Just the same, if I showed off my Christianity and southern accent too much up here, I would get an immediate blacklist as one of "those people". I have to admit I kind of hate it that I live in a world now that assumes Christianity comes with being small minded, homophobic, and a bigot. Just the same I can't help but feel that the people who assume that this is always true are just as shallow as the people they despise.

But... where do I stand now? I've been turned into a succubus, a being of a damned, a demon. How... how do you cope with that? As I look down at my blue hands, I realize if I concentrate a bit the fingertips form claws... that's a monster thing. I'm a monster. I'm not the little girl daddy raised anymore. I'm this creature...

Oh my, my father... I wonder what he is going to say?

I hadn't even thought about that. How on earth can I tell my family about this? Just go "Hey mom, I sprouted horns and wings and now look like one of those stripper signs!" that'll go over great... Here's hoping I can have a rational conversation with my local pastor, sort things out.

I wonder if he'll even see me? I'm hoping I can get my friend Olivia to talk to him on my behalf, after all she's his daughter...

It's amazing... when you think about it, on how fragile your relationships with other people can be. One wrong thing done, another thing said, and a long relationship can go down in flames.

"...Natalie..." Professor Agnew called politely, snapping me out of my thought bubble as I looked around to see the other girls kind of staring at me...

I must have not been paying attention for a while.

"Oh I'm sorry did you need me?" I asked, tilting my head to try and be as apologetic as I could.

"Oh no honey, you look a little preoccupied. But we need the piece of equipment you're sitting on. We're going to see what's inside Kayla..." Dr. Agnew explained.

"What!? Inside!" I said suddenly hopping up to see what I was sitting on, I just picked a hard flat surface and well... since I'm so light now I can sit on pretty much anything. I turned to inspect the machine that I had been sitting on. It looked like a standalone generator with a long silver tube looped in a glass case, as everything else did in this lab, it sported the silver star of the Silverlight Corporation.

"So what is this tool and why do you want to see what's inside us?" I asked the professor, curious.

She explained quickly, "Well you see Natalie, you are fascinating, absolutely fascinating. As we can see with Kayla here all of you possess fangs of a carnivorous nature, down to the molars, yet none of you have any desire to eat meat."

"Yeah… actually no desire to eat anything really…" I admitted. My friends all nodded to show they felt the same way.

Kayla chimed up to join in the group conversation, "Well Professor, Vivian and I both had some hard candies given to us by Officer Morel and Lea last night on our way to the cell, but we never really felt hungry but the candy certainly tasted good. It's not that we don't or can't eat, we just really feel no desire to do so."

The professor looked around at all of us.

"Is that how all of you feel?" She asked.

We nodded, that's exactly how I felt. I could probably go for some lemon meringue or perhaps an orange soda flavored cream popsicle. But those were favorite comfort foods of mine. Not something I need for sustenance. I don't know what it is I eat anymore… I hope it's not something disgusting, like blood.

"Well, I do have a couple ideas then… here Kayla are you willing to be my volunteer again?" Dr. Agnew asked as she opened up the device I was standing by and pulled out the long sterile metal tube.

"Whoooaah… where's that going?" Kayla asked, her yellow serpentine eyes going wide as the professor raised the pipette end to Kayla.

"Oh my goodness, in your mouth silly. Now say ahh. This is a medical snake, it has a camera and will allow us to see inside you." Dr. Agnew explained as she cleaned the end again before putting it towards Kayla.

"Oook… AHHHHHH" Kayla playfully opened her mouth wide and flopped out her tongue. Hah, I didn't know that our tongues narrowed, almost like a snake's. Thankfully they didn't fork or I'd have a whole new issue to worry over.

Dr. Agnew put the snake camera down into Kayla's mouth, who winced, expecting a bad choking experience but found it was really easy to let the tube go down.

"Wahu! Nob gab weefwex!" Kayla admonished with a happy tone.

"What did she say? Am I hurting her?" The professor spoke up, concerned.

"No gag reflex." Claudia translated, sighing as she looked over at Kayla. Claudia likes things to be taken seriously, which makes me wonder why she likes Vivian so much. I also notice she never gets mad at Vivian being silly, but as soon as Kayla does something funny Claudia immediately disapproves. I wonder if people are aware of how they act? I wonder if I am? Huh. I don't get to see how I am seen by others, I bet my opinion of myself and how I interact with the world is totally different from what other people see. I wonder if they see me as a deep thinker with a love of the profound? No… probably not. They probably see a dumb cheerleader who never pays…

"…attention." Vivian finished a sentence as I shook my head to concentrate on what they were talking about.

"Oh, there she is!" Vivian perked up as she looked over at me. "Hey Natalie do you want to see what's in a Kayla?" She asked me kindly as she backed away from a monitor so I could have a turn.

I nodded, still partially thinking about human perception. Making Vivian smile as I sort of absently I walked over to the console and had a peek, and what I saw I couldn't understand right away.

"There's nothing…" I said to the room. "I don't see a thing here, there's absolutely nothing."

"That's right." Dr. Agnew patiently explained to me. "That's because there doesn't seem to be anything down there, you're hollow inside Natalie, all of the Succubae are."

I felt my ears move up and down as my tail and wings stood on end in sheer surprise. I drew back my hands to press the backs of them against my chest as I recoiled.

"Ww-what!?" I shouted in disbelief, backing away from the monitor before hopping back to it quickly with a flutter, grabbing onto the monitor to really focus on what I was seeing. I looked to Kayla with the pipe still in her mouth, and seeing the cable still leading to this readout... it's definitely what the camera's showing me... I could see the wall of where her skin began along the outside, but there were no organs, no blood, no... anything.

"Yeah, we're seriously hollow, look, and if you press fast enough..." Vivian assisted me as she pressed really hard on my stomach, causing me to make a rapid sound like a squeaky toy. I shot her an incredulous glance. She shrugged.

"Man..." I said aloud, testing it myself to hear the squeak... and it did...

"I'm squeaky."

"Hey waitaminute." I said in surprise, letting my southern accent slip. "Kayla said she had hard candies last night... if nothing's in there shouldn't they still be rattling around in there, probably somewhere around her feet?"

The group of scientists around me all looked at each other with a dumbfounded look. I guess no one thought of that one. I guess the cheerleader's not so useless after all.

"Wholy wap! Wets chetkit owt!" Kayla excitedly answered, still with the tube in her mouth.

"Well... ok then." Dr. Agnew agreed with interest as she began to move the camera around to inspect for the missing hard candies, but they were nowhere to be found. Even down in her feet.

"Noffin!" Kayla noted excitedly at seeing no sign of the candies anywhere. "Festmeh!" She ordered as she pointed to her little purse left from last night. I walked over and grabbed it off her computer desk.

"What does she want?" Dr. Agnew asked.

"Test me. She's looking for food I think." I said as Kayla nodded in agreement. I reached into the purse and pulled out a couple peppermint candies she had stashed away in her purse. Kayla motioned greedily for me to bring them to her, as she fidgeted to make the interior camera point up at her cavernous mouth. Honestly, still seeing that she was hollow made me shake my head in disbelief. I mean… that means I'm just skin right now… or something… Anyway, I handed off the candies to Kayla who quickly unwrapped one of them and then handed it to Dr. Agnew to place in her mouth as she held it open. Dr. Agnew took a deep breath in a slightly awkward moment and pressed the candy into Kayla's mouth. We all looked at the camera with deep interest as it slid down her throat.

The peppermint was swallowed, and as one would expect from already having a *tube* down there Kayla choked and gagged a moment in a move unexpected by no one. But once the peppermint started to fall into the open interior of Kayla it picked up a flash of light around it, and as suddenly as it started to fall, it was burned up like an object entering the earth's atmosphere with a brief fiery conclusion. Everyone observing made the same, surprised face in almost unison, I have no idea what we were all expecting, but it certainly wasn't that.

"Whoah…" Vivian leaned forward to press as close to the screen as possible as she blinked twice as that now probably no longer existent brain processed what was happening. "So… wow… so if we eat, it just burns up in… stomach orbit. Like I got a stomach oven or something!" She attempted to classify what was going on, but no one really had a solid grasp.

"That's very descriptive Vivian…" Dr. Agnew attempted to answer without trying to belittle Vivian's grasping-at-straws too harshly. "But it does appear that you have quite a few secrets that would be worth exploring. If you would like, I'm willing to cancel my classes for the day to stay with you and continue studying you girls, that is if it is all right with you."

I felt a calm, warm feeling wash over me as she offered to stay with us. I was comforted by her presence, and having Dr. Agnew want to stay with us, and not be afraid was the most reassuring thing I've had since I turned. I've been so scared, since the very first moment. But the feeling of love and comfort from the professor seemed to provide so much warmth to me that I felt as if I just had a good meal or a full night's rest.

"Of course it's all right Professor. Right girls?" Claudia answered for us as she looked around, we all nodded in agreement.

To my surprise, Dr. Agnew quickly took a breath as she reached up to wipe away a quickly forming tear. "Girls… I've been thinking it for hours now and honestly I can't bear to keep it back any longer… I'm so sorry." She apologized to all of us. Leaning back against the lab table as she said it, letting the weight of the world rest on her shoulders as sighed.

Vivian was the first to react, rushing up and laying a dark blue hand on the professor's shoulder while supporting her back with the other, Vivian's tail flicked as her long ears raised slightly. "What!? Why? Why do you have to apologize? You've done nothing wrong!" she defended on Dr. Agnew's behalf.

"This…" Dr. Agnew explained, "This is all my fault. I dragged you girls into this, I left you unattended to go on a stupid date with someone who never did show up anyway then only found out about what was going on when I saw you being arrested on the news! I'm a terrible teacher and I don't deserve to be your caretakers… Earlier today when Damien told me that you were my responsibility now… I realized that I lack the capacity to really care for you… I… I just…" And she just plain started to cry.

I stood up as everyone went to move to support the professor. Dr. Agnew wasn't really all that much older than us, maybe five, six years tops… she shouldn't be expected to carry all that burden herself. "Now it's all right professah…" I said with my Georgian accent slipping as I felt her love as well as her pain wash over me, something I'm beginning to understand is a part of what I now am. "It's going to be all right, you're doing just right by us. Don't worry 'bout it." I hugged her and brought her in close, one of the nice things I guess about being hollow inside is that you're awfully soft, and it was very easy to be a comforting shoulder for our professor in a time of need. I pulled her close to me as she let herself lean. Her dark reddish brown hair falling out of its short ponytail as she wiped the tears from her eyes. "I'm sorry girls…" she apologized again "It *is* my fault. I knew there had to be something special down there in that ruin… I knew it might possibly hurt you. It is my fault…"

Claudia sighed and went to get a warm cup of tea for the professor as Kayla looked on with a worried expression. Vivian withdrew, thinking, as Kayla stepped in to help me support the professor.

"Oh don't be sad!" Kayla supported with her cute and much more rambunctious tone. "You rock Dr. Aggie! Don't be down on yourself. After all… It's my dad's company that set this all up. If anyone is to blame its more likely me. You're just being a good professor of a research school. We can't fault you for that." Kayla explained as she waved her hand dismissively, passing off Dr. Agnew's emotional claim in attempt to make her feel better. I felt the professor's heart rise a bit in spirit from Kayla's comfort, but just the same I knew Dr. Agnew was still blaming herself.

Then Vivian stepped in.

Vivian looked up after several moments of thinking, pondering, and mulling something over.

"No." Vivian said sternly, hands clenched at her side as she looked down, not making eye contact with anyone as she trembled. Her little black horns shimmered from the overhead lighting as she made a bold statement to present company.

"It's not your fault Dr. Agnew…

It's mine."

I looked to Vivian with a surprised tilt. How could it have been Vivian? If anything she was the first victim in this. I couldn't see how she came to that conclusion. Claudia returned with Dr. Agnew's tea, appearing just as equally baffled as she passed the cup to Kayla, who in turn gave it to the professor. Vivian looked like she had more to say, so we all politely listened, as the dark blue succubus with the bright red hair raised her serpentine yellow eyes to us…

"You may have known some details to the temple, Kayla may have turned the key. But I made the conscious choice." Vivian began to explain, "I walked up to Rosier, I was the one who tempted the demon, unleashed the parasite Azazel, and transformed us all. I messed up everyone's lives, and I did it because I wanted what that temple had to give. I… I want this. I wanted to turn into this, I didn't know that Rosier would do this to me, but I knew I needed something more. More than the ordinary, more than human. I chose this, no one else did. Dr. Agnew, Claudia, Natalie… Kayla… I accept responsibility. It's my action, it's my fault…" She looked up at me, locking eyes with me, the one of us with the most regret as she stated an even bolder sentence.

"But I'm not sorry I did it. Only sorry that other people got involved in it." Vivian said bluntly.

We murmured a few remarks as Vivian went to explain herself. "I like being a succubus. I think this new body is amazing… we can fly… and well, look at how pretty we are. Look at how we can sense each other's emotions, and we can even feel Dr. Agnew's love. Just now we were able to feel and empathize with her on a level not possible back when we were human. There's just so many benefits… I don't consider this a curse… it's a gift. Don't feel bad Dr. Agnew, these past 24 hours have given me what I've always wanted, and if in part I have you to thank for that, then I am very fortunate."

I found myself looking down, at my sky blue hands, staring at the pointed fingertips. I'm a monster, a creature… how can this be what Vivian wanted? Kayla stepped forward as I thought to myself, offering her own perspective.

"I'm glad I'm not the only one who feels this way." Said the other dark blue succubus, at that moment I realized that the two dark blue ones were ok with being succubus, while Claudia and I, light blue, felt strange about it. Maybe our colors have something to do with the way we feel?

"This new form is incredible, I mean, look at how dang good I look!" Kayla applauded herself as she twisted sideways to see more of herself, "But besides that, it's like Sonya said, we're going to cause a change. A shift in this world. But where she's wrong is that the change doesn't have to be a bad one. I think it was Ghandi that said 'be the change you want to see in the world, and let the world change with you.' And that is what I feel can happen from here." Kayla put her hand on Vivian's shoulder, shaking it slightly to show they were in the same camp.

"Let us hope so." Claudia added, "I second Kayla sentiments, there's no reason to be upset Dr. Agnew, I still can't thank you enough for all the help you've given us already, and the very fact you're willing to stand by us in this hour shows a compassion that few will ever have. That is something to be proud of." Claudia supported the professor as we all kept in close proximity.

And the feeling that washed over, was one I simply can't describe.

"Oh… thank you girls… I love you all…" She said as she finally picked up.

It was clear that we all were enjoying that feeling coursing through the room. I felt full, like enjoying a home cooked meal after being out in the cold for so long. Like returning to someone you love after being far away… and then I realized…

It was love.

We were consuming the feeling of love experienced in this moment.

And for the first time since my transformation.

I realized that maybe what I am…

Isn't so bad.

We enjoyed a momentary group hug, but before anyone else could say anything, we felt a new feeling come rolling in from the hall. One that certainly was not that feeling of love and invitation. Kayla immediately recoiled as she darted back her long ears and in a reflexive motion growled an animal growl. Vivian stood in front of Dr. Agnew, getting between her and the door as the light to the hall was obscured by darkness. The locks Silverlight put in should keep whatever this now frightening force was out… but soon after the shadow arrived at the door I heard the click of the lock, they were in.

Two suits of jet black armor with gold trim, both standing at about 6 and a half feet tall with the enhanced hydraulic systems found in modern military power armor came striding into the room. One moved left the other right as they parted ways. Both held a futuristic type of assault rifle I had never seen before, a glowing blue light in the chamber gleamed off the glossy finish of the armor plates. The helmet was one like a fighter jet pilot's, with a mask in the front that went into the rear tank. The legs flared out, giving a heavy pad like shoe. This was the *Striker* power armor I had seen on recent military shows… This was a US Government force…

Next entered a man and a woman. The man was older, probably in his 60's with salt and pepper hair a square jaw and many wrinkles across his suntanned face. He wore a black t-shirt with black and grey military camo pants and heavy combat boots. To his side stood a woman, beautiful, blonde, and with bright blue eyes that seemed to glow, they were so piercing that I couldn't look away. Her frame was thin, her ponytail long and tight. She carried a datapad under her arm and as she smiled…

We saw fangs.

"Ladies and gentlemen…" The older man began as another even larger suit of armor entered the room, turning and shutting the door behind him, checking the door and standing before it to lock us all in. We were now trapped at the mercy of this military team.

"This operation site is now under the protection of the Department of Paranormal Investigation, I'm going to need everyone to stay calm, we don't want an incident." The man explained as he motioned for the two armored soldiers to fan out more as he motioned the large one to stand by him. As the soldiers complied we felt trapped, encircled, as we backed up to the professor.

"So this was Silverlight's game…" The man looked around before turning his attention to the floating temple in the room.

"Well no longer." He noted, waving his hand dismissively. "It's now the duty of the DPI."

Chapter Five

Kingsport University Archeology Lab

Kingsport, Maryland

United States of America, Earth

The Journal of Dr. Cynthia Agnew

August 16th, 2011

2:13 PM

Damien warned me about these people. The Department of Paranormal Investigation… DPI for short… a hidden government agency tasked with sequestering and eliminating nonhuman threats… if they thought for a moment that they could harm my girls and get away with it, they would have another thing coming. Before I even began to speak, before they would have a chance to do anything at all, I leaned back on my desk and pressed a small button underneath the counter. An emergency call button to the Silverlight Special Forces Private Military Contractor, Damien's team. For all our arguing and strife between us, I knew he would never let them harm Kayla. And right then and there that was good enough for me.

"Stay away from that building… I don't know who you are but this is private property…" I cautioned to the armored soldiers approaching the Temple of Rosier. I walked over to get in the way of the soldier, but the strong, cold fusion powered suit just pushed me aside, nearly knocking me to the ground as Natalie quickly flew and caught me, righting me on my feet. Kayla immediately took off and landed in front of the soldier, getting in the way of the temple.

"This is the property of Silverlight LTD, trespassing on this ground will result in immediate action. I suggest you leave…" Kayla growled, giving the proper phrase her father taught her as she put her hands to her side, clearly upset. I didn't want her to get involved, but the older man stepped around his soldier as he glanced down at Kayla, who was coiled and ready to strike.

I didn't know how to react… I mean, this was the US military barging in on our lab… but just the same, Kayla is no longer just your average girl… I didn't know who was in danger and who would need to be protected.

The military man calmly and slowly raised his hands as he motioned for his soldiers to stop advancing on the temple. "Now calm down there little Miss Gilden, we have no intention of messing up your day any more than you've already gone and done experienced… we're friends ok?" he said without getting to fussy over Kayla's open threat.

"That's to be determined…" Kayla defended, still on edge.

The man put his hands on his hips as he looked Kayla over, "Well look at you!" He said with the raised and slightly southern pitch one might expect from your classic American 'good old boy', "Gosh, they keep getting prettier, I keep staying the same! Now were you that pretty before the blue set in or was that all aftermarket?" He asked bluntly and boldly, deflecting the conversation to an entire new track. Kayla didn't know how to answer that one, immediately becoming indignant as she backed up. I heard the blond woman sigh as the gentleman made a shrug.

I stepped up to stand between the man and Kayla, as I reassumed my role as the girl's protector.

He looked at me for a moment before hanging his thumbs on his pants' belt loops and letting air pass his lips as he pursed them slightly before offering me his hand, "Man! Look at the teachers too! I think I was born in the wrong generation! Major Raymond Howell, commander and chief of the Deeepartment of Paranormal Investigation, the major bit is just something I can't shake. Glad to make your acquaintance, Miss…" He introduced as he extended his hand out to me. I carefully extended mine to shake his hand. He was firm, but not overbearing. The man had control, I can admire that. However, he needed to understand, he was not in charge here.

"Doctor." I corrected.

"Doctor Cynthia Agnew, Archeologist."

The man finished shaking my hand and put his hand over his heart before fluttering his sky blue eyes a moment in an over-exaggeration of sincere apology. "Well, well, well I do deeply apologize Miss Doctor Cynthia Agnew but you must excuse me, I hail from a more Neolithic time as your archeology would uncover. But today I believe that you and I need to talk." He pointed next to Claudia and Natalie, who had begun to shirk back to my side, seeking protection. I couldn't help but put one arm around the back of both of them, providing what comfort I could. "About these lovely women." He continued. Pacing around to look over Claudia, who quickly fussed with her shirt to ensure she was properly covered.

Claudia stepped forward from me and took a slightly indignant tone with the Major, "Then why not speak to us directly? We are not animals to be bartered for."

"You must be Miss Brashear." The major said with a nod and a lowering of his pitch. He made sure to make direct eye contact with her while they were talking, and his eyes showed a level of sincerity I had not seen in a man for quite some time. "And you're absolutely right. If possible I'd like to talk to all of you. As you know, most people don't normally encounter demons on a daily basis. They're rightly liable to respond irrationally, in a less than admirable fashion, and possibly even get a couple people hurt. So please..." he said as he hopped up on one of the lab tables and turned to face us once more as he slapped his knees.

"Let's talk."

The blonde woman made a couple quick sharp steps up to "Major" Howell's side as she tapped at her datapad with the back of her hand, "Major we do not have time to play coy with this. The live broadcast begins at 3:30 and we all well know that Silverlight is likely on its way. Please be courteous and allow these women the dignity they deserve, you do not need to be so crass with them. Imagine if it were one of us sir." The woman with the impossibly blue eyes and very pale skin rebuked him with a voice that seemed to echo and ebb through the room as if we were surrounded by a broadcast system rather than simply speaking from herself. She had to be something other than human, and I found myself staring at her mouth as she spoke to look for glimpses of her fangs.

I, like Vivian, have a deep and lasting fascination with the supernatural… it's why I started this project to begin with… yet now that I am seeing it for myself first hand, I find myself increasingly afraid of what it is I've found. It's safe when it's on the page of a story or an idea far away. It's an entirely different tale when it's in front of you.

And if I myself am afraid… what about the general population? What about the girls?

"Aww Val, have a heart!" The major remarked with a slap of his knee and a chuckle looking up and away, unwilling to really admit to being chauvinistic. The woman sighed, clearly not enjoying the Major's comment. After clearing his throat, the very tall soldier at the door spoke up, his voice carried a tinny quality through the headset speaker but a thick Texan accent permeated through.

"Major, I don't think that's really appropriate sir. We're not really makin the right first impression here, we're here to help the girls, not piss em off." The huge soldier stated with concern. I saw Natalie react to his voice. A small smile at the southern gentle tone, but quickly replaced by her prevailing nervous concern.

The major sighed and tilted his head towards the extremely tall man in black armor, "Oh Trigger you're right as always, I'm just givin the girls grief. Miss Doctor Agnew, my team is right and I do apologize to you and yours for my less-than-refined way of being. Let me just get things underway then I can shut my trap and everyone can go on with their lives. This beautiful and talented lady to my left is Colonel Valerie Hawthorne, commander of Squad 28, a Striker Unit. These brave men and women are tasked with responding to supernatural disturbances and handling aggressive visitors from some of our lesser known realms. Behind Miss Hawthorne we have Clayton Zelinski, ex USMC, Katie Deras MIT grad, and of course the large opinionated gentlemen at the back is Mr. Trigger Valentine. Please believe us when I tell you we mean you no harm." His tone carried a solid honesty to it as he looked back at me with his aged yet kind blue eyes and as he relaxed his forehead he carried a genuine quality that despite his initial entrance, did make me wish to trust him. He completed his thought with a simple phrase.

"Ma'am, we're here to help."

"In what way?" Claudia asked defensively as she stepped forward from my left and placed her hands on her hips, staring at the Major as her tail's heart shaped end curled upward in a disbelieving curiosity. "Forgive my incredulity, but I do not believe the words of a man with a gun so readily. If you were here to win us over by word alone then the gun would be unnecessary."

The blonde woman stepped forward up to Claudia, placing out her hands to show that she was unarmed as her tight fitting dress pants and jacket showed no signs of being armed, "Then believe me Miss Brashear. As introduced, I am Colonel Valerie Hawthorne... like you, I have found myself on the outskirts of human society..." Her flighty tone was strong and empowered, devoid of emotion, but her words for their context carried sympathetic concern. Valerie outstretched her hand to display the other soldiers that assembled behind her, all covered in their black power armor.

"In more ways than one, the DPI has been a safe haven for those who have gone beyond the human veil. Like you, we are still understanding what lies beneath, and beyond our comprehension of this world. What we suggest is a combined effort. We have the laboratory and facilities away from prying eyes where we can study the temple and its purpose. And perhaps find something of value to all of you in the process." As the woman completed her offer, she unintentionally opened her mouth all the way, showing a most telling pair of fangs on her upper jaw. I already knew what she was, but apparently some of the girls finally put the clues together.

"Ah!" Natalie gasped, scooting back on her laboratory stool that she had sat down in during Valerie's exposition. "A-a-a-are you a vampire?" She asked sheepishly, tucking in her hands to her chest as she allowed her big yellow eyes to open wide and ears to drop back in fright. I had a hard time not coddling the girl as the succubae form was exceedingly endearing when expressive.

"Yes." Valerie replied with that same cold tone. "And like you I was not originally one, but a human being. You will find you are not alone in your transformations away from humankind, if that brings you any comfort."

Natalie nodded a bit, still obviously a little afraid of Valerie, "It does, thank you." She nodded as she continued to hide behind her hands. The room fell silent as the conversation arrived at a sudden end. Vivian stepped to stand alongside Natalie as she cautioned Valerie and her men.

"Please don't go in there. That temple isn't safe, there's so much in there we don't understand. And there's so much we can't seem to decipher. I don't think you should play around with it. I think it was made to hold something back." Vivian attempted to be cryptic in the way she presented her perspective on why they shouldn't meddle with the temple, but that only prompted a more pointed response.

The Major walked back into Vivian's view to get back in the conversation. He hopped back up on another lab table as he folded his arms and cocked back his head, "Now… what would make you say that little lady? Did you maybe *find* something that was supposed to stay locked away?" The military officer asked in a tone more suited for a father trying to get his daughter to confess to staying out late more than an official investigation.

Vivian immediately turned away from Major Howell, grabbing her upper arm with her other hand as she leaned forward, allowing her mismatched blue and red hair to fall over her eyes. "I… I don't want to talk about it." She answered with sincerity.

I myself had only seen what had occurred through the security cameras, but from what I could make out… it was awful. I understand, Vivian and the others had been violated by a parasite, forced to attack and harm their friends while being aware of what was happening, that is not something easily forgiven, or forgotten. The experience in itself must have been highly traumatizing.

But to my surprise, the Major didn't press the matter, and in doing so gained my respect.

"That's fine Miss Maybell." Major Howell said with a much more gentle tone as he hopped off the table to walk up to Vivian, carefully and gently placing a hand on her shoulder as she looked up to him.

"She didn't hurt you, did she?" He asked with sincerity, clearly speaking about Azazel without saying her name.

Vivian shook her head "Nothing I can't heal." She answered with a meek and wavering tone.

"I'm not talking physically." Major Howell returned with his stern tone, but said in a way that sounded defensive of Vivian. "Is Marian all right?"

Vivian looked up quickly, "My mom!? How do you know my mother?"

Major Howell put his hands up as he stepped away as he let the professional veneer slip for a genuine tone, "Vivian, Miss Dr. Agnew, I can't go into every detail right now, but I want you to know that we are friends. No matter what happens after the news airs today, you have the DPI protecting you. You have my word. I'm ready to fly these girls up to Arkham and keep them in our finest remote facilities if that's what it takes to keep them safe. I know you love these girls Doctor. That's clear as day to see, and like you, I don't want to see them hurt. That is the only reason why I'm here today. Silverlight can keep their temple, they can hide in their lies and secrets, but I want to make sure that tomorrow still has at least four United States Citizens that can check 'other' in the ethnicity box. You get me?" He finished his promise by placing his hand over his heart, as he turned back to me before waving back his most curious soldier from the temple to prove he wasn't operating on ulterior motives.

I felt the blood drain from my face when I finally realized the Major's, and by extension, Damien's concern. They were not afraid of Vivian and the girls harming others...

They were afraid of others harming them.

"Do... do you think it's going to be bad? When the people find out?" Natalie asked in a frightened tone.

No one answered, as the room's residents looked to one another with that same somber gaze.

"I think we've hassled these ladies enough for one day. Let's pack it up team. We've got to get ready for security detail." The major turned and waved to his squad, as the group fell in to go. As the soldiers filed past without a word, the tallest and most powerful looking suit of armor stopped before Natalie, who had begun to fall into a deep depression at the well of emotion that befell her. The tall man laid an armored hand on her shoulder, as she glanced up with her big yellow eyes to meet the black abyss of his visor. No words were exchanged, no gestures made, but in that moment, something must have transpired. Because after a second, Natalie smiled.

The soldier removed his hand, and proceeded with the others towards the door.

Before they could leave the door opened by itself, as a more familiar site entered the laboratory. Several suits of *Silhouette* power armor belonging to the Silverlight Private Military Contractor organization entered the room. Each armor set extremely form fitting for maximum movement, with a base grey material that looked like motorcycle leather. The seams of the inlaid armor plates were sewn with teal string, silver hard plates made up the boots and pads on the joints. Each of the six soldiers that entered wore the same blank facemask with a teal manteaux. The mask was designed to hold electronics, but I doubt they paid much concern to the unsettling effect it had on those who observed them.

The mask had a blank, almost porcelain like quality to it, with two yellow eyes that glowed with a very expressive moving sculpt. You could see if the wearer was thinking, if they had narrowed their eyes or had them wide, it was the only emotion the mask offered. Other than that, it was utterly blank, with no other markings or designs. I realize in the minimalist thoughts of Silverlight, it was ideal, but when you are supposed to be working with civilians, I don't find it appropriate.

The soldiers filed past the DPI squad without a word, clearly focused and concentrated on defending the tall and imposing man at the middle of their group. A proud, six foot seven man in a black business suit with a silver tie and very well groomed blonde hair came striding into the room with his guards arrayed around him. His beard and mustache blended together, all cropped and kept tight with a neatly groomed appearance. His bright blue eyes seemed to stare through you, not at you as he fixed his hawk-like stare on the Succubae in the room. Everyone froze, realizing who it was that stood before us.

Even the DPI stood back to give the Silverlight group a wide berth. Simply allowing the man to do what he pleased before attempting to leave through the door he was now impeding. He looked to me, and as soon as he did I found myself averting my gaze, scared. He turned his attention to Kayla, who shrugged her shoulders as she looked down, tucking her hands behind her back as she swung her upper body back and forth, making a small circle with her foot in the floor as she fluttered her wings. Her tone dropped to a very cute and innocent tone as she batted her yellow eyes at him.

"Hi daddy." Was all she said.

And to those in the room that did not yet know…

Daniel Gilden, is here.

Chapter Six

Kingsport University Laboratory

Kingsport University, Maryland

United States of America, Earth

The Journal of Vivian Maybell

August 16th, 2011

2:55PM

Daniel Gilden.

I don't know what emotions I should feel, I didn't know what to experience, what was appropriate, what was justified. I mean… after all, this is the man that's behind it all. He created this company, this University. He even got Baltimore to give up part of its zoning so he could create the Kingsport Municipal area…

He's likely one of the most powerful men in the entire world, so who am I to come against him?

And I mean… what do I do? What do I say, do I scream at him for subjecting me to Azazel, for making students go and do the work now clearly meant for his private military? Do I thank him for giving me the opportunity to see all this? I still haven't decided if this is for better or worse. Can it be both?

Instead of deciding anything at that moment, I found it best to just bite my tongue and allow the events before me unfold.

Mr. Gilden walked right through his group of soldiers, they instinctively parted without ever looking at him as he neared. Without any notice or care he breezed past the DPI, not even recognizing their presence in the room as he approached the professor, looking down on her as she sheepishly turned her gaze upward at him.

"Thank you for picking up Kayla, you've done a good job keeping her safe up until now, and for that you have my thanks." Daniel Gilden said with a tone of voice that was imposing, almost echoing, but at the same time, I felt an honest emotion wave off of him.

He clearly had a deep well of rage and upset hiding in his voice, and I could feel the deep emotional stress emanating from within him with my empathetic sensitivity, but it wasn't directed at the Doctor, no. He was mad at someone else.

Dr. Agnew bent her neck down slightly as she tucked her shoulder length dark red hair behind her ear before nodding quickly to Mr. Gilden. "You're welcome, thank you for letting her study with us, she's a pleasure to have in class." She attempted to casually answer, not knowing how best to respond in a situation like this. Kayla walked over to stand close with the professor, trying to act as a buffer between Dr. Agnew and her father.

"Dad." Kayla bravely addressed her father, "This isn't the professor's fault-" She began to defend.

"I know." Daniel Gilden cut his daughter off.

"Where is Carter's daughter?" He asked directly, his voice now bordered on anger.

Kayla let her wings flip back as she coiled her tail close to her. "Wh… you mean Sonya? I don't know dad, she left us and we got arrested right after…"

"Who called the police?" Daniel Gilden cut his daughter off mid-sentence again.

Kayla shook her head as she tried to put everything together, "I… I don't know, I mean it wasn't any of us… right Claudia?" She asked Claudia with upturned palms. Claudia quickly nodded to show she never called the police in. We all knew that when dealing with secrets like this, you don't involve the cops.

"Maybe one of the students that saw us when we went outside?" I asked, trying to support Kayla.

"Impossible. The speed they arrived compared to the amount of time required to drive from their location proves they had to be on their way before…" Daniel Gilden turned to me quickly and angrily, fixing his bright blue eyes on me, prepared to ream at me but as he saw me, he just dropped off. I felt a wave of emotions roll off him that I could not even begin to comprehend. It was everything, love, hate, confusion, joy, and another I just couldn't place.

"Vivian." He said in a deadpan tone.

I nodded, "Yes sir… Vivian Maybell, official thing messer-upper… at your service…" I answered with a small attempt at a curtsy, trying to show deference to him while accepting my blame away from Kayla and the professor.

Daniel Gilden actually stood at a loss for words for several moments, before breaking off entirely as he walked towards the computers. The tall man stopped short as he looked at the holo-display of the local time. The small 2d holographic square that hovered off the holo-computer table showed 2:58, he nodded to himself before turning back to everyone in the room.

"Damien, have your men search the recordings, find her. Find Carter. Bring them to me. I don't need any more surprises today. Do it quickly." Daniel Gilden ordered to the masked armor suit closest to him. The suit bowed and lowered its yellow eyes.

"It will be as you say, sir." Damien Focht answered from his armor.

I knew it. I knew he had to be paramilitary. Just in all the time he was with us, all the months on the ship. He was just too cryptic and cautious not to be. I wanted to blurt something out but Dr. Agnew stopped us all.

"It's almost time." She said with a deep intake of air.

"I know." Daniel Gilden answered.

The Silverlight soldiers bowed and exited the lab without another word. The DPI soldiers decided to stay as Major Howell and Valerie turned back to join us once more.

"Y'all going to be ok?" Major Howell asked with concern.

"I'd appreciate it if you stayed with the girls for a while, Raymond." Daniel Gilden said as he turned to face Major Howell. The two older men exchanged a gaze of knowing, they clearly had met several times before.

"This ain't part of your plans, is it?" The major asked directly.

"I would never place them in so much danger…" Mr. Gilden replied in a much quieter tone.

The DPI soldiers in armor collected folding chairs off the wall. I flew over to help them as Claudia did the same. We got our mismatched viewing party together, sat down, each of us willing to put aside whatever inclinations we had for one another to just watch, and allow the news broadcast to unfold.

We're about to be worldwide news.

"Which news should we watch? ANN? BCN? Or the local broadcast at KPLN?" One of the black armored suits of the DPI asked with a higher pitched and cute voice. I jumped a little in my chair when I heard such a kind tone come out of such imposing looking armor.

"ANN. I need to see the worst of it. The politicized news will show me where we stand." Daniel Gilden stated boldly, folding his arms and refusing to sit as the DPI soldier changed the holographic image before us over to a large widescreen projection large enough for the whole group to clearly see.

"Colonel Hawthorne? Can I please take off my helmet?" The young voice asked from her suit.

"Yes Katie, this goes for the rest of you as well." Valerie stated in her cold tone.

Katie Deras removed her helmet, I was surprised to see a cute and petit Asian girl with a short pixie cut with dyed purple hair. Her narrow face and kind smile seemed to accent her harmless and kind demeanor. It seemed strange to me to think that she was just a faceless armored soldier a moment ago.

"Thanks." Clayton Zelinski, the other armored suit around Katie's size stated as he pulled off his own helmet. He was a fit looking young man, a little older than me and definitely looked more travelled than me. His shaved head and stubble covered chin leant towards a more classic soldier. That's more what I expected to see from this group.

"I'll keep mine. Thank you." The extremely tall suit of armor said from the back.

"Suit yourself Trigger." The Major answered as he took a seat nearby.

I heard the music of the news opening broadcast, as I watched the symbol of the American News Network scroll past. I found my hands reaching out, scared, I realized at that moment that I didn't want to be alone, and as quickly as I did that, I found a hand in each. Claudia on my left, Kayla on my right. I reached back my tail, as I felt Natalie grab the arrow point end and hold on for comfort. I let the prehensile end curl over her fingers, providing what comfort back that I could.

3:30…

Showtime.

The opening graphic gave way to a clean and sterile, beautiful but not threatening pair of news anchors that excitedly waited behind their news desk as the world watched. The tall dark haired, fair skinned Asian man on the left seemed to match with the shorter blonde woman on the right, as they smiled an artificial grin. They took a breath, looked to one another, as the woman began the presentation.

"Good afternoon everyone I'm Susan Braille with my special guest anchor from the National Security Agency Adam Yama and this is the American News Network's special edition, your source for true and honest news." The woman spoke in a tone too excited to be a normal presentation, as she quickly turned to Steven, her co-anchor, as he took on a more serious tone and expression.

The man sat back in his chair as he looked directly at the camera, concerned but stoic in his delivery, "Ladies and gentlemen, we have an… incredible, story for you tonight. We have, once and for all, discovered that we as the human race. Are not alone."

The anchor let the words sink in for a moment before he continued, pausing for obvious dramatic effect.

"That's right ladies and gentlemen, at just after midnight last night on August the sixteenth, 2011, we encountered beings from another species. Creatures like us, yet unique. There is still no word on if these creatures hail from another planet, or where their true origin may be but one thing is for certain, this is not a hoax. We warn you now that some of the footage we are about to show may be graphic and disturbing to younger viewers. We caution parents at this time to have your children turn away from the device being used to broadcast this program. We will now go to the footage of the creatures themselves."

Creatures.

That's the word being used to describe us, creatures. Are we really that different? My different skin and a few little parts are enough to make me a creature? Well, I guess when something as mild a skin color can be used to segregate and disenfranchise, I shouldn't really be surprised when this would label me a monster away from society.

The footage came on, and as soon as it did I knew I wasn't going to like what was shown. The footage was of Sonya and Natalie running scared across the front lawn out beside the laboratory dome.

"Now… here comes one of the creatures." The man passively described as Claudia, under control of Azazel, swooped down from above to grab Natalie to convert her.

"This is where this might get graphic." The male anchor warned the audience a second time.

Claudia's tail impaled Natalie on camera, as Natalie began to convert to a succubus.

I heard Claudia gasp and place her free hand on her mouth. Natalie let go of my tail to lean forward and pat Claudia's shoulder to show she bore no ill will.

The anchorwoman gasped as the video ran, "Oh my God…" it was clear you could hear her fidgeting in her chair in discomfort as the camera continued to film Natalie transforming. Near the end of the process we saw Kayla and myself land to try and take care of the situation. The camera feed expertly ended before it showed us comforting and caring for Natalie. The camera went back to the anchors as the man took over the presentation as the blonde woman was clearly in distress at seeing the footage.

"Now, we have confirmed the identity of the woman attacked on film as 22 year old Natalie Rayborn, daughter of a Marine captain currently serving in Afghanistan. We also know that shortly after this footage, the other woman pictured, 24 year old Sonya Shannon, was killed in a fatal car crash caused by one of the creatures. We are now joined by Miss Shannon's father, Director Carter Shannon, as representative of the Silverlight Corporation and Kingsport University affairs." The man calmly looked up to allow the graphic to switch to the multiple side by side face shot pictures common in modern news.

On the second square a very clean shaven man with a narrowed chin, green eyes, and very well kept, dirty blonde hair perfectly combed in a right part took a deep breath as he steepled his fingers in front of his black suit with silver tie.

"Shannon…" Daniel Gilden stated coldly with narrowed eyes.

I stiffened in my chair, thinking of the moment Sonya's car crashed, and where Kayla and I were in relation to the scene.

Oh my god… they're going to say I killed Sonya.

Kayla's fear darted through me as soon as I felt my own release, she quickly turned to her father and shook her head, "Dad I didn't…" She started to explain.

"I know." He answered.

Carter Shannon, one of the directors of the Silverlight Corporation and Sonya's father, leaned back and took a deep breath, very clearly trying to look distraught but wasn't. As I focused on him, I realized I could feel his emotions too… right through the video feed. There was happiness, there was mirth, and a deep and lasting layer of satisfaction…

This was on purpose.

This was a plan.

"Thank you… for having me on your program in such short notice." Mr. Shannon thanked the anchors with a solemn nod. "As much as it pains me to confirm the death of my only daughter due to these creatures, my duties to the company are firm. I am here to provide what answers I can to the chaos of last night." He feigned being helpful as he batted his eyes and wiped away a tear before resuming a more stoic stance, attempting to look like he was remaining strong after suffering an incredible emotional blow. I could feel the studio audience tensing and feeling a deep sympathy for him as Carter Shannon shifted his weight in his chair and looked down before turning back to the camera. He played a good wounded man.

"No, thank you. And we appreciate the Silverlight Corporation being willing to discuss the details on such short notice." The woman anchor, Susan Braille, thanked him as she stepped back as control and moderator of the conversation.

Behind me, Daniel Gilden could not hold back a comment, "This is bold Shannon… very bold." He scoffed at the image display.

"Director Shannon, and Agent Yama…" The Anchor began, "Where do you think these women came from? Where do we even begin? What are they and why are they here?" She asked with a barely professional tone. She was simply scared, and searching for answers.

The NSA agent just took a breath as Mr. Shannon went right on ahead and began to explain his version. "Very recently in our studies into the matter, we have determined that what was once thought of as fiction, as mythology, religion, or stories, seems to be in actuality… true. These are not aliens, at least, not aliens as we know them. They hail from a world and realm like ours, but under our own in a dimensional plane." Carter Shannon looked to the man, who did a good job at looking distressed at the confession of information.

"This information was deemed highly speculative until the night prior." The government agent added. Covering his position quickly.

"And, you must forgive the government in this one, I mean, how could we possibly think this was true? The thought of a world or worlds outside our own that we cannot see because they exist on a different plane or medium from our own is fantastic at best." Carter defended the government man quickly, giving a sympathetic bow to him before he continued, "I mean, certainly physicists have discussed the existence of alternate dimensions for years, but they were only theories, speculations, not fact. Now we know that there are worlds outside our own, and now a few of one of these world's denizens have come upon us… and their intent is clear."

The anchorwoman was now completely enthralled at Mr. Shannon's story. "Wh… what is it? What do they want?" She asked it more like a scared child than a professional woman, I guess I really overestimated how professional people would handle this.

Of course, Mr. Carter Shannon was very fast to provide her wanting answers, "To answer that, we are going to have to step outside the bounds of science… but Miss Braille, these are the Succubus, the demons of lust and envy. If legend continues to be true their intention is to spread among the women, as we have just seen in the video footage you procured, and to eliminate and capture the souls of men. They feed off emotion, and will drain away life from this world."

The other two faces on the split feed quickly jumped at the revelation, the agent leaned forward as he took a quick stand, "That will not happen, as we speak Director Alan Westfield of our department is working closely with the military in order to maintain a safe and contained zoning of the current demons, we will respond quickly and accurately with this situation…"

As he postured and provoked in his tone, I watched the social media stream at the bottom display the kneejerk thoughts of the people. Messages of hate for us scrolled across the bottom, people demanded we die quickly, others sent out fearful messages about conversion with prayers for the students we shared a campus with.

I started to hyperventilate, I could hear my own gasps echo in my hollow body, drowning out the news as they continued to villainize us on national television. I heard a sharp bang on the doors of the archeology lab, people were trying to get in. The DPI soldiers stood up and immediately put on their helmets, drawing out their assault rifles as they prepared to act as a buffer. Daniel Gilden shouted to turn off the news. I turned in my seat, scared, to Kayla and Claudia as they hugged me. Natalie sobbed in her chair as Dr. Agnew kept her close. The situation escalated as we heard police sirens and the thrum of vans… news crews, here to capture live footage of us.

The door swung open to the lab and quickly locked, as Damien returned with a young man around our age, the two of them leaned against the door together until it locked, shutting out several news teams that had tried to barge in.

Damien reached up and removed his mask as he pulled back the cowl of his hood to address all of us. "It's a madhouse out there, news media and gawkers have gathered en masse. They're literally crowding in from every angle, the dome is completely surrounded." He clipped his mask to his belt as he looked back at Kayla. Kayla quickly looked away from Damien to focus on the young man I just now started to pay attention to. He was a very lanky early twenty something with an Arabic skin tone, black hair kept in a short spiky gelled up front to resemble a realistic attempt at anime hair, and a frumpy grey KPU sweatshirt with blue jeans and converse sneakers. His nerdyness was confirmed by the video game controller belt buckle. Kayla flew above the chairs and lab chairs to soar out to him.

"Tooobeeeeeeeeeeeeeee" She cooed as she hugged him, "What are you doin here?" Kayla asked as she pulled away. The relaxed sigh on the boy's face told me he lived for those fleeting moments of Kayla's affection.

"Oh my gosh, Kayla is that you?" Toby asked as he put his hand to his forehead and scanned her over.

"Yep!" Kayla answered, proud of herself as she put her dark blue hands on her hips. "Guys, I want people to meet my best friend from since ever, Toby Malak, neighbor and fellow anime watcher." Kayla introduced.

I started to wave when Daniel Gilden quickly stepped forward and cut off all conversation, "We don't have time for this. Toby I don't know why you're here but you need to leave, Raymond, I'm taking the girls out of here, they're going to Kayla's home on Ruxton. Cynthia I'll need you to stay with them. Damien, since you're here I'll need you to clear a way, we aren't staying here a moment longer, if they discover the temple as is this situation is only going to get worse. We need to go, *now*." Daniel Gilden gave no room for argument as he motioned for us to leave.

"I'm keepin him." Kayla demanded as she pulled in her friend, Toby nodded happily, just wanting to be near her.

Daniel Gilden strode towards the door, realized the futility of arguing with his daughter in this matter, then turned to look at the dark blue succubus and her nerdy friend.

"Fine, don't fall behind." Her father cautioned.

We were going.

I couldn't have been more frightened if I tried.

Trigger, the tall man in armor, led us out of the room with a hard push on the laboratory door. As soon as he opened that seal the hallway erupted with a series of high flashes and that roaring wave of conversation as a crowd struggled to get a glimpse of us. Cell phones, smart phones, computer tablets and new Silverlight Holo-Video recorders glimmered and whirled as people held up their devices over one another to try and capture pictures, recording, and wavering glimpses of us. I tucked in close to Claudia, who in turn grabbed onto the professor for comfort as we made our way into the crowd. Katie and Clayton, now back in their fully covered armor suits, closed in tight to us to form a physical barrier, Katie was even kind enough to raise up her rifle to shield my face from the paparazzi.

"We're gonna get you out of here." Katie placated Natalie as she reached behind her with her free hand and helped push the barely moving Natalie up behind us, I reached out and grabbed Natalie's hand to keep us together. Damien strode up in front next to Trigger, as soon as he began to walk with his intimidating, and dangerous looking gait, even news teams moved back. Silverlight has been an American private military contractor for several years, and during that time, it was never known for it's kindness to anyone it deemed a threat. The news knew better than to directly crowd a Silverlight soldier.

But they certainly wanted a statement out of Kayla's dad. The questions flew at us from every angle. Valerie leaned in close to us and told us to only look ahead, the Major stood to block us from being seen completely.

"Mr. Gilden! Are these creatures somehow affiliated with Silverlight!? Did you make them!? Is this a product of the Nucleo-Genetics wing? Possibly the new Nanotechnology development?"

"Is this the secret project Silverlight was involved with in 1991?"

"Mr. Gilden, can we get a statement? Why are you defending these creatures?"

"Do you believe they represent a threat to American society?"

"Hey, they're hot! Gimme your number baby!"

I instinctively reached up to my shirt collar as if I wanted to shield myself even more despite the fact I was wearing a T-shirt. I didn't like being stared at. I didn't like this kind of attention. People either feared me or wanted me, from what I felt from the majority of them, both at the same time. We were exotic, new, and frightening, we tapped at the very essence of what people wanted and hated all at the same time. We were their subject of allure.

And I didn't like it.

"Almost out... Everyone clear the way! I'm not going to say this again!" Damien ordered as he stepped around in front of Trigger to raise out his hands. Four more Silverlight soldiers suddenly appeared at the door as they disengaged the *Silhouette*'s cloaking system, making the armored soldiers suddenly appear, scaring back the crowds outside and making the cameramen at the news vans back up. The Silverlight team held the door for us as we were ushered through. With the appearance of more armed guards, the carousing crowd had begun to back off a bit more, allowing us more breathing room. As we started to spread out a little more, Natalie picked a face out of the crowd as she immediately started calling to him.

"Stephan! Stephan! It's me!" She started running to the edge of the guards as she tugged on the letterman jacket she had worn for comfort. The black and white Kingsport University Knights letterman belonged to him, and she pointed from the jacket to herself to try and make the connection.

I had never seen Natalie's boyfriend before, and stereotypically for a football player he was a fit young man of decent height with dark hair and a thick brow that seemed to cover part of his eyes. I never really found that attractive at all but other women seem to go crazy over that. Never understood why. The athlete stepped back a bit as the excited and relieved succubus skipped up to him, obviously wanting calm and comfort. She smiled up at him and let her long ears lower a bit as her tail flicked happily, awaiting his love and comfort.

But that's not what I felt out of him.

"N-Natalie?" The young man asked with a slow shake of his head, pulling himself away in disgust.

"Ye…yeah?" Natalie answered, quickly pulling in her hands close to her as her eyes widened and her form drooped in fear.

"Y… you're a monster…" Stephan stepped back again as he gawked at his girlfriend. Kayla immediately started towards Natalie to get her out of here as Claudia and the professor gasped at Stephan's complete lack of concern for her.

Natalie held her breath in surprise as she trembled, unable to answer him as she let a small squeak of disbelief pass her lips. The news ate it up as they recorded the event from every angle.

The tall armored soldier stepped in, overshadowing both Natalie and the football player as he leaned over. "Only one monster here." Trigger said as he stepped in for Natalie, getting between them. "And he's going to leave if he knows what's best for him."

Stephan narrowed his gaze, "They killed her, the demons destroyed her. Made her one of them." He parroted the news broadcast as Natalie started to cry.

"…no…" Natalie whimpered, clutching onto the jacket.

The football player looked at the jacket on Natalie and waved his hand, dismissing it "It's probably contaminated now anyway." He said as he turned and disappeared back into the crowd. Leaving poor

Natalie gasping and crying as she struggled to stand. Trigger shielded her from the crowd as he wrapped an armored hand around her.

"Miss y'all able to walk? It's best we go…" Trigger kindly whispered to her through his armored visor, giving a tinny sound to his statement through the microphone.

Natalie couldn't answer, she was simply overcome with grief.

Then things got worse, at Natalie's show of weakness, the news got bold. They swarmed in again, putting the microphone in her face as they shouted questions.

"Is that true? Are you no longer yourself? Can you think on your own?"

"What's your religion? Would you identify yourself as Christian?"

"What does it feel like to not have a soul? Can we get a statement?"

The DPI and Silverlight started to come in to stop the crowding, it was getting bad. I wanted to help but if I got in there it'd only make it worse. People started to recognize Kayla, the crowd got even more fevered as they realized that one of the demons was Gilden's daughter.

Then, out of nowhere, a news camera was suddenly slammed to the floor with a loud bang and a clatter, the crowd pulled back quickly as the cameraman backed away.

The crowd parted for a girl.

A human girl.

"What the hell is wrong with all of you!" She shouted as she reached up and pushed aside her heavily dyed jet black hair. Her piercings on her ears, nose and upper lip glittered as she sneered at the crowd with her black lips, her bright blue eyes seemed to burn on their own level of anger as the goth girl, garbed in dark jeans and a short leather jacket with a black and white striped tee underneath, turned her back to us as she shouted at the crowd.

"These aren't monsters! They're us! As soon as you see something different you go all crazy and start acting stupid! Get a grip you petty bastards! Leave em alone!" The girl was probably my age, but the gravel tone spoke of years of cigarette use, and her rage that I felt spoke of a long time of torment.

"Violet… what are you doing?" Another goth girl in a white graphic tee with a long leather jacket and tight jeans worried as our defender pushed back a couple news groups, forcibly driving them back. She was attempting to look tough with her bracelets with spikes and matching choker collar, but her cute and fragile skinny frame and long blonde hair made it quite obvious that this second girl was very much the more reserved.

"I'm doing what no one has the guts to do Charity." Violet, our unexpected savior said through gritted teeth, "C'mon, poke and prod at them I dare you! I'll put you down before you even get out your half-assed question!" She challenged the crowd as she tapped her hands off her chest and extended her hands outward to egg on aggression. Right away people in the crowd began to boo or throw nasty phrases and comments at Violet. But I couldn't help but find myself smiling at her bravery.

Daniel Gilden looked at his phone then back to the Major and Valerie, "Take them with us, we'll use two limos if we have to, I don't care. We're leaving, now." He demanded as two black Silverlight LTD limos came screeching up to the curb, their powerful Cold fusion engines roared with an ominous purr as the news teams were once more parted for our exit. More Silverlight personnel got out as they formed a barricade, the DPI soldiers made a wall and let us get in. Natalie begged the DPI to come with us, but Trigger explained that the armor was too heavy, and they would see us later. Violet and Charity, the two girls that stepped up for us, were ushered along with us.

And with a slam of a door and the electric whine of the new tinted window system being activated, we were once more sealed away from the world.

As we pulled away towards Kayla's exclusive mansion, away in a gated community that would keep us away from prying eyes. I took my first exhale of relief since we first turned. As I did, I thought about all of those things that linger in the back of your mind yet only come to light when you have a moment's peace. I thought about my future, I thought about where we can go from here... then I thought of my mom... my mom! She's probably seen the news! She might think I'm dead! Or injured, or worse!

"Oh my gosh!" I said aloud as the rest of the car turned quickly to look at me. "I... I need to call my mom!" I demanded. To my surprise, Daniel Gilden seemed to agree.

"Yes..." He stated with a calm nod, "When you get to safety, contact your loved ones using the secure phones in the building. I know if I was in your parent's positions, I would want to hear what happened to Kayla from *her* perspective, not the news. Don't let the lies and smokescreen of the media be all they know of you. Tell them yourself." He said as he looked back to me.

"What is she going to say?" I worried aloud, thinking of the possible implications.

"I'm sure Marian will understand." Mr. Gilden said to me.

I looked up, "Why does everyone know my mom's name?" I asked him honestly.

"It's a long story Vivian, perhaps when we have the time." Mr. Gilden answered politely before looking back to his phone.

Claudia looked to me as I reached forward and grasped her hand, I feel like ever since I turned that I stepped into another life. Like Alice through the looking glass or so many travelers in fiction that I've entered a world more fantastic than I was used to...

And I wasn't welcome.

Daniel Gilden thought for a second before glancing up again. "Yes... that's what we will do from here. Tonight, you rest at my daughter's house. But first..." He turned to make sure he was making eye contact with all of us.

"You must call your parents."

Chapter Seven

Kayla's Personal Mansion

Ruxton Road, Baltimore, Maryland

United States of America, Earth

The Journal of Vivian Maybell

August 16th, 2011

6:40 PM

Quiet.

Calm.

Peace.

These words have been elusive the past 24 hours, but for the moment, we had rest.

"Tea? Vivian?" Claudia asked politely as she stepped out of the kitchen area carrying a beautiful Chinese cast iron tea kettle. The saucer shaped water vessel was fascinating enough, but the woman carrying it was equally as inviting.

Claudia had already run the gambit and ordeal of calling her parents, afterwards she decided to go upstairs to her new bedroom and get cleaned up, and now that she's had a moment to settle into her new self…

She was beautiful.

She wore something I had only seen her wear in the most formal occasions, when she was representing the university at a lecture or was attending some important event. She wore a yellow and red Indian dress, called a Sari. The bright colors matched well against her sky blue skin, the silk and satin fabric was wrapped in a way that let her shoulder free, showing a bit of her black sports bra underneath on one shoulder. I caught myself staring at her large yellow serpentine eyes as she politely waited for my response.

"Oh!" I said suddenly, snapping myself out of the moment. "Yes! Please, I'm sorry, it's been a long day…" I answered her as I took a cup off the tray she carried as she poured the tea for me. Claudia just calmly comforted me with her soft Indian accent and a kind tone as she turned to motion to the two human girls that had tagged along to us. They both sat together on the sofa across the coffee table from me, they looked so out of place in their punk attire in such a fine mansion. Violet didn't want a cup but Charity politely accepted the tray as she poured herself some tea. Claudia sat down on the plush brown recliner on my left, reached back to let her long braid out from behind her back, folded her arms, and sighed.

"No worries Vivian. On another feather, have you contacted your mother?" She asked me as she tilted her head slightly to emphasize her concern for me.

I shook my head as I scooted back on the sofa, pulling in my legs as I tucked them underneath me, leaning all my light weight on the arm rest of the matching mocha colored couch. "No… not yet. I let Natalie go ahead of me, since my mom's on UK time I figured it was for the better. I've just been admiring and gushing at Kayla's home. Who knew she lived in a place like this?" I glanced up at the high vaulted ceiling with recessed lighting and a u shaped second floor walkway that looked down on our present area. It was such a large and beautiful home, a stark departure from what I was used to.

"Y-yeah…" Charity Fahnestock, the cautious and meek blonde of the dark duo commented in a slightly gravel voice that came out as barely a whisper. She took a dainty sip of her tea before brushing her long blonde hair out of her eye line, tucking her hair behind her ear as she took another sip. "This is the nicest place I've ever seen…"

Violet Townsend folded her arms and rolled her eyes, unwilling to grow accustomed to the luxury. "A gilded cage is still a cage. So everyone's trapped here until this blows over?" She asked as she picked up her feet and dropped them on the coffee table, stretching her arms out to tuck them behind her head as she stared skyward. Charity leaned forward and slapped Violet's boots. Violet glanced back to Charity with a shake of her head before lowering her feet back to the ground.

Claudia answered for me, "I imagine since you are human and only briefly on the news, you will be free to go. However, it will be much safer for us to remain here. After all, this 'cage' as you so call it is acting more like a shark cage, keeping us safe rather than in open water. So yes, until things calm, we shall be here."

And I have to admit, if I was forced to be trapped somewhere. I'd rather it be in a beautiful mansion.

Violet huffed in response, folding her arms. "Only human." She said with a disappointed tone.

"What do you mean?" I asked.

She tilted her head and looked back to me. "Well look at you, you're a succubus, the fabled demon of lust and envy. You're gorgeous, powerful, and should be beholden to no one! You're a demon for crying out loud. You should be out conquering things, not teaching anthropology and hiding from the news or whatever." Violet waved her hands as she finished to parody my frantic way of doing things. In response I folded my arms and turned my head, flicking my tail up in the air as I did so.

"I'll have you know I teach Greco-Roman Archeology, you keep your soft science out of this." I retorted.

"Whatever." Violet answered. "The point is, I'm envious that you got to be so lucky and get turned into a demon. I've always wanted something like that. I used to be all into witchcraft and stuff, trying to summon demons and supernatural stuff… I know it wasn't real or nothing, but just the thought of it ya know? It was cool."

Charity set down her cup of tea to politely provide supplemental information, "We practiced, Wicca, not merely witchcraft or some satanic type of worship. Wicca was actually not about summoning demons but getting in touch with the base spirituality found within each living…" Violet cut her off.

"Whatever!" She waved her hands again, dismissing Charity's correction. "What I'm saying is, you're cool. Being a demon is cool, and I don't know why the world doesn't see that."

"Well… thank you." Claudia answered, taking a sip of tea herself. "I feel very privileged to be one in actuality, and it's nice to see others carry the sentiment." She said as she looked back with her bright yellow eyes and smiled a warm smile.

I sat up on the couch, leaning forward on my knees as I let my knuckles prop me up as I put my arms between my legs and perked my ears and wings, "You mean you like being a Succubus Claudia? I thought you hated it? When did you change?" I asked with curiosity. As I did, the professor came into the room. She had… hehe… changed to a more comfortable selection of clothing. Our dear professor was now wearing a very warm and very large set of flannel pajamas, complete with fuzzy slippers. She took a seat on the far end of the sofa from me as she poured herself tea and sat back in her state of deep comfort. It was only then did she realize her entrance had not only derailed our entire conversation, but everyone present was now focused on her.

"What?" Dr. Agnew asked as she held the saucer and cup of her tea a few centimeters from her lips, "I'm allowed to wear something other than formal attire when at a place of rest, thank you…" she answered indignantly as she took a sip. I couldn't help but giggle.

"So that's where you were." Claudia said as she sank deeper into her chair, coiling her tail as the brought in her legs with a sly smile.

"No, not just primping for the evening, I'll have you know I needed to make a few calls myself. I know my own mother would have been worried sick if I didn't. She will have assumed I've died or one of you girls have somehow devoured me." She laughed a bit as she thought of it, sipping tea as she smiled with her eyes at the thought.

"Well you know we still just might, rawr!" I joked, making gnashing motions with my teeth. Our conversation was once again invaded by another member, as Damien Focht, once more in his black slacks and silver button down dress shirt with the top two buttons unfastened, came striding in to take a seat at the unoccupied recliner across from Claudia, already carrying coffee and a biscotti.

"I hope everyone is all right and unharmed." He stated plainly with his deep voice and stern, serious tone. He took a sip of coffee and immediately inquired, "Have any of you seen Miss Gilden recently? Is she well?" He asked out of honest concern… then it dawned on me.

He had feelings for her.

How did I not see that before? I guess now that I can detect emotion I can cheat, but I should have seen it. All today, he was scared *for* her, he was worried about her. That's… actually very sweet.

"She's upstairs with Toby, last I saw they were playing video games and yelling about who was going to be what character." Claudia passively dismissed as she waved her hand before pouring more tea for herself.

Damien nodded and laughed to himself slightly, "Well then it's situation normal. Those two will likely be up all night doing that. They've been inseparable, ever since childhood. I've had to watch over Miss Gilden for a very long time, and that boy has always caused me so much trouble in doing so." He waxed nostalgic for a moment as he leaned back. Everyone seemed interested in hearing more about the shadowy man from Silverlight.

Violet was the most abrupt, "So you've been watching Kayla for a while then? Are you her guardian? A sort of bodyguard? I know rich girls usually have one, but you two are around the same age, so that's gotta mean something else." She was blunt, direct, and without tact. Damien looked back at her with a passive stare, and turned to speak to Claudia.

"Have you called Mumbai yet?" He asked the Indian demoness. She politely smiled, hiding a laugh at Damien shutting down Violet's question so directly, and answered as best she could.

"Yes…I already called my parents…" Claudia stated apathetically, dropping her kind candor for a decidedly empty tone.

"In India? How did they take it?" I asked, sliding up beside Dr. Agnew as she put her arm around me and let me rest and steal warmth from her flannel attire. Damien politely listened for a moment before his radio on his belt began to crackle, he was being called for by other

Silverlight soldiers he politely excused himself as he let his coffee rest on the table, stepping off into the side room.

"They were upset at first, and confused; I had to upload photos of myself for them to get it. I heard Mom fainted, but Dad was only worried that it would inhibit my ability to produce children…" Claudia snorted. She turned to look away for a moment. I could feel she was on the verge of screaming aloud, but she turned back, folded her hands, took a deep breath, and continued in a somber tone.

"I told him women normally pay a lot of money in America to get their body looking like this, and it actually seemed to placate him." She said with a sneer and a blast of air from her nostrils, running her hands down her curves almost in self-disgust, her voice trembled like she was holding back tears of anguish. I felt the need to reach out to her, just anything to comfort, but found myself unable to do so.

"Wow" I answered, unable to really come up with the right words.

"That's terrible." Charity gasped, "Claudia that's awful, I'm sorry…" she cradled her teacup as Violet folded her arms, her feelings of empathy were incredibly strong, but on the outside she showed nothing.

Claudia continued, shaking her head quickly, then looked over at me with a wincing grin, "That's my dad, so traditional, women are for making babies… you know he only sent me out here so I can marry a young doctor?" Claudia asked, her tone wavering.

My preconceived notions of Claudia were shattered.

"I-I had no idea, I always figured you were here on some amazing scholarship for managing to never make an academic mistake…" I joked to try and make her smile, honestly though, I was only half kidding.

She laughed. "That's sweet of you but no, I never actually received a formal education. Most of the women in my family were home schooled, by my father and older brother. I pretty much figured that I was going to end up a housewife to some idiot when I was first sent out here, but I that's when I met the professor…" Claudia looked over with an expression I could only explain as grace. As she spoke to me I could see the deep well of pain just underneath that sky blue skin, but she worked through it like a champion. I was honestly in awe of Claudia. For the first time, as she for once was truly honest with me about her guarded feelings. I felt something I had never felt about a woman before.

I realized, she was truly beautiful.

I held back a gasp as I knew my emotions could be detected, I glanced up at Claudia, as her yellow eyes flashed back to me. We hung in a mutual stare for a moment. I didn't know what to react with, or say. Oh my gosh… what does that mean? About her, about me? Did I always feel this way? I didn't know how to react, or what to do. So I froze. Thankfully, the Professor broke the silence by joining back in on the conversation.

"Claudia, you're an invaluable member of this team. I could never have completed my research without Vivian or yourself. I don't consider you just another intern, nor any of you here. In many ways, you're my family, so we're seeing things through to the end." The professor answered in the kindest way possible.

I was touched, the professor's kindness and my ADD jumped my mental track as I focused once more on Claudia's tale.

"Thank you professor, I feel the same of you as well…" Claudia nodded and thanked before continuing, "She was the first person to really see anything other than a middle class Indian girl in me, and I learned a lot in our time together. Then I realized that if I stayed in school, I didn't have to go back to a life I didn't want, and if I got all the way through school, I might have enough prestige to get a job soon enough that I can just stay here in the United States." Claudia explained with a smile and a shrug.

"What did your parents think of that plan?" I asked as I adjusted my sitting position, fluttering my wings to keep myself righted as I crossed my legs in my lap. I realized something in that moment, Claudia was never arrogant… she was scared. All the things she corrected, all the careful attention to detail, she was worried about failing. I understood her and felt more connected with her than I ever had before; I had to know the rest.

"My parents..." She looked away "They said that if I never loved them in the first place I should just stay here, and then cut all my funding."

"Harsh." I answered. "Claudia I'm so sorry."

Once again Claudia took it all in stride, smiling back at me, "Yeah, but I saw it coming, and so did the Professor, that's why I'm her TA. The money from the TA ship pays the rent, and as you well know TA's get free tuition. I am truly happy with the opportunities I have been given, and am grateful for Professor Agnew and everything that's happened so far." Claudia stated, nodding to herself in reflection.

"Even this?" I asked, showcasing myself.

"I'd go as far to say especially this." Claudia added "Despite the looks and comments, which by the way, I got anyway being anything other than white in America, I feel better; both about myself and about my previous decisions. I can't explain it, but the transformation has made me stronger, and I do not mean in simple strength. I feel like I am more secure as a person, the person... I would rather be."

"That's funny... I thought the same thing earlier today..." I said honestly.

"Yeah, and I noticed you're a pretty decent person when you're not constantly complaining and worrying over everything. Your kindness suits you; you're a good person Vivian. I'm glad to see you finally realize that for yourself, as I always have." Claudia complimented kindly with a smile.

"Thanks, you're not so bad yourself now that I know you're not perfect." I replied, stopping as I realized what I said was not really a compliment, feeling serious foot- in- mouth sickness soon after. She saw my ears and tail droop at my regret. I jutted my bottom lip forward in an ogre-like dumb face I often do inadvertently when I've done something stupid. I can't help it. Claudia just giggled a bit as I did.

Damien once more entered the room, now clad back in his power armor, holding his mask in his hand as he smiled. His assault rifle was strapped across his back, he was ready to fight at a moment's notice. He looked to me and suppressed a chuckle, as he explained my intentions on my behalf.

"I believe she meant to say you have many admirable qualities, which you do, Claudia. I have thought of you as a valuable partner in our months at sea." Damien corrected for me.

"Yeah… like that… I'm sorry." I apologized.

"Ha, don't beat yourself up, no one is perfect, but I think that's what makes us all unique." She smiled, fully letting her former emotional guard down to my surprise, her tone was serene, her yellow eyes radiant, as she thought over her next line.

"We are occasionally defined by our strengths, but much more often are we made up of our weaknesses. One should not feel bad about having weaknesses, but in awareness of what they are, strive to lessen them. After all, it's our shortcomings that really make us… human…" Claudia told me with an almost savant like wisdom, smiling and staring downward at her tea as she said that last and fateful word. Taking a sip to hide the emotion that rolled off her.

"That's one of the most profound things I think I heard in all of my time in college" I said honestly. "That's right up there with 'Show me your boobs.'"

The room laughed at the comment.

Claudia kept smiling as she motioned over to me, "So, what about you Vivian? What's your story?" Claudia asked, she set down her tea and folded her hands on her knee to show her undivided attention. I turned from my present position to meet her directly as I began to explain, patting the professor's hand to thank her for letting me hug. Violet and Charity gave their rapt attention, fascinated to hear about the lives of the succubus.

"Well, it's just me and my mom. I never met my dad, but she tells me he still lives in Arkham, up in Massachusetts, and I grew up there until I turned 13 when my mom decided she needed a change of pace, packed her bags and moved to Dunwich, England, with me. Dunwich was horrible though, kids made fun of me. Everyone thought I was dumb because I was American." I sighed before continuing.

"It seemed like everyone decided to give me crap. So I decided to give a little of it back. I suppose that's where I started the complaining and fussing all the time." I mused; never really thinking about it before, realizing that was probably the total truth.

"Were you mad at your mom for ripping you away to another country? I'd have been pissed." Violet scoffed as she leaned back, starting to put her feet up out of instinct but stopped as she glanced over at Charity, who arched her eyebrows in concern and after a moment Violet complied with her friend's wishes, lowering her boots.

"No, I never told her how I felt, and I wasn't mad at her. I never let my mom know anything…" I answered with an elevated pitch and a wincing smile "I made sure that every day I got home from school as chipper and happy as when we were back in Arkham. I know it sounds really dorky to say this but my mom… was my best friend, and still kinda is." I smiled, remembering some of the things we used to do together, suppressing a strange sigh as I waxed nostalgic "I remember playing through *Super Mario Brothers* on the *SNES*… We were terrible. I couldn't seem to figure out how to get Mario to fly with the cape on, and it was clear my mom never really was into video games…" I sighed and licked my lips to stall for time as I worked through the memories, "She tried so hard to reach out to me, it was only natural to try just as hard to reach back."

"That's very noble of you, it sounds like your mother loves you very much." Claudia thoughtfully replied.

"You had a similar situation to myself, actually." Damien answered. I turned, surprised.

He suppressed a smirk as he saw my reaction, "Oh? Surprised? Yes even corporate soldiers have families too."

I shook my head. "No, it's not that, I just realized I can't possibly imagine you as a little boy."

He laughed a little at that, "Well believe it Vivian. I once was a boy, and a teenager, and I even went to college like you. Imagine that." He chided. "But yes, I actually grew up alongside Miss Kayla Gilden. Our homes were next door, my father was Daniel Gilden's personal protector and friend. Now that mantle rests with me, as the Knight Commander of Silverlight's Private Military Company."

"So that's what you really do..." I mused, the term 'Knight Commander' sounded really cool, I admit a small amount of jealousy.

"They call their soldiers knights?" Violet scoffed, "So do you like have to swear loyalty to Daniel Gilden, and do you hold land somewhere and titles?" She laughed to herself at the thought of a 21st century knight, but Damien's answer stopped her cold.

"Yes. I do, and I did." He answered, surprising Violet immediately, "We abide by the code of the Silver Light. Noblesse Oblige, we care for those who cannot care for themselves, and lead those who need to be led." He answered.

Violet shut up.

"That's really cool." Charity noted.

"So, you were always a soldier? Even when you were on the boat with us?" I asked Damien, curious to hear more of his tale.

"Yes, but I had to deceive you when I did, I apologize, but now I am tasked with defending not only Miss Gilden, but all of you." He answered, nodding politely.

Claudia turned her head and smiled a knowing smile, "You have a healthy amount of respect for 'Miss Gilden', don't you?"

Damien looked down, cradling his mask in his hands as he sighed. His dark skin hides a blush well, but we can feel his emotions.

"Kayla Gilden is a very capable woman, she's forthright, strong, and knows what she's doing. Just like her father." He took a breath before continuing.

"I still remember my father taking a hold of my shoulders as a young man and said to me 'that woman is the most precious thing this company has, it's Mr. Gilden's future. As my job is to protect Mr. Gilden, it is yours to protect her. When she falls, be there, when she is thirsty, you provide water…' until yesterday, that promise was never broken… Now it has been." He let out the kept up air as he spoke, letting the weight of his own words settle.

"You love her, don't you?" I asked with a voice barely a whisper, as I came to realization of his intentions, his hanging around, and his loyalty to the company.

Damien did not answer, I listened to the shouting and cheering of Toby and Kayla playing video games with each other upstairs, absolutely enthralled by each other's company, I could feel the deep emotions of love and affection between them, it was undeniable. By the time I looked back to Damien, he had affixed his mask. Showing only a blank white armored face, and two yellow eyes.

"Miss Gilden's heart, and its decisions, are her own."

And with that, I understood Knight Commander Damien Focht.

The room hung in silence for several moments, until a jarring, wailing southern voice screamed for absolution through the walls of the room adjacent.

"THAT'S WHAT I'M TRYING TO TELL YOU DAD!"

The shout echoed from the high walls of the mansion, we all turned to the study where the secure phone was located, peeking through the double paned glass doors to see Natalie trembling as she growled into the tiny phone, the current source of all her torment.

"No Dad…" she continued, trying to fit a word or two in between her father's upset tirade.

I know it's not polite to eavesdrop, but… devil's ears I suppose…

"No, it's… I've been changed… I'm different now." Natalie sighed and spoke softly as she attempted to explain again, dropping down into Mr. Gilden's chair in the office with frustration, looking like a small child with his oversized desk and office furniture surrounding her.

“No… no of course I’m not gay Dad! No I don’t have sex with women!” she shouted, as her father seemed to steamroll ahead in his berating of her. I felt Claudia bristle at the conversation, I couldn’t help but feel empathy as well.

I couldn’t make out all of what Natalie’s father said, but I certainly heard the words *condemned*, and *hell*.

“Oh my goodness, I still wanna go to church Dad! It hasn’t even been a Sunday yet, this happened YESTERDAY!” Natalie tried to reason, but it was clear it was not working. Finally, Natalie snapped, letting go of not only of her temper, but apparently her repressed southern accent…

We could hear an intense grumble on the other line. She sharply responded.

“Then fine dad, fine! You know what, yeah, that’s what happened, that’s me now, I’m a demon from hell now, I got turned into a succubus! It’s apparently some servant of the dark lord and I’m stuck like this forever so you go right on ahead and disown me because shoot, God right out and tells you to drive away the devil as you so see fit, EVEN IF IT’S YOUR OWN DAUGHTER! Oh no wait! No he don’t!”

Natalie moved to throw the phone but halted as she realized the phone didn’t belong to her, keeping true to her noble charm even at this point of anger. She looked at the receiver for several seconds trying to think of something to do with it but just sat it in the cradle and began to cry. Natalie sobbed as she hid her head in her arms on the desk. Claudia and I rushed to comfort her, but we were apparently the last people she wanted to see.

“GET AWAY FROM ME!” She shouted, shaking us off of her, her voice crackling with her very southern accent wailing. “It’s both of you that done did this to me! Now I’ve lost my friends, my family, and the eternal love of God!”

She turned to run outside, but Damien was right there.

“Natalie. I heard what your father said to you… he’s incorrect.” Damien attempted to placate her but an armored man in a suit provides little comfort at a time like this.

"It don't matter if he is or ain't, he's my father and that's what he feels! I'm alone now! From him, from my friends, my family, from God, ALONE!" she shouted as she charged away back up the stairs, and slammed the door to her new room, as she did, the door was ripped off the frame like it was made of paper. She looked at the destruction she caused, and teared up again, but the corporate soldier just followed up the stairs after her.

"I… I'm sorry…" Natalie apologized, still crying as she handed the door to Damien, but the masked man raised an armored hand and took it from her gently.

"There's no need, I'll have a repair team attend to it in the morning, if you would like we can reposition you into another room, it is of no concern to us." He gently offered with the calm demeanor worthy of a 21st century knight. Perhaps it's not just a name after all.

Natalie tried to respond to Damien's kindness, but was too distraught. She threw herself on the bed and wept in the dark.

Damien just stayed outside her room, keeping watch through his visor, just in case she attempted to hurt herself.

That's also when I realized maybe corporate spook Damien wasn't such a bad guy. Perhaps somewhere beyond all the lies and secrets, he does actually look out for us.

Nothing's really that easy anymore. Is it? I've been trying to pin down who's right and who's wrong in this. Was Silverlight bad or good? Is the DPI good? Are we?

I looked at the clock… half past seven… mom should be available by now.

"It's time…" I said with resolution, standing up, glancing to the office room before looking to Claudia.

"May peace be upon you" Claudia blessed, only half kidding.

I hesitated as I went to dial the number. How would my mother respond? Would she disown me like Natalie, dismiss me like Claudia, or play it cool like Kayla's dad just did?

As I walked I thought of my times with my mother, I thought of how important she was to me. I didn't know if I was ready to give that up, to give up the only person that's ever truly loved me...

But I had already dialed.

The phone clicked.

"Vivian? Is that you" I heard my mom ask on the other line.

"Yeah mom... it's me." I answered, my voice nearly trembling as I spoke.

"Honey... what's wrong" My mom asked, recognizing instantly...

And suddenly, as I heard my mother's voice... it all came out.

I explained ***everything***, and I mean everything...

I blurted out what happened to me and how it happened. I explained how I didn't even have organs anymore, about Sonya, about Silverlight, the strange men in armor... I even spilled the beans about what kind of people I had been hanging out with, telling her their stories as well as my own. Complete and utter disclosure...

I was so scared that I had unfurled far more than I had ever hoped to divulge. After realizing this as I finished my tale, I winced to myself and prepared for her ultimate judgment upon me. The phone rattled in my hand as the top of the receiver bounced against my horn.

"Vivian..." My mother said to me.

"I love you."

"Mom..." I started to say, tears gathering as I spoke.

"Vivi, you're my little girl" She cut me off "No matter what you say or what you do or did, no matter what you look like nothing will ever change that fact to me. Now you sound like you're in good company, with good friends, you watch out for them, as they have watched out for you. You have a good head on your shoulders, I trust you to do the right thing. I love you very much Vivian, I just want you to know that. I'll be out as soon as I can… you say you're with Daniel Gilden?" My mother asked, I numbly answered.

"Mmhm… and Kayla." I replied.

"… Kayla…" My mother seemed to gasp.

"Mom is something wrong?" I asked her, hearing and feeling a strange churn of feelings from her.

"No… nothing's wrong, I love you Vivian." My mother said to me.

"I love you too mom." I said, trembling, unable to hold back the feeling of relief and love I felt for my mom at that moment.

"I'll hug you as soon as I see you, and I will try and see you soon, goodnight" She whispered with a smile I could almost feel over the phone. I looked up through the glass doors to the armored sentinel upstairs.

Yellow eyes flared behind a pale white mask. I knew Damien was listening.

"Goodnight" I whispered back, tears welling in the corner of my big yellow eyes, and hung up.

"Vivian… are you ok?" Claudia creaked the door open and asked me as I turned to her, unable to hold back emotion any longer.

"Yes!" I said as I started to sob in emotions I could barely fathom. She rushed forward and hugged me as I leaned on her shoulder. She just gently held me in her arms.

"You know what Claudia?" I said, taking a breath of fresh air between the tears.

"I think we're going to be ok." I said with mirth.

"Yeah…" Claudia answered, patting my back, "We're going to be ok."

"I think… I think it's time I get cleaned up and ready for bed… Tomorrow's a new day." I said with a renewed smile and the feeling that I was loved. Not only by my mother, by my friends and coworkers, but even new companions like Violet and Charity. I might be exploring a brave new world, but I have enough support to make it through.

"That sounds good, have a good night Vivian." Claudia said as we walked back out into the living room.

I looked back to Violet and Charity, "You guys… thank you so much again for helping us today. I'm glad that we got to meet you… I hope you'll stay for a little while if you can." I asked as I folded my hands at my waist and fluttered my wings, turning on the charm to keep our new friends for a while still.

Charity smiled as Violet rolled her eyes and looked away, "Yeah…" Violet let her shoulders raise and fall a bit, "I 'spose we can spend at least a night in this bourgeoisie palace…"

I bowed to say thank you, said my good nights and bounded up the stairs. My room was beautiful, soft, and with my own private bath I could enjoy a hot shower in comfort. With the rise of the steam on my dark blue skin I felt the troubles of the world wash away. So I'm a succubus, a demon… that's not so bad. If the world doesn't like me, then they need to meet me. If you think I'm evil, you should say hi. I'm Vivian Maybell, girlventurer. I just might even make my own archeology show after all.

Perhaps it's like Kayla and Claudia said, good or evil isn't defined by what something is, it's by your perspective. Perhaps one person's sin is another person's salvation. It's not the demon that's evil, it's what he or she *does* with the time they are given.

It's all a matter of Prolecto,

A subject of allure.

Chapter Eight

Kayla's Personal Mansion

Ruxton Road, Baltimore, Maryland

United States of America, Earth

The Journal of Vivian Maybell

August 16th, 2011

8:49 PM

The hot shower became a bath as I really just wanted to unwind. I relaxed, spent some time just looking at myself, getting used to what I now was. It's strange, you know, to look down and see someone else. To glance in the mirror and see you, but… not you. If that could possibly make any sense. I enjoyed the many hotel-like mini bottles of bubble-bath, bath salts, and an imaginary basketball session with the spongy loofah and the shower faucet as the imaginary net. After I had my bath-time fun playing in bubbles and pretending to be a sea monster as I swam around in the palatial Romanesque tub and used my tail as the serpent's head, I got out to cut my hair.

I finished dying my roots back to the bright fire engine red color that I enjoyed, and with my dark blue skin, it looked fantastic, I think I'll keep it that way for some time. I cut my hair to regain the same just past the shoulder length, and made my front hair choppy and jagged, letting it frame my face for when I put back my ponytail.

I had begun to feel like myself again.

I wiped my dark blue hand against the foggy screen, seeing my yellow eyes look back at me as I smiled with my pearly white fangs in my KPU black and white pajama pants and a white tee shirt. I was me. And that was that.

"At least I know I'm not a vampire!" I said to no one in particular as I played with my reflection, cutting my hair carefully while using the mirror's reflection. I batted my yellow eyes at myself in the mirror, liking the view I saw as I recognized myself once more. I pulled up my hair and made my ponytail, for my finishing effect I reached into the medicine cabinet to grab out a hair tie to make the look complete. I had dyed my hair back to my bright red, I have my bangs back and they look great with the blue skin. I just got the little black tie, closed the cabinet…

And there she was.

"Hello Vivian." Sonya Shannon purred as she stepped out of the shadows made by the bathroom door. Like literally stepped *out* of the shadow, there was only a wall, and she went right through it.

She was fully enjoying her new succubae form. Standing tall at six foot three with her hair now white and cascading down her back with a long front strand flipped forward to hang partially over her left eye. Her bright green serpentine eyes glowed against her midnight violet-almost black skin. Her ample chest was barely contained in a white button down shirt, showing off her lacey undergarment without a hint of shame to her, the cross on the matching white lace choker collar seemed only to remind men "hey my boobs are down this way".

As much as she was still Sonya, she came with a few new and deadly additions.

She slowly tilted her head as she smiled a wicked smile, allowing her teeth to start to stretch and change. To my abject horror I watched her pretty face morph as her teeth became long six inch metal daggers, flayed and jagged like knives married to shark's teeth. I froze, staring at her reflection in the mirror without being able to even scream.

I was so, so, scared.

She grabbed the back of my head with her hand and rammed my face through the porcelain sink, shattering the faucet and sending water spraying into the air like a fountain. I whimpered in pain but before I had time to react she gripped harder on my head and hair and dragged me back up onto my feet, pressing my face against the fractured tiling on the wall as she continued to make deconstructive art with my head in the Gilden family guest bathroom.

"Oh isn't it amazing Vivian!?" Sonya shouted with a crazed tone as the hurled me through the bathtub's side, causing me to land in a big shattered porcelain pile. "If you'd have been human you would have died some time ago, but we're stronger now, oh so much stronger! The humans were right to fear us, I'd be afraid of me too… now… where's Kayla?"

I gritted my teeth as I felt the horrible throbbing pain in my head, realizing I had a bit of sink stuck in my skin as I ripped the piece out of me, "Sonya! Why!? Why are you doing this? Seriously what is *wrong* with you, woman?" I shouted at her as I lifted my head to see what she was doing now. Sonya stood at what was left of the mirror, keeping an eye on me while looking at herself, testing her teeth as she switched the blades on and off.

She turned back to face me, smiling with a confident smirk as I watched something move under her clothing, before I could ask what the heck it was a black tar began to creep out and across her skin. I recognized it instantly.

How could I have possibly forgotten about that?

"Azazel! Oh crap that's right! Sonya it's taking you over you have to fight it!" I shouted, trying to see if I could appeal to Sonya within the monster.

But, in hindsight, I should have seen this next part coming.

"Oh no! Azazel the parasite! What shall I do?" Sonya said in very much her own voice as she put a hand on her chest and feigned fear in the most overdramatic way as she swooned with her other hand on her forehead. Before she could go further, we heard shouting from the hall, Damien and his soldiers were on their way. Sonya stopped mid jest and opened her left eye, arching an eyebrow as she realized she could be in trouble.

"Let's take it outside." She said in a more back of the throat and gnarled tone as she dropped her hands to her side and spun around quickly as I started to stand at the worst time. She brought around her foot and kicked me hard in the gut with her heel. I sailed through the wall and clear outside as I felt the cold wind whip past me as I took a long drop down into the large and flat Maryland lawn out front of the mansion. I dug a small channel with my body into the otherwise perfectly uniform grass as I slid to a stop. I realized at that moment despite what Sonya just said, even if I was stronger, that didn't mean it felt better to be beat up by any means. I groaned and struggled to do anything as I felt waves of pain wash over me.

"H...help..." I weakly groaned as I attempted to reach out from my self-carved rut. I heard Sonya's clawed feet land with a thud behind me as she leapt out of the hole in the second story. No sooner had she landed on the front lawn a series of metallic clicks and whirrs echoed from the ground. I craned my neck to see what the sounds were and promptly gasped as I watched portions of the perfectly level grass slide back to reveal several hexagon shaped holes about two feet wide across the grass. The whirring continued as double barreled Gatling gun turrets popped out of the ground, a chain of assault rifle bullets trailed out of each device as the barrels began to turn in place. A red eye like diode in the bottom right of the barrels on each turret illuminated as they whirled around to face Sonya and I. I clenched my teeth and shuddered as I stared down a turret barrel, when suddenly every gun on the lawn turned sharply to face Sonya.

"Oh Daniel... that's not an HOA approved home modification." Sonya purred as she smiled at the many red tracer beams flickering off her shiny black skin. She tucked her lips into the corner of her mouth as she pulled back her leather jacket's sleeve and revealed a gleaming metal device on her arm that looked like a small gauntlet with a diamond shaped glowing cyan light on it. I could see the Silverlight logo sparkle as she slapped down on the large glowing diamond. A sheer moment after the turrets converged fire, pouring hot lead towards Sonya at a speed that appeared to be a steady red stream of molten lava as the phalanx systems mounted into the Gilden family's lawn. Sonya's device let out a vibrant and powerful light that encapsulated her in a bright cyan gleaming bubble, causing the bullets to ricochet off her into the ground, I scrambled out of my hole in the ground to avoid the deadly fast shrapnel that rained over the area. The sheer shockwave of the ground fire caused the grass to ebb and wave like the heavy pulse of air from a stereo speaker at full blast.

I ran for the trees at the edge of the property, hoping to use the thick underbrush to hide me as Sonya was distracted by the turrets. Damien Focht appeared, standing with a full squad of Silverlight soldiers in the upstairs bathroom hole. I could see him motion with his hand for Claudia and Natalie to stand back as they tried to come in after him. He locked his *Mauser* assault rifle in place as his glowing yellow eyes narrowed at Sonya, who smiled up at him as the guns ceased firing, cooling before they could barrage her again.

"How are you still alive…?" Damien coldly asked as he let his glowing eyes on his mask become slits as Sonya placed her hands on her hips and smiled a gleaming metal smile of dagger teeth.

"Silverlight Reactive Kinetic Ferrier! You should know Damien! After all it's *yours!* Hahahaha!" Sonya cackled as she slapped the side of the device with a wicked grin and looked back at him as her bright green irises began to glow until they became a solid gleam that consumed her entire eye with a malevolent light. It was clear that she was about to attack. Damien wasted no time as he immediately raised his rifle and fired.

In the instant the bullets from Damien's rifle took to travel from his rifle to Sonya's location, Sonya… I guess she moved, but I couldn't see it. All that I saw was a series of small black wisps that looked like Azazel's Ichor, but they quickly vanished like rising steam as they flipped away into nothing. I looked up to Damien to see that Sonya was now standing *behind* the squad of Silverlight soldiers. The soldiers were completely unprepared for the Sonya's sudden arrival, the soldier at the back started to move when Sonya's fingers extended into long blades as she lanced forward and drove her hands through the man's back and out his chest.

I gasped and screamed in fear as the team of trained soldiers turned to face her, but she used the stabbed man as a shield as she dragged him around to take the bullets of another soldier's assault rifle before spinning once to throw the man at another soldier, causing the body to push Damien out the open hole in the upstairs window. As Damien and one of the other soldiers fell, Sonya once more teleported to below where she awaited them with extended blades, reaching her hands high to impale them. Damien turned in the last moment and bent down his wrist, letting a powerful high tension wire shoot forth from his armored suit and grasp into the side of the building, letting him swing out of Sonya's clutches, the other soldier was not so lucky, and was lanced through the chest and out the front with a spray of blood that I can't help but remember as the glittering globules left an imperfect scar on the pristine white building's siding.

"C'mon Damien! We both knew it'd come to this! Where's little Gilden? I know you're hiding her!" Sonya shouted as she pulled off the dead man's assault rifle and held it in one hand as she fired it without any sign of trouble from recoil. Damien activated something within his power armor as he suddenly sprinted with a speed I could barely see, running outside the bounds of her bullet barrage as she raked the rifle across the front of the house. I gasped as I realized the professor and the girls were probably still downstairs! I hope no one was hit!

"Backup! We need backup! I'm calling in the DPI!" One of the Silverlight soldiers shouted as he realized only him and Damien still lived. The man chickened out, running backwards and away from the fight back into the house.

Damien stepped back out of the shadows of the far tree line as he reached behind himself, pulling out from his cloak a small metal bar. He flicked his wrist as the bar extended out into a long pole with two very sharp ends, the ends split open into a triangular hook as they ignited a large spark of what looked to be cyan lightning, concentrated in a wave like an active Taser.

"You will never have Miss Gilden." Damien coldly promised as he slowly walked towards Sonya with an intimidating and direct path. Completely ready to fight the demoness head on as she recoiled back and smiled, letting her teeth turn once more into blades as she flicked her tail. Outwardly Sonya looked like she had control of the situation but from what I could feel she let slip fear…

She's afraid of Silverlight.

"Ah… going to fight me one on one? What a brave little knight…." Sonya purred as she let her claws extend and prepared to receive Damien's charge.

"You're as dumb as your father. Does he really think we don't know he's pulling your strings?" Damien coldly replied.

"So you figured it out did you? Why the big revelation then? I thought Silverlight liked to keep secrets." She snidely purred as she brought her long claws around to fight him.

"Because dead men tell no tales, or women, for that matter." Damien retorted in a lackluster voice as he let his glowing eyes drop to half open as he stood upright and let his weapon down at his side.

Sonya stood upright and withdrew her metal as she realized what he meant. All of the turrets on the lawn had cooled, their laser sights focused once more on her as they opened up. The heavy and constant roar of the massive amount of gunfire rippling through the night. Sonya was absolutely rocked by the gunfire as streams of bullets riddled through her body. I heard her scream amongst the gunfire as her demonic form shuddered and violently jerked from side to side as the force of impact from the dozen or so guns unleashed from every angle, tearing fabric and skin all the same. After about 10 seconds of sustained fire the guns stopped, leaving Sonya, or what was left of Sonya, lying face down on the grass. Damien pressed a button to retract his staff and put it back in his cloak as he looked down at the very dead demoness.

"Garbage in, garbage out." He said emotionlessly as he turned away from her and grabbed out his phone, raising it up as he looked skyward with an exasperated hand on his hip. The turrets retracted. "Situation handled. It was Shannon's daughter. She's carrying the Nexan. Yes sir… Yes we can have a team extract it. Miss Gilden was never involved sir. Thank you sir. Yes, I'll have an architect look at it in the morning I'll transfer Miss Maybell to another room. Good night sir." Damien clearly caught up with Mr. Gilden, filling him in on the details as I came trotting up to him from the woods.

He turned around to face me as he glanced over my now dirt covered pajamas and messed up hair. "Miss Maybell are you unharmed?" He asked me with courtesy. I nodded as I glanced myself over…

All my cuts were healed.

"I'm… wow I'm fine." I said as I looked at my hand where moments ago I had a massive gash from Sonya's attack. It was perfectly fine now, no hint of even a scar. I pressed down on the area to see if it was still tender… nothing. I had healed completely.

Damien reached down and grabbed my hand, holding it up and looking it over himself. "That's a very useful ability. You're just full of surprises Miss Maybell. Are you going to be all right?"

I nodded, I heard my friends come swooping in.

"Holy crap! I was thrown in the panic room and couldn't hear a thing! What the heck went on here!" Kayla shouted as she flew from the hole in my room down to us. Claudia and Natalie quickly followed behind her. Toby, Dr. Agnew, Violet and Charity came running out of the front door and joined up with us. Damien quickly raised his hand to stop them.

"Please this is a dangerous area don't go any…" I started to say, but when Natalie saw the bodies from the fight, she screamed.

Damien sighed as the light blue succubus scooted to Dr. Agnew's side as the professor hugged her in comfort, looking at the body of a soldier with a wincing expression. She turned back to look at Damien, "I'm sorry Damien… what happened here?"

Damien walked over and knelt at one of the fallen soldiers, placing a hand to the soldier's neck, trying for a pulse. He stood up and shook his head, "We were attacked by Miss Shannon. She was dealt with but not without leaving a few scars. These were good men." He turned back to look at Kayla, "You're not safe, she was here for you."

Kayla rolled her eyes, "Here for me? I could have taken her Damien, we both know that." She replied in a calm and very nonchalant tone. Two things surprised me at once about that statement. The fact that Kayla was so calm after what just happened suggested that this has happened more than once, and the thought that she could fight something as powerful as Sonya…

What am I getting myself into?

"So… is everything ok here?" Toby asked Damien. "Are you going to be all right man? Are you ok?" The kind boy asked the soldier. Damien waved his hand to dismiss.

"I'll be fine Toby. Just get Kayla back inside, I'll cleanup here but you tell me if anything strange starts to happen ok? I'm not kidding if Shannon wants Kayla, I doubt he had only a single plan. Stay up all night if you have too don't let her out of your sight, you understand?" Damien instructed Toby as the young man nodded, thinking over how serious Damien's instruction was to him.

"You're trusting me? We're that screwed?" Toby asked, only half kidding as he said it in a joking tone.

"Yes." Damien answered directly, "The media will already be asking about the shots, we're not about to bring in more units. It's just us for the night now and I heard one of our less sterling members has run to get the DPI. For now we just need to..."

Damien stopped short. Everyone froze.

I heard the whirr of the electrical turrets.

We all turned to see the turret grid rise out of the ground again, this time the red beams focused on us. I backed up to Damien as everyone shirked in together around him, Damien quickly tried a series of commands on the computer mounted in his armor's left arm, but had little progress.

"The system's being overridden... I can't control it. It says I'm unauthorized from my own network..." Damien commented out loud, trying to put together what was occurring around us when we suddenly received our answer.

"... maybe I'm not as dumb as my father..." Sonya's voice growled in a menacing tone. I turned to stare at her corpse.

Sonya, like me, had healed. She stood, at first slowly but then with a sudden jerk as she snapped upright, her wings cracked as they extended, the holes from the bullets sealing as she smiled a wicked grin.

"Checkmate." Sonya purred, I could see tendrils of black ichor running from her lower back stuck into the ground, likely rewiring the turret system, "I needed to find a decent interface to override local electronics, and you just gave me one. Why should I bring weapons when you'll provide them all for me. Now give me Kayla Gilden." She demanded as she dropped her tone, "Or I kill every one of them, including you." She challenged Damien as she adjusted her frayed clothing to fit back on her, letting her green eyes glow at him with a menacing stare.

I heard Damien clench his teeth and let off a frustrated grunt as he contemplated a way out of the situation. I looked to Kayla who balled her fists and stared Sonya down. Toby held onto her, looking outward at Sonya.

"Why do you want me so bad? What do you intend to do?" Kayla asked directly in attempt to spare our lives. I realized that if Sonya could survive the bullets maybe the other succubae could as well... but Dr. Agnew, Violet, Charity, Toby and Damien would all be killed for sure... I couldn't lose a single one of them.

C'mon Kayla...

"It's simple really, I need your power. I want you and the other Succubae to join me in a move towards cultural upheaval. Nations don't topple themselves you know. If I am to succeed then I'll need support. You're going to be that support. You all are. It's as simple as that, now be a good girl and come over here or your precious boyfriend and teacher die." Sonya stated plainly, I took a deep breath and let a wave of anger come and pass. She thinks that I would help her murder people? That's horrible! I'd never...

Kayla wasn't having anything of it. "And if I don't join you? What makes you think that I'd listen to you. I'm Kayla Gilden, the daughter of Silverlight. You come into my house, kill my guards, and expect me to follow? You're a fool Sonya. You always were. Now you're just a fool with wings." Kayla stated boldly for someone at gunpoint.

Sonya raised her hand and wagged a finger at Kayla, delivering a snide retort, "You just don't get it do you? An object lesson is in order then. I have Azazel, you do not. She's a highly adaptive nano-ichor parasite. Your consent in this issue is not required, because I'm taking it. You don't have to be you in order to serve me, you can be anyone I want you to be. You get the picture?" She purred as she let her eyes fade to glowing green as she sneered.

Nobody liked the sound of that.

To my surprise, Violet stood before Kayla, putting out her hands to barricade her as she called Sonya out.

"I don't know who the hell you are or what you're doing here, but you can't have her. I see what you're doing, you're giving the media what it wants. You're being the monster they want to see. I'm not stupid. I can see you're catering to their fear. Why? What's in it for you? The whole world's going to come after you, you know that. So why?" She stood up for us as she bought time. C'mon… maybe the DPI can get here before Sonya does anything.

Sonya raised an eyebrow at Violet, "That… is actually pretty smart coming from a little goth like you. Hmm…" She pondered for a second, then in a sudden flash, she acted.

I heard Charity gasp, calling out Violet's name.

She pushed her friend aside as Sonya immediately closed the gap, running her bladed tail through Charity's back as the thin blonde girl shielded her friend from the incoming blow.

"Charity!" Violet shouted as Sonya leapt back with the girl still impaled on her tail. Violet started to run towards her, but Kayla put out her hand, stopping Violet's sudden movement. As she did the turrets clicked.

We were forced to stand and watch.

"Now… I want you all to watch very closely…" Sonya's grin grew wider as she pulled Charity back towards her, lifting Charity up using her tail embedded in Charity's back. The frightened girl reached back towards us as Sonya pumped in the changing venom, turning her into a succubus before our eyes.

"I…" Charity turned her head to look at Violet as Sonya held her aloft, already I could see a color creeping across Charity's back, light blue… like Natalie and Claudia.

"I'm sorry…" She apologized to Violet. The sweet girl was more worried about endangering us than herself… if I could feel any guiltier about the situation, I would, but I couldn't.

"No… you're going to be ok Charity, Damien! Can't we do something? I'm not going to just sit here!" She screamed at our soldier as Charity's form began to flair. Her hips surrendered their bony physique as her form began to stretch and swell with her new succubae body. Her shoes fell away as her feet transformed. Charity's tail extended from her lower back, she was completing her change.

"I can do something…" Damien said as he raised his pistol from its holster and aimed it at Charity's still human head. I realized what he was going to do when I pulled his hand down sharply.

"What are you thinking! You're going to kill her!" I shouted at Damien, I can't believe he'd even *think* of doing something like that.

"You heard Sonya she's going to infect her! It's only a matter of time!" Damien shouted back.

"Ahh… help… please…" Charity politely whimpered as her wings extended and her white T-shirt strained as her succubae form continued to emerge. Her face began to shift as her fangs grew in, her skin now blue as her yellow eyes enlarged. Her horns emerging at the end as her blonde hair faded to a beautiful dark blue. She was let down, complete.

"Charity!" Violet shouted again.

Charity looked down at herself, seeing her new hands and her new and extremely curvaceous form. "Whoa…" She gasped. Sonya raised an eyebrow as she looked down at the new, very beautiful, succubus.

"You're welcome. Don't say I never did anything for you." Sonya sneered. Charity just backed away from Sonya, still very afraid.

"I…" Charity trembled as she looked over herself, patting at different parts of herself as she glanced back to Violet and the rest of us. "I'm still me… guys… I'm still me…I think I'm ok…" Charity tried to placate us as she got her bearings, trying to figure out what happened to herself while still carefully trying to scoot back towards us.

Sonya tilted her head as she held out her hands to make a picture frame with her fingers, "Now, pay attention. Here we see this girl, who she is, what she wants, irrelevant. I like the new buxom thing she's got going on, let's work with that. Taller I'm thinking, let's up the power, and I need a good yes-girl who can bring the muscle. So let's go with that."

A sound somewhere between an active helium tank and gurgling water echoed from within Charity's hollow body as Azazel's ichor turned active. I recognized the noise from when I saw Claudia turn the night before, or when Azazel exerted herself while inside me. Charity gasped as she started to fill, her chest heaved forward as Sonya made good on her promise, she made Charity's waist synch in a bit as she flared her hips, made her taller and taller, growing up to the seven foot standards that Azazel had made us the night before, as Charity grew her feet turned into hooves. Her horns grew longer and curled back across the top of her head, turning up at the end and pointing more. As she changed Charity clearly was uncomfortable with the act. She held onto herself to try and keep herself covered, looking between us and Sonya with worried eyes.

"Hmm… You have a cute face but your hair is awful and I think your chin's too wide, pinch that in… and the attitude sucks… let's fix it." Sonya stated quickly as she waved her hand. Quickly, Charity's hair changed length and style to turn long and flowing down her back, while in the front cute jagged triangles of hair framed her face as Sonya crafted a perfect feathered series of layers by whim alone. Her chin narrowed as her cheekbones altered to give her a more ovular like face from her more rounded features and finally at the end Charity flared out taller and bigger in every way as her eyes contracted all the way as she gasped then dropped her hands to the side as she calmly sighed and rolled her neck, suddenly becoming comfortable with herself.

As she completed she gasped a contented gasp. Closing her eyes and stretching her wings as she took a deep breath, like she had just awakened from a long and peaceful rest. "Mmm… thanks… I like the hair. Now… what do you want me to do?" Charity complemented as she finished transforming. She stood alongside Sonya, flicking her tail playfully as she turned her profile sideways and calmly stared us down.

She was completely overwritten. I couldn't feel a single feeling I experienced from her before. She was a new person, belonging to Sonya.

The polite and calm girl was gone, this was Charity now…

Sonya with Azazel's power is truly terrifying.

"What did you do to her! Let her go!" Violet shouted as Dr. Agnew held her back, the professor tried to keep her calm as possible but given the circumstance that was impossible.

"Oh shut up." Charity scolded from her new lush lips and pretty smile. "Relax Violet. This is what you wanted. You'll be a demon soon and we'll be able to do everything we ever wanted." She barely attempted to placate her friend with a dismissive wave before she turned and asked politely to Sonya. "So, do you want me to start converting the other humans or just get Gilden?"

Sonya passively shrugged as she seemed to focus her thoughts elsewhere, "Neither. Just sit tight a moment I'm seeing if I can make this any easier… Did Azazel leave any bits of herself in… ah… of course." She stopped, walking at a still considerable distance from us as she paced to the side of the group, we slowly turned to face her. Natalie tucked in towards Claudia as Claudia put her arm around the girl, pulling her in defensively. I watched Damien as he continued to do something secretly behind his visor. I put my faith in his ability to be sneaky. In this case it just might work in our favor.

"Natalie…" Sonya began, motioning for the girl to come to her.

"No." Natalie refused immediately, clenching her fists as I felt a wave of anger roll off Natalie.

"Aww why not? We're friends aren't we? I see there's a teeeeny little bit of Azazel in a couple of you… and I just need that to grow. You're afraid of me aren't you? Well let that fear feed her, let her grow.

When there's enough, I'm sure you'll see it my way." Sonya purred happily as she smiled a metal smile, her glowing green eyes reflecting off her own teeth with an effect that made them seem to glow all the same.

Natalie was somewhere between rage and fear as she stared down Sonya, trying not to feel heavy emotion but unable to stop in the turmoil. Fear turned to anger as Natalie quietly cursed her fate. You know, that's the problem with fear, that's the problem with a tyrant. There's only so far someone can be pushed, there's only so much a person can take. Eventually the bully bites off more than she can chew…

And someone hits back.

But it wasn't Natalie, it wasn't Damien, it wasn't Violet or even Kayla.

It was Claudia, and no one saw it coming.

With a flash of yellow the beautiful silk Sari flew across the crowd without a wearer, the fabric landing on Sonya's face and chest, obscuring her vision. Before anyone had time to act Claudia now clad only in the black yoga pants and sports bra she wore underneath the Sari leapt with an incredible force across the professor and Violet as she landed with a gymnast's grace before spinning around and delivering a hard heel under Sonya's chin as the un-expecting succubus was very firmly knocked off her feet.

The turrets, under Sonya's control, wavered from their position, knocked off operation by the master being interrupted. Damien took full advantage of the situation as he ignited small jets in his armor along the back of the legs, dashing across the surface of the grass as he pulled back his hand in a punch, causing a violet blade of what looked to be electrical light shoot forth from his forearm as he stabbed it into a seemingly unimportant patch of grass. As soon as he did the turrets sputtered and failed across the lawn, slowly sinking back into their hiding spots.

"Don't just sit there! Do something!" Sonya ordered to Charity as she reeled from Claudia's attacks.

That was all that was needed for Kayla to start taking charge. "Toby! Get the Professor and the girls inside! Damien get my father!" She demanded as Charity came charging at us. Charity threw out her arms to the side as her fingernails extended then overtook her fingers as they formed and morphed into blades just like Sonya had done. I froze, afraid of the incoming strike, but Kayla appeared in front of me in a move I just couldn't see and stopped Charity's bladed slash in mid action with her bare hand. Her succubae hand just held onto the sharp edge as Charity continued to apply pressure in attempt to get through but Kayla's grip was steady as a rock. The shorter dark-blue succubus let her long turquoise hair waft in the night's breeze. Her choppy raver's bangs fluttered across her face, obscuring her eyes as her emotions churned between a deep upset I had never felt from her…

And a strange calm that frightened me.

"Mistake Shannon… Mistake…" Kayla said to no one in particular as she looked back up at Charity. The large transformed demoness now tried to pull her bladed hand away from Kayla, but was unable to escape her grip. Kayla, in a rapid motion that was difficult to see used her free hand to attack Charity in where her ribcage would be, striking a multitude of times before knocking Charity into the air. Kayla leapt into the air and let her wings extend as she brought around her heel. As she did her clawed succubae foot suddenly was enwreathed with an azure light that trailed for a moment as she flipped around and brought down her heel hard on Charity's head, striking her with such a force that she bounced off the ground and hurled her back a few dozen feet.

What…

What was I getting into?

"C'mon don't stand there Vivian! Help Claudia!" Kayla shouted to me as I immediately glanced around to see that Toby had started to run with the rest of our group back for the house but stopped as Sonya and Claudia's fight blocked them from the door. Sonya and Claudia were locked in an intense spar out in front of the entrance's steps as Kayla flew after Charity. Violet was still locked on Charity, trying to see if she could do something for her friend.

Claudia didn't look like she needed help though. She had assumed a fighting stance by throwing forward her front knee as her back was locked in a low and extended way to stabilize herself as she stood on the front steps to the house, flicking back her long black braid over shoulder as she held out her hands in a way that her index and middle fingers formed a hard point with her thumbs out. The forward hand had her fingers pointing skyward while the back hand was pointed right at Sonya. The firm stare on Claudia's face inclined that she intended harm if Sonya dared to get any closer.

Sonya dared.

Sonya came flying at Claudia, wings stretched and claws forward. As she neared zero range Claudia bounced up into the air with a spinning leap before bringing down her pointed fingers into Sonya's neck and shoulders before flipping around and digging into her back. Sonya's arms went limp as Claudia attacked, her face went immediately from anger to surprise as she found herself being lifted off the ground as Claudia flipped Sonya end over into the pavement of the sidewalk.

Go Claudia!

"What the hell!?" Sonya shouted from her personal crater in the pavement. Seriously confused on why she was losing so heavily to Claudia.

"I learned everything from my father and older brother. My brother is a champion Indian martial artist, and I would have beaten him if I was allowed to participate in his tournaments!" Claudia informed as she flipped around and landed a hard drop kick on Sonya's back. Sonya wailed in pain and frustration as she was ground harder into the dirt. As if to add insult to injury as Claudia delivered her last blow to Sonya's gut she was rewarded with a succubus squeak.

"And another thing!" Claudia scolded in her Indian accent. "If you're just going to kill or control people, do it! Don't talk about it, don't gloat!" Claudia finished with her hands on her hips and a shake of her head. Sonya groaned as Claudia turned to face me as I came running up with our group right behind me.

"That was amazing!" I applauded as I came to a stop, my ponytail bobbing with every happy step as I thoroughly enjoyed Claudia's victory.

Claudia tilted back her head and fluttered her wings with a happy flit as she let her tail wag slightly. "Thank you. Miss Claudia Brashear, demon beater, at your service." She suppressed a giggle as she made a quick bow to me, making me laugh a little as I smiled and let my wings make a few happy flaps.

"We should all head inside." The professor warned to us with a concerned tone. We nodded and turned to do so when the ground nearby erupted as Sonya came crashing through the sidewalk and grabbed Claudia by the face, holding Claudia by the mouth as she held her aloft, smiling up with that crazed and fevered expression.

"You should listen to your own crap!" Sonya sneered as her leathery sleeve undulated as something moved underneath her skin. Claudia's eyes opened wide as she struggled against Sonya's grasp. It took me but a moment to understand what was going on when a bit of black ichor splattered from the top of Claudia's lips as she tried to struggle against Sonya's hold.

"NO!" I shouted as I rushed forward and tackled Sonya with a force I didn't know I had. I rammed her hard, feeling her hollow insides give way as I knocked her sideways, letting Claudia drop to the ground. Sonya was thrown through the side of the house, crashing clear through the window into the study. As soon as I got Sonya off I ran to Claudia as she picked herself up on her knees.

"Claudia! Are you ok?" I asked with fear and concern coursing through my voice like a worried mother. Claudia coughed as she reached up and pushed me back from her.

"No, Vivian, everyone! Please get away! Sonya's going to…" Claudia cautioned before letting out a surprised gasp like she had been winded from within. She tilted back her head and arched her back as I heard that gargling and churning sound I had heard from Charity. I winced out of sheer dislike as Claudia began to grow and stretch, turning taller as her form flared out within her stretchy yoga wear. Her wings extended as her feet morphed and popped into hooves. Her horns grew longer and curled like Charity's as her face made a scrunching sound as it turned away from the girl I knew into a much more blank yet pretty form. She lost her beautiful Indian facial structure as Sonya clearly tried to redesign her from memory. Claudia's braid came undone as her long and flowing raven hair wafted in the night as she gasped a contented and happy gasp as her stretching form slowed to a stop, complete.

Claudia rose to her feet with a sultry wave of her new sinuous form. Her big yellow serpentine eyes rest half open as she calmly smiled and stood in our way at the door. Her shoulders were much wider now like she was remodeled to someone of a more Nordic or possibly Russian persuasion.

Sonya climbed back through her hole in the wall, happy with her handiwork.

"There we go… I was thinking like a female Bruce Lee with some Chuck Norris on this one… I kind of like it." She stated contentedly. Claudia turned her head and nodded before looking back to Dr. Agnew's group.

"Yes… oh… and a new accent too…" Claudia said in an American tone. I didn't know what to make of it… Sonya just took Claudia from me.

Sonya sauntered up to Claudia, "Ok Natalie, enough playing around, I've got mooks now come be my number two you know you wanna and that rage of yours is ready to go. C'mon… I'll even make ya look like something almost as good as me, you can be the funny one." She sneered as she looked to Natalie. I looked to Natalie as poor Nat gritted her teeth as she tried her best not to have an emotional response but honestly Sonya was extremely talented at provocation. Natalie.

"No! You don't control me anymore!" Natalie shouted as she threw her hands out to her side. Trying her best to avoid the confrontation but was just pushed to the point of response. You just wanted to hug her in support as she flared her wings and tried to look tough as she wore a matching set of flannel pajamas to Dr. Agnew.

"Really? I can seem to tick you off pretty easily, that seems like control. Now let's fix all your flaws sweetie, taller, obviously I need that bigger form strength, but could you lose all that morality and constant worrying about life choices? Because… yeah that would be great." Sonya parodied a boss scolding an employee as she quickly made a swirling hand motion with her left hand as Natalie gasped and coughed as Azazel violently exerted herself from within Natalie. Natalie tried to reach for someone as her form suddenly flared, turning taller as her outfit turned tight, she shot up to the seven foot stature of the others as her horns grew out. Sonya clearly had her own designs as she switched around Natalie's facial structure to take on an almost Barbie doll look with a very pretty feathering to the edges of her hair. Natalie struggled with herself for a moment before relenting as her pajamas lost a couple buttons here and there and her lips switched over to a happy and toothy grin. Natalie's eyes had an empty quality as the clever and good natured cheerleader was reformed into a waifish sidekick.

"I'm back Sony… what do you want me to do?" She asked in a much more playful tone, smiling and tilting her head in a subservient way. Trotting happily up to Sonya as she gave a very empty hug to Sonya before gleefully bouncing in place and smiling at her other converted companions.

"Aww it's like Cheer squad all over again, makes me choke up." Sonya laughed to herself as Claudia and Charity giggled a supporting chuckle with her. "Who says I can't make friends? Now, the rest of you, come quietly, or kicking and screaming?" She motioned to the rest of us.

I had reached the point that I was so scared, so worried, and so distraught, I could handle my stress in the only way I knew.

Humor.

I held one finger aloft as I stood in the way of Dr. Agnew and Toby, "Let it always be known that I died as I lived, kicking and screaming." I stated in a very calm and out of place tone as I closed my eyes and pointed skyward to drive my statement home. As I did Claudia snorted as she laughed, putting a clawed hand to her pretty face as the statement touched a nerve like I always do.

Claudia continued to giggle in response to my joke, hiding her laughter behind her hand as Charity and Natalie both rolled their eyes at Claudia for looking so un-cool.

"Stop." Sonya scolded Claudia, "It's not that funny". Sonya continued to scowl at her minion as Claudia sat on the stoop to the building and held out a clawed hand, explaining her predicament.

"I know it's just that it was funny then not funny, but then because I realized I was laughing at something that wasn't funny that made it funny. So then I started to laugh more and…" She laughed again at the explanation. I smiled as I felt Claudia's feelings stir within her. That's still Claudia in there… I know Natalie, and by extension Charity must still be in there as well. Claudia's laughing at my unfunny jokes was like her way of telling me she's still in there… if there's still a bit of her, she could be saved… or well… I can sure as heck try!

Oh! Or Damien could step in, that works too.

Damien jetted into the area with Kayla flying in close behind him, he brought back his electrical staff and slammed Sonya in the side, the shock reverberated as Sonya gasped at the hit. Kayla followed through by picking up Claudia and tossing her back a distance as she swooped and scooped the unaware succubus.

"Everyone! Inside! Into the panic room!" Kayla ordered as she landed and took a fighting stance. Dr. Agnew ran as Natalie awaited orders from Sonya, unwilling to lash out at us from her own volition.

I decided to stay.

"Vivian! What are you doing?" Kayla shouted at me as everyone ran inside.

"I'm gonna save them." I said with a confident nod. Firm in my commitment to not run and hide in the panic room.

Kayla put her hands on her hips and looked sideways at me as Damien grunted as Sonya launched an intense counterattack.

"Oh yeah?" Kayla said with an incredulous tone. "How?"

I opened my mouth and raised a finger, but realized without any sort of plan, I didn't have much to say. I then closed my mouth, pressed my bottom lip into my top lip, and tilted my head upward.

"That's what I thought. Panic room, now." Kayla ordered.

"I'll take her!" Violet shouted as she grabbed my arm, she yanked me off the ground without any trouble! Ah I forgot! I'm hollow inside! That makes me super light!

"Heeyyy I need to save the people!" I complained as Violet dragged me away. Kayla immediately went back to fighting as I was pulled along by Violet. Before going inside, however, Violet leapt off the stairs and landed behind the bushes by the entryway, dragging me along for the ride.

"Owww!" I complained, Violet put her hand to my lips and shushed me.

She narrowed her eyes as she pulled me close, "Ok… now I need you to make me into a succubus." She commanded with a firm whisper. My eyes went wide as I flailed my arms in protest.

"What!?" I shouted, once again she crept closer and cupped her hand over my mouth, I licked her hand to get her to quit. Something that clearly surprised he as she immediately let go.

She shook her hand before wiping it on her dark jeans, "Ick! Stop! We're trying to be quiet here, I need you to focus!" Violet scolded with a loud whisper. "Seriously Vivian, turn me into a succubus, I know you can do it, you just gotta stab me with your tail or something." She stated as she grabbed my tail, pushing the point against her stomach as the little arrow point end folded against her skin, soft and velvety like how my skin normally is.

"Why? My current experience of being a succubus is that you get arrested and everyone wants to murder you, why do you want that?" I asked Violet.

"Because, I think that together, we can save our buds. You lost Claudia, I lost Charity, I say we get 'em back!" Violet clenched her fist and made a proud and brave stare of conviction. "Plus look Vivi, they're not going to win this like that, they need backup." Violet pulled aside the bushes as we looked out on the lawn.

Damien leapt over Kayla's head as he brought down the electrical staff on Natalie who blocked it with her metal claws, something that quickly backfired as Natalie became the plug to Damien's electrical socket. Claudia broke the current, sparing Natalie from further shock as she rolled across the grass before hopping back to deliver a powerful hooved kick and a downward punch that rocked Damien so hard that he bounced off the grass and back into the air for another hit. Sonya and Kayla sparred at a speed I could barely see as they continuously hopped around the area, chasing and diving at each other.

I looked back at Violet, "Ok, you have a point. But for serious, you can't go back. You're perma-demon, is that what you want?" I asked, making sure.

"More than anything else in my Goth heart. Scout's honor." Violet said with nod and one hand held aloft with crossed fingers to suggest that her answer should have been obvious. Which now that I thought about it, yeah… I suppose being a succubus would be a Goth girl's prerogative.

"So gotta ask, is it for the…?" I asked as I put my hands under my succubae chest and moved down my body to kind of show the succubae form.

"Only partially. Now quit stalling we gotta save people!" Violet slapped my arm as she demanded conversion.

Now, before I go any further. In my defense, I have never *tried* to convert anyone before, so she should have cut me some slack. I brought back my tail, Violet lifted up her shirt to expose her stomach, and I lanced forward my tail, wincing a bit at not wanting to hurt her. The little arrow point coiled against her gut as the internal compressed air from the lancing motion made me give off a cute squeak, failing to stab anything.

Violet sighed.

"I'm trying!" I whispered loudly. Trying to concentrate on how I make the arrow point all pointy.

"Need help getting it up? Should I get like a magazine or something?" Violet chided me as she waited impatiently, slightly lowering her grip on her shirt as she looked over at me with her scowling black eyeliner.

"Shhh… Stop you're making me laugh. That's not making this easier, I'm a new demon I didn't get the demon manual of demoness…" I complained, trying to see if it was some sort of muscle memory as I tried doing several things. I could make my wings stretch to flight mode, but the tail was remaining elusive.

"How about if I go get Claudia over here?" Violet smirked. "She really seems to jive your dri-ugh!" Violet's sentence was suddenly cut off by the introduction of my tail to her abdomen.

"Why is everyone so on about that?" I asked as I folded my arms and looked away. I heard Violet beginning to convert as the popping and filling sounds of her succubae conversion began to become apparent. After the first couple seconds, the pain subsided, allowing Violet to talk again.

"Vivi, it's kind of obvious you two are super into each other." Violet explained as she continued to turn. I looked back at her to see purple spreading across her, the new color immediately derailed my conversation.

"Whoa purple flavor succubus." I gawked.

"Yeah… whoa…" Violet looked at her bulging hips and changing legs, making a small gasp as her tail popped out, growing long with a different end from any we'd seen. Hers had a narrow point with a dagger edge that looked like a small sushi knife of mini meat cleaver with a pointed end.

"Whoa." We both said together.

"You better not turn evil on me…" I warned, narrowing my yellow eyes at her as she sighed and rolled her eyes.

"I thought you were the one all on about how it's the person inside and all that?" Violet defended.

"Yeah, then Sonya turned my best friend into a seven foot tall demon beach babe who hates me." I replied.

"Touché'" Violet pointed to me as she spoke, her hand turned into the succubae clawed hand as she did. She pulled her hand to clearly look at herself, obviously happy with the turn of events.

"Hey Vivian, what makes the different colors?" She asked. I shrugged.

"Like I said, no manual." I answered honestly. We just listened to the sound of the intense fighting going on outside the bushes as Violet turned.

"So..." Violet casually stated as she looked down at her body as she turned, the color was now moving past her chest, making changes as it moved to her neck. "Was this... just as awkward when you turned?"

I shrugged, "She was unconscious, I was screaming, I dunno..." I answered apathetically.

She shrugged. I shrugged back.

"Ok... so plan of attack, when we're done here, ooh... woah that felt good." Violet started to say before her transformation made it to her head, turning her eyes into serpentine blood red eyes, her black horns protruding from her head as her hair grew out and her fangs grew in.

"Yeah I like that last bit. Oh dude you're cool." I said, looking over Violet. "Anyway, you were saying?" I asked as I pulled out my tail, Violet was now complete. She... looked like your classic succubus you'd see on a motorcycle jacket or WWII fighter plane. She was now buxom, strong, and clad in leather. She looked like she might be able to do some damage, I hoped that damage would be directed at Sonya, not back at me.

"Ok... yeah. Oh this is so cool." Violet was distracted again by flicking her tail and trying her wings. She snapped back to attention, looking at me, "Right I don't wanna fight Charity, and you don't wanna fight Claudia. So I say we fight *each other's* best buds. We figure out how to get 'em back, and we help the other, got it?" She asked, I nodded.

We both looked through the bushes again.

Now Kayla and Damien were in serious trouble.

Sonya had managed to pin Kayla, Claudia had Damien in a hold on the ground and Charity and Natalie stood at Sonya's flank waiting for her to convert Kayla. Now, I'm pretty sure I couldn't fight an evil Kayla, so I didn't want to let that happen. We needed to act, and quickly.

"Ok so Violet we need to…" I turned to look at my partner in arms, to find that she was already gone.

"WHAT HAPPENED TO THE PLAN!?" I shouted out to her as she flew across the front yard, flipping around backwards at the end to bring both feet hard into Sonya's side, knocking her back off Kayla, freeing the turquoise haired succubus from involuntary conversion.

"Nice! Who are you!? Damien hang on!" Kayla shouted, as the rolling to her feet. "Oh crap Violet!? Is that you? Sweet look!" Kayla complemented, giving Violet the thumbs up before tackling Claudia off Damien, freeing them both.

"Yeah! And oh my junk this is fun!" Violet shouted as she performed a rapid backflip with her new acrobatic form, parrying Natalie's Claws with her own and kicking her back.

"Oh yeah…" Violet purred to herself as she threw out her fingers and let the nails become full blades.

"I can get used to this… bub." She tried her best to copy a classic super hero.

Damien and Kayla got to their feet and stood back to back as Sonya closed in with Natalie alongside. I realized if we were going to help, we had to stop them from ganging up on our not converted friends, so I came running in to see what I could do, running up alongside Violet as we cut off Claudia and Charity from joining

Sonya's fight. The two tall and beautiful succubus stopped to look at us with a condescending gaze. Well… more accurately looked to *me* with a condescending gaze.

"Really?" Claudia asked, pulling out her original voice to sound as pleading as possible, "Vivian you're going to fight me?" she asked with a chesty sigh.

I jutted out my bottom lip and tucked it around my top lip in a pouty and pathetic way, looking up at Claudia… I realized I just didn't have it in me to harm her…

"No… just please stop being evil…" I asked politely.

"I'm not evil Vivian, you know that. Sonya makes many good points, you'll see, plus I think you'll look cute all tall with hooves." She purred in her new voice as she got closer. I realized this was bad.

"Plan! Remember the plan!" Violet shouted as she jumped forward and punched Claudia in her left cheek, sending my companion tumbling. Charity leapt for Violet, I instinctively jumped over Violet to get in the way, intercepting Charity and grabbing her hands as she grabbed mine.

"Right!" I shouted with conviction as I pushed Charity back a bit in our grip. She sneered as she pressed harder and crushed my hands. I yelped in pain as she started to extend her claws into blades, digging into me, I couldn't pull away.

Then I realized… can I do that?

I tried concentrating, how does one simply turn their fingernails into deadly death blades? I don't know… I gripped onto Charity, wrestling with her as I tried to focus.

"GAH! Get off!" Charity demanded.

"Hang on!" I shouted, elbowing her and concentrating on the claw thing again.

"What are you doing back there!?" Charity shouted as she managed to stand up and lift me up as I held onto her neck.

"I'm doing claws… hold on." I explained.

"Go, go gadget death blades!" I said as I threw out my fingers and expected claw-ness… but I just flared out my fingers like an idiot.

Charity just stood and sighed with her new cute haircut, man… why didn't Sonya just become a hairdresser instead of a murdering psychopath?

I tried a series of things to attempt to get into succubae battle mode.

"Blade cutty fingers a go go!"

"Strike laser claw!"

"Mastodon!"

"Quarter circle back and b!"

"Well… frick!" I worried as I just flanged my fingers while thinking about if I could figure out any way to make the blades come out, and with an absolute amount of surprise they came out… they ALL came out. I had blades on my hands, my feet and my teeth went into crazy metal Sonya like death teeth. I accidently impaled Charity and in the surprise I let her go. She backed away and nursed her wounds as she tried to let them heal.

I looked down at my bladed hands… those aren't just blades, they're like little machetes! I should *not* be entrusted with such deadly weaponry in my fingers. Or my feet… oh and look the reflection of my teeth in my finger blades, I look like pure crazy!

Violet saw me extend my blades and tilted her head with a curious expression, "Can we all do that?" She asked as she smiled, making her own teeth morph. "Oh sweet…" She purred as she playfully flicked her purple, knife-edged tail and charged back in on Claudia. Claudia's claws clashed on hers with the sliding steel twang of entwined blades. I felt it best to look away and focus on my target.

Charity narrowed her yellow eyes at me before rushing forward, blades out. I tried to think about all the things I could possibly do to fight her, but I thought of so much that I ended up doing nothing but getting a blade in my gut and thrown up in the air. She brought around her claws to slice me in half as I fell, but I stretched my wings and took off skyward before she could land the blow. She took off right after me, chasing me into the sky. I retracted my claws and teeth to focus… at least now I know how to do it!

I flew up above the mansion and trees, looking out on the city of Baltimore from my bird's eye view before Charity came gliding up. The city's many lights along the waterfront glittered like gems among the churning late summer bay. The sight was beautiful and I appreciated my ability to fly for a moment as Charity shrieked before running her blades inches from my face. I flapped twice and backpedaled in the air, narrowly avoiding the swing as I attempted to negotiate.

"Charity it's me! I know this isn't you! Snap out of it! You're a sweet girl, I know you!" I tried to get through to her as she continued to swipe her claws in the space I was a moment ago as I flapped from left to right on my demonic wings, narrowly avoiding every slash as tried to talk her down. I'm not going to hurt her unless I have to, and I don't want to have to.

Charity responded with a frustrated roar as she spun in place and brought a hooved foot around towards my head. I ducked under in the last second, letting her hoof fly just above my horns, making my ponytail shake from the shock force. It was clear she wasn't going to hear me, or couldn't. So I used the moment to fly forward quickly and put a regular, un-bladed fist under Charity's chin to get her to stop attacking me. She was knocked back a bit, I realized I could fight her without doing any real harm. If I could incapacitate her, I could get her in a position where perhaps Dr. Agnew or Silverlight could save her. I had to try.

I gave my all, focusing on Charity as she brought around her light blue fist. As she did, everything seemed to slow for a moment, I actually felt things I normally would never feel, like my serpentine eyes dilating and clenching, or the pressure caused by Charity's incoming punch. I turned my head slightly as I saw the shot incoming, automatically getting out of the way with as little movement as possible. As I did, everything seemed to fall back into time, as everything sped back to normal.

And there floated Charity, and me, flapping in place in the air, her fist resting on my shoulder, where my head had been a moment ago.

"Whoa…" She admonished, "H…how'd you do that?" She asked with sincerity.

I couldn't focus on her, I saw something else. I saw opportunity. Something within me told me that if I attacked her right side of the abdomen, she would bow in a way that would let me knee her in the chin, then I could break her jaw with my elbow, then lead into striking her down to the ground. It all came so quickly, my movements almost automatic.

Before I realized what was happening, I had hurled the succubus ground-ward. She grasped for air as she hit terminal velocity, slamming into the ground with a solid, crater carving, thud.

The fighting below stopped as all parties turned to see me land at the edge of Charity's crater. I've never hurt anyone before, I never got into a fight… not a real fight anyway, I've been bullied many times but never lashed back…

I didn't like the feeling of causing someone so much harm.

"Vivian… won?" Sonya asked with curiosity as she backed off of Damien and Kayla, retracting her claws.

I turned to look as Sonya.

Sonya disappeared with a flash of her power.

She had tried to grab me like she did to Claudia, but I actually saw her coming. In her moment of teleportation time seemed to dilate again. I backed away, fluttering my wings. My mind told me to bend down, so I did, I let her hand pass over my head, I reached up my palm, and thrust upwards under her chin. I knocked her skyward. I spun around, and kicked her in the waist, sending her tumbling to the ground.

Time came back.

Kayla's eyes widened as she looked over to me, "Impossible..." She muttered in barely a whisper. Everyone froze as they looked to where I stood.

Sonya picked herself up on her back, propping herself on her elbows as she scowled at me.

"How... how am I doing this?" I asked, coiling back my tail and putting my hands to my chest in fear of myself. I... I've never done anything else like this in my entire life. I immediately chalked this up to being a Succubus thing. But from the surprised looks from everyone else...

This was something else.

Kayla fluttered to my side, standing beside me but forward enough to appear to be defending me. "Vivian, that's not important right now, what's important is you do not let Sonya get you. If she gets you or I there will be no stopping her do you understand? There's some things that are better not known..." Kayla almost explained as Claudia, Charity, and Natalie closed in around Sonya. Violet and Damien stood beside us as we took a stand against them. Everything's been happening so fast. I could barely take a moment to understand what's been going on the last 24 hours. But for some reason, I felt that I had tapped into the core of it. So as I took a fighting stance without fear against Sonya. As Kayla stood by my side, as Damien and Violet backed me up, as I saw the passive stare in Claudia's eyes and the scared and wavering feelings still fighting inside of Natalie, I closed my eyes, and listened to the world around me.

My name is Vivian Maybell, I'm just a girl.

I discovered a temple that flies, I found other life beyond our own. I lost my humanity and was turned into a demon. I've discovered I have abilities and strength I didn't know I had before. I didn't ask for any of this, but I wanted something more. I didn't want this responsibility, I'm just a dreamer. One who wanted to dream about something other than the normal life...

I didn't expect it to become real.

And now that I have it.

I'm afraid, I'm not perfect, I'm no hero.

But I'm not afraid of *her*.

"Fear of power is natural for those who are not meant to wield it." Sonya answered my emotions, smiling a wicked grin as she stepped forward. I opened my eyes, letting my yellow pools settle on her green stare, "Just come to me Vivian, I can make it better. I'll take care of you. I'll manage things. Just let yourself follow me and everything can be all right." She beckoned with a steel clawed finger. I tensed, I wouldn't waver. As I held my ground, Kayla, Violet, and Damien stepped forward slightly, ready to defend.

I don't understand this world anymore. There's so much to know and so much mystery that I'll just have to figure things out one at a time… but I knew then. As I saw my companions defending me, as I saw my friends no longer themselves staring coldly at me from across the lawn. As I saw a small red dot move across the grass and settle on Sonya's head…

I will *never* give up.

A gunshot rang across the lawn, Sonya gasped and dropped back, her minions turned in surprise to see her fall. From behind us, above the trees, the soft purring wind of a new Cold fusion engine parted the treetops above the skies behind us. An electronic flicker of an angular, triangular shaped, rotorless craft coming into visual spectrums resounded as a military *Nighthawk* VTOL craft pulled sideways, a very tall armored man in black armor held a rifle in the open side door.

The DPI was here.

I felt comfort from the DPI squad as they leapt out of the open bay and fell in around us. Rushing forward with their guns lowering as they hit the ground. I felt the rush of wind from the black power armor suits charging past, I saw Clayton and Katie draw out devices that looked like a respirator with an intricate metal box along the back of it. They rushed forward and cupped the facemask of the respirators on Charity and Claudia as they tackled them in their heavy armor. The tallest one, Trigger, was so large he could pick up Natalie even in her altered form and hold the device against her face as he gently bent one knee to support her as she struggled momentarily. The vehicle set down behind us as the Vampire, Colonel Valerie Hawthorne, hopped out of the side and finished zipping up her jacket as she took a glance at the fallen soldiers on the lawn with a passive stare. Internally I could feel her sympathize for Silverlight, as she slowly stepped towards Damien.

I ran forward and knelt by Claudia as she began to shrink back to her normal Succubae form, the black Ichor of Azazel was being pulled from her by the device, there was a moment of violent shaking followed by short period of calm. Finally Katie pulled the device off Claudia, who awakened back as herself with a loud and surprised gasp.

"Oh my God Vivian!" Claudia quickly shouted as she turned and hugged me. I wrapped my arms around her and clamped hard as she patted my back. "I'm so sorry Vivian, I hope I didn't harm you." She asked with sincerity. I shook my head and just held her back, not able to answer through all the relief I felt. I just cradled her in my arms, holding her like a doll and not letting her go.

"Wheew!" Katie excitedly shouted through her helmet with the tinny grain from the microphone. She flipped open her visor and smiled with her eyes as she turned back to see her companion, "Zelinski how we doing?" she asked with her clean yet very east coast accent over to Clayton as he held the beautiful and now very curvaceous Charity Fahnestock in his arms.

"Oh don't you worry about me." He replied happily from his current vantage point utilizing his southern drawl. "I'll manage somehow." He said with a surly tone as Charity slowly woke up in his arms, Violet knelt down beside her friend.

"Hey Charity, it's me…" She said as she ran a hand along Charity's cheek to get her to focus. Charity fluttered her eyes and wings as she took in Violet.

"Oh my crap what happened to you?" She asked with a weak yet surprised tone as she looked over at Violet's new form. The purple demoness was having trouble not smiling a happy, toothy grin as she looked down at her fellow gothic friend with serpentine blood red eyes.

"I turned into a succubus and saved your life from being a cheerleader's dumb sidekick. But look at you!" Violet defended, pointing at Charity's new form. Charity

The light blue succubus did not really have a comment, she just nodded and looked back to Violet. Then realized she was being held by a man. She made a face that suggested that this was suddenly no longer comfortable and her wings politely pushed her out of Clayton Zelinski's grip.

"I... I think I'm ok to walk now..." She politely suggested for Clayton to let her go as she tapped on his armored hands. He sighed and did so as Violet helped her to her feet. Clayton stood and put an armored hand on the back of his helmet, letting the black visor flip up so they could see his face.

"Well I hope you're feeling better and hey if you ladies aren't doing anything later..." he began. Charity quickly deflected, but in a polite enough way.

"Oh I think I have a headache right now, probably from all that mental domination and bloodshed. I think I need to lay down and rest for a while..." She put him down immediately but as gently as she could. But nodded before saying, "And thank you very much for saving my life. I really didn't want to hurt my friends."

Major Howell, getting out of the pilot's seat of the VTOL, laughed as he walked over and slapped the back of Clayton's helmet, letting the visor clamp shut. "Oh don't mention it. It's just doin our job, After all you think all that tax money goes to roads and wetland preservation? Hah!" Major Howell laughed to himself as he shook Zelinski's shoulder and turned to see Dr. Agnew and Toby coming out of the house.

"Is everything all right?" Dr. Agnew asked with fear still in her voice as Claudia and I came sprinting across the grass to her. Dr. Agnew went to check on Natalie, as Claudia and I walked over to see our southern succubus being held gently in the tall armor clad soldier's ours.

"You… you saved me again…" Natalie barely whispered up to the tall warrior.

"Again?" The tall soldier asked with a polite yet obviously recognizable Texas accent.

"Yes… just now… and when you calmed my heart earlier today… I thought that I was alone, but you gave me comfort without needing a word. That meant everything to me. And you even showed us the way through the crowd. You're very brave… and I don't even really know your name. And I've never seen your face… But I like you… thank you." Natalie smiled as she reached up and felt the side of his helmet. The tall soldier set Natalie down gently and let her stand, Dr. Agnew put her hand on Natalie's shoulder as Natalie turned back to face the man.

"Natalie…" The tall man said with polite southern tone as he put a hand to his chest, "I wasn't always this way, I was like you. Well… not all pretty and cute like you but ex human, like you. I used to think that losing your humanity meant losing your path with God. But that's not true. Ultimately what you are in this world is superficial. It's who that person inside is that makes it up. Now, I'm jus' a soldier and I can't claim to be a good preacher. But I know for a fact that if God won't accept someone like you then he ain't no man worth prayin to. And I know the God I serve is a man worth prayin to…"

He reached up and let the clasps open on his long and angular helmet. The lot of us seemed to collectively draw back a moment as we saw brown fur where we expected clear skin to be. Long, dog like pointed ears atop his head, and a long, and easily recognizable snout with iconic long teeth. He smiled a toothy grin as he moved the helmet under one arm, reaching into his pocket as his bright golden brown eyes looked at Natalie calmly. He pulled out a rolled up hat and flicked it, letting it return to its normal form. A classic Texas tradition, a tan cowboy hat.

"Allow me to introduce myself." He said as he gave the hat a spin, resting it atop his head as he moved one ear up to make one side of the hat fold upward.

"Trigger Valentine,

American werewolf."

We were all stunned. A live werewolf. I mean… I know I've met a Vampire today and well, I'm a succubus but… he was the most far out there thing I've ever seen! And he was awesome!

Trigger shrugged slightly as he looked over to Natalie, "So… yah still like me?" He asked with his sweet and cocky tone.

Natalie smiled as she nodded her head, hiding her smile behind her hands but her dimples gave it away. I had to hide a smile of my own, happy for Natalie to feel anything other than the constant pain she had suffered since her conversion.

I glanced over to see Toby and Kayla exchange a hug on the grass. Kayla started to fuss over the scene around her, looking to the dead soldiers and the destruction across the grass when Toby put his arm around her and gave her phone back and got her to focus on less tiring things. He was a good friend to her, and I hope she appreciates having someone like him. Probably not. Before I could go any further headlights flashed on the horizon as a black Silverlight limo came pulling into the long driveway, stopping before us all.

The car doors clapped as Mr. Gilden stepped out with a small entourage. A tall dark skinned man with a salt and pepper beard and the most steeled eyes I had ever seen stood at Daniel Gilden's side as a woman with grey skin and long white hair strode up alongside them in a lithe black suit. Her fingers were amazingly long, probably 9 inches in total length. Crazy long. Her eyes were milky white and she had a very, dead, stare on her face, but her pretty lips seemed to carry an arrogant air of intelligence to her as she calmly observed the scene.

"Kayla…" Mr. Gilden said as he put his cell phone in his pocket and knelt to hug his daughter as she came running up and hugged him. "Are you all right? Did Azazel touch you?" He asked with sincerity.

Kayla shook her head and held him back. The tall man beside Daniel looked to Damien.

"My son." He stated in a voice that was much more experienced than heard. The deep quality coupled with an African accent spoke volumes to the amount of strength that this man must have.

Damien's father looked at the bodies of Damien's squad members. "You did what you could. And Miss Gilden is defended." He stated without any other need for conversation.

"I understand." Damien returned, bowing slightly to his father.

I realized I was staring at Damien and his father's conversation when my train of thought was derailed by the strong southern shout of Major Howell. "Get her bound, she'll be up soon!" he ordered as he flung his arm and pointed to Sonya. Katie and Zelinski clapped on what looked to be very large and strong cuffs on Sonya's arms and legs then placed something around her neck. She started to stir as her body healed from the gun wound.

Sonya groaned before trying to move her hands. As she did she realized she was stuck and pulled quickly. Realizing she was being retrained she flailed with Azazel's power, making tendrils of black fly off her and try to attack the bonds, but as she did the collar on her neck flickered a green light and a deep shock coursed through her body, causing her to groan and stop, her ichor appendages retracted as she slumped in defeat.

Clayton reached down and grabbed the chain on the cuffs, lifting the light succubus up as he walked towards the Major, who was now over by Mr. Gilden as Claudia and I joined in on the conversation.

"Boss what you want me to do with her?" Clayton asked with sincerity.

"Put her in holding, we'll take her back to Arkham with us." The Major answered without a hint of remorse for Sonya. Looking back at Mr. Gilden with a concerned stare.

“She didn’t do this alone…” He boldly informed Daniel directly.

“No.” Daniel Gilden returned with a expressionless tone, the undercurrent of anger rolling off Daniel was frightening, even Kayla took a step back.

“Find out what she knows, then inform me immediately.” Mr. Gilden demanded from the DPI’s commander.

Major Howell shook his head, “Now I know you’re used to getting your way…” He began as he put his hands on his hips. The two soldiers in black armor marched Sonya onto the VTOL craft, she turned as Clayton put his armored hand on the back of her head, shouting back towards us.

“This isn’t over Gilden! The truth is in the open! The wheel has begun to turn! I won’t be one of your DPI puppets, I’ll be free once more. We’ll meet again Kayla, and I’ll see you soon Vivian Maybell…” Sonya shouted before Clayton pushed down her head and shoved her inside before slamming the door.

“Target captured.” Valerie stated coldly into her phone.

“Understood, Director Westfield will want a debrief at 0900 hours.” The voice on the far end of the phone replied before hanging up. Valerie tucked away the slim black phone in her jacket pocket and stared back at the assembled group.

“Damien.” Mr. Gilden turned to order, “Take a team to inform Mr. Shannon that his services here are no longer required. Then find out who paid him. Who’s he working for. He’s smart, but not that smart. Someone is pulling his strings. Find out then come to me.”

Valerie looked to Gilden with curiosity in her glowing blue eyes.

“I suggest a trade.” Daniel Gilden informed to both DPI officers, “Up until today, I believed that the only people that had something to gain from defeating me was you. But now, we see there’s another player. You give me the information I want, and in turn I’ll tell you what’s going on here. We’re all on a timetable now. Each and every one of us. The world knows we're not alone. Even now we have standing before us today Succubae, a Vampire, Dr. Toft is a zombie and we of course have Mr. Valentine here. How long do you think that is going to stay safe? How long do you think that will go unnoticed? Humanity is not an understanding race. There will be blood. We both know this. This is the beginning of a new era. Do you think that the average American can comprehend what is right or wrong in a world like this? Do you believe for even a moment that people will be able to keep their faith in the face of fear? Do you think that they will turn to you and your government soldiers for answers? Or will they believe the first thing they see on a sensationalized TV?

War is coming.

I don't know the sides, and I don't know the outcome, but we're sitting at a beginning, a genesis of something greater. We may have different goals and ideals, but right now we're all humanity has. So we work together. And that's what's right today."

Mr. Gilden finished by offering his hand to Raymond Howell. Who contemplated his words carefully, but never returned the shake.

"We'll see Mr. Gilden. For now, we have to both retreat into the night. It's almost dawn, and I doubt people will wake up to find a peaceful scene.

It's going to be up to the people now, it's up to America, no… it's up to humankind.

Are they going to accept the new change, and let people different from them live among them? Or are they going to fall prey to petty fear, and let their emotions rule over what's right? I guess the question you gotta ask yourself is are you an optimist or a pessimist in this Mr. Gilden?" He shook his head as the DPI team reassembled in the VTOL, Major Howell rest his hand on the door frame as he turned back to look at the tall man in black.

"What do you think the people fall back on in a time of crisis?" Major Howell asked as Valerie started to make the craft take off.

"Faith…Or fear?"

Epilogue

Abandoned Textile Factory

Camden, New Jersey

United States of America, Earth

The Journal of Christine Angela

October 4thth, 2011

4:23 AM

Echoes,

Echoes,

Footfalls on pavement.

I knew that with every step I was giving away my position. I knew I should just stay still, let it all blow over…

But I was so, *so*, scared.

It all seemed so romantic when I was first offered it, immortality. A life eternal with a man I loved. He was cute, and I already loved vampires so much from the books and movies that I had read. I even became beautiful through the process, and when I first turned I spent hours looking back at my glowing blue eyes…

I never expected it to be like this.

I ran, arms flailing and legs continuing on with the relentless pace of the undead. The eerie state of an abandoned building the early morning made my no longer beating heart leap at every noise that was not mine. I stopped suddenly as I realized that the floor in front of me was no longer there, my blue and white sneakers skittered to a stop with several quick squeaks.

"Up there!" Shouted one of the men as several flashlights on the end of assault rifles turned skyward, reflecting off my pale white skin as I pulled my grey hoodie up over my long brown hair to try and hide myself from the light as I covered my face. I ran backwards away from the hole as the concussive sound of gunfire ripped temporary spears through the concrete flooring and stucco walls, causing dust and shrapnel to rain from the glowing blue tracers that meant to end my life.

Eddie and I were just having dinner, nothing creepy, just normal dinner at a small Italian place just down the street. The butcher there was a friend of Eddie's family, and he always provided and saved animal blood for us, we weren't bothering anyone. It was exactly what I always wanted. It was the kind of life I dreamed of having, anything better than growing up in Camden as a poor girl. This was something amazing, and I went for it.

But they came.

It was only a few moments ago. I leaned in to kiss him he smiled at me, and the floodlights of a DPI *Nighthawk* came flowing into the restaurant. He turned to see what was wrong, standing and putting out his arm to shield me as glowing blue tracer bullets came flying into the restaurant, shattering the glass, the table…

And my Eddie.

The butcher told me to run, and I ran, I ran so fast I didn't know I could. I found the first place to hide from the helicopter thing, and that was here…

Voices below…

"Did she run back the other way?"

"Get a couple people on the walkway, I'm too tired to chase this thing, send her in."

The second man's voice was confident, cocky, and self-assured. I held the tassels tight on my hoodie. I reached up and wiped the falling mascara from my face as I let the tears soak into my sweatshirt.

I heard the *Nighthawk* land, and the door slide open. I crept along the floor as I peeked into the open crevice to see what waited for me down there. The DPI soldiers in their black armor with gold trim waited at the edge of the building as another soldier hopped out of the side of the craft with something small that I couldn't see clearly from the window, could be a dog from the fact it was obscured by the window frame I was peering across from my vantage point upstairs.

"Spooky's already complaining, they're saying call off the mission." The approaching man scoffed as he shrugged.

"Friggin bleeding hearts, of course they would say that. Then we'll have Vampires all over the city and then where would we be? It's bad enough they let Hawthorne live. Major's getting soft in his old age." Another soldier propped back his helmet to smoke as he leaned on the door frame, lighting a cigarette as he offered the box of them to the approaching soldier who waved it away with an appreciating gesture.

"I agree man, nip it in the bud, that's why we're letting her do it." The first soldier said as he reached over and seemed to work with something I couldn't see.

"Protocol: Vampire, Female, Age irrelevant, TOS." The DPI soldier told whatever they were talking about then pressed something. I heard the electronic whine of something activating.

"That's still creepy as shit." The smoking solider laughed in a nervous laugh.

"Yeah man you tell me, at least we don't gotta go in there. OK, ok, now gimme onea them smokes." The other soldier motioned as he too leaned on the building, sharing a smoke break with the soldiers as they waited for something…

Then she stepped forward.

A girl, a little girl. Probably around 14-15 years old. She was small, Asian, around four and a half feet high. She stepped into the building, looking downward, never up, never at anything. She just stared. Something about her made my no longer flowing blood thin. Maybe it was the dead stare she gave, the innocent look of the black knee high socks or her almost catholic school girl like ensemble. Or maybe it was the collar around her neck, a small digital device with a flickering green diode and screen on the back. I could see it glowing through her long black hair. Suddenly she looked up, directly at me. I shirked back.

She was here for me.

And so I ran.

And did I run…

I pulled back and leapt across the gap from my current vantage point, landing with a thud as I heard rapid tiny footsteps, I knew she was coming.

I saw the staircase on my left was missing the first three steps, so I jumped and grabbed onto the next stair as I pulled myself up. The rapid tap-tap-tap of the girl's running pace kept up behind me, I knew she was getting close. I scurried up and then bolted with all my vampire strength up the stairs, getting to the next floor as I heard the rush of wind of her jumping the gap. She was closing faster than I could have anticipated. I got to the top of the stairs and saw a fire door, so I grabbed and slammed it and left down the lock, hoping that would keep her out.

I looked around at the open windows and fluttering plastic drapery of the upper textile floor. Three old fabrication machines were left over, they looked like they were meant to spin cobwebs these days more than anything else. I ran towards the far one from me, dusty footprints marked my path along the open and echoing work floor as I heard the rapid taps of the girl reaching the top of the steps. I looked out the window as I reached the far end… I was now about four stories up, seeing over the buildings around me. At least I could see the *Nighthawk*, I knew they weren't waiting for me at the top.

I realized… I was a vampire, I could leap… but where? A sharp and sudden noise distracted me as I heard two loud bangs followed by a sharp snap, I saw the fire door fly off the hinge and screech along the work floor. She's here.

Up, I had to go up. I figured I could fool her by leaping out the open window frame, grabbing onto the piping outside as I began to climb. Eddie's last gift to me was helping as I found that I could climb quickly, pulling myself up higher and higher as the night's wind breezed past, my ascension framed by the half-moon above the dingy city. Several footsteps from the floor below were punctuated by abject silence. I knew the girl had rushed in and stopped, scanning for where I had run to. She couldn't follow my footprints anymore, I wasn't leaving them. I could hear every movement of my superfluous breathing, the adrenaline and fear were permeating everything as I continued higher. I needed to escape, I needed to keep going…

I won't die to here, not like this! Not now!

I pulled higher, finding the fire escape as I leapt across onto it with inhuman strength. I managed to land in relative silence, leaving only a slight tap as I made my footfall. I saw across the way… the old RCA building! I if I made it to the roof I could leap across! And then I would be free! I knew that building from field trips back in school! It's like a maze! I had a plan, a way to escape! I ran to the roof…

And there she was.

The girl stood on the bald and reflected rooftop, stoically waiting for me, one hand behind her back as the little girl stared with cold, dead, eyes.

"W… what do you want from me!?" I shouted as I backed away from her, moving back over the top of the fire escape again, hearing my heel clatter against the old wrought iron railing.

"Vampire… Female, age irrelevant…" The girl mimicked what the soldier had ordered. I gasped as she spoke, hearing a warning from Eddie's father, a cautionary story we should have paid attention to…

But now it's too late.

"You're… You're Clara…" I stuttered.

She raised a pistol to me.

"Clara the demonkiller."

And now, the great mystery.

UNTIL WE MEET AGAIN DEAR TRAVELLER~

-BO-TAN

TO BE CONTINUED

WRITTEN AND CREATED BY MATTHEW MACDONALD

Prolecto: Genesis

Volume II: The Kingsport Incident

Episode 3

Faith and Fear

On sale now

Want more Prolecto? Visit us at **www.prolecto.net**